Bandit's Bride

by

Gail MacMillan

Riverhaven Rogues: A North American Regency Series, Book 4

Bandit's Bride

Cover Art by *RJ Morris*

The Wild Rose Press, Inc.
PO Box 708
Adams Basin, NY 14410-0708
Visit us at www.thewildrosepress.com

Publishing History
First Tea Rose Edition, 2017
Print ISBN 978-1-5092-1347-4
Digital ISBN 978-1-5092-1348-1

Riverhaven Rogues: A North American Regency Series, Book 4
Published in the United States of America

"Awake at last." Her words were soft, gentle, soothing.

He struggled to focus. Golden-red hair, a delicately beautiful heart-shaped face, that voice... He knew them from somewhere, somewhere.

She stood and moved away. Again his thoughts reeled incoherently. Cold, so cold, and pain, so much pain. Memories straggled back...

She returned, kneeling beside him, a cup in one hand, raising his head with the other.

"Drink." She held it to his lips.

The liquid trickled into his mouth. He tried to swallow but was overcome by a fit of coughing. She put the cup aside and drew him more upright until the spasm subsided. As she lowered him gently back into his former position, he realized that he was in a bed. Somewhere nearby a wood fire crackled out warmth and light.

"Where...am...I?" he croaked. "What...?"

"You arrived at my door during a blizzard." Entrancing green eyes looked down at him. The thought again staggered across his mind that he'd died and gone to heaven. Surely no angel could be lovelier than this mysterious stranger. But why did she look familiar—why?

"You were wounded." She was speaking again. "You're in my cabin...and safe."

"Wounded." His thoughts were clearing, lining up with a bit of remembrance and logic. "Aye, I'm beginning to ken. Fox!" Gritting his teeth against pain, he tried to jolt upright. Her hand, surprisingly strong on his shoulder, restrained him.

Praise for Gail MacMillan

"I love, love, loved this book [*HEATHER FOR A HIGHLANDER*]! It…begins in England with a murder, and ends with a fiery romance in British North America. And it's all because of a horse bet between brothers. I mean, isn't that how all good stories begin?"

~*Romance Novels for the Beach*

"Truly engaging. I would definitely pick up another book by this author."

~*a judge at TransCRW competition*

"Be prepared to be hooked on the first word of the first page and go on to the next with anticipation."

~*Rebecca Melvin, Publisher, Double Edge Press*

"Gail MacMillan's stories delight the senses and brighten the dark days of winter like a candle glowing on a windowsill."

~*Sue Owens Wright, author, newspaper columnist*

"I love this little adventure [*HOLDING OFF FOR A HERO*]!…surprises…one light, wonderful read."

~*The Romance Reviews (4 Stars)*

"Not sure who I like better, [the] German Shepherd, the Pug, or the sexy next door neighbor."

~*Matilda, Coffee Time Romance & More (5 Cups)*

"Not your typical romance story [*SHADOWS OF LOVE*], but I couldn't put it down."

~*Michelle, Cocktails and Books (4 Cups)*

"If you are looking for a historical starring pirates, er, privateers, some subterfuge, and a woman showing the men what is what, then [*PRIVATEER'S PRINCESS*] is it."

~*Llaph, Coffee Time Romance & More (4 Cups)*

Dedication

In loving memory of my husband Ron,
who passed on September 1, 2016.
He made my life an adventure.

Also by Gail MacMillan, from The Wild Rose Press

Non-Fiction:
How My Heart Finds Christmas
To All the Dogs I've Loved Before

~

Historical Romance:
Shadows of Love
Caledonian Privateer
Lady and the Beast

~

Other Riverhaven Rogues books:
Privateer's Princess
Heather for a Highlander Harry (winner of "Best
Heroine" in the 2014 Canadian Romance Writers
Maple Leaf Contest, with the hero taking second best
and the ending awarded an honorable mention)
Highland Harry (winner of "Best Opening" in the 2015
Canadian Romance Writers Maple Leaf Contest)
Backwoods Bride

~

Contemporary Romance:
Phantom and the Fugitive
Rogue's Revenge
Ghost of Winters Past

~

Cowboy Country Connections Series:
Holding Off for a Hero
Counterfeit Cowboy
Cowboy and the Crusader
Cowboy Confessions
Cowboy Country Christmas

Chapter One

"Uncle Brodie, come and see! The witch is at Harper's store!"

Brodie MacMillan turned to the thirteen-year-old tugging at his arm and frowned. "Witch? Samuel, I left you to unload the wagon, not go makin' up fairy tales."

"Come on!" The boy's tugging became more persistent. "Her wagon is right beside ours! She's loading up. She might leave any minute!"

"Best go with the lad." Franklin Miller put broad hands down on the bar of the Riverhaven Inn and shook his head slowly. "The creature comes to town but twice a year—spring and fall. You'll not get another chance until April or May."

"Frank, you're not tellin' me you believe in witches and the like?" Brodie stared at the man as the boy ceased his yanking at his arm to listen, wide-eyed, to the innkeeper's words.

"Not in general, but when it comes to Louisa Abbott..." He drew in his lips and shook his head again.

"Uncle Brodie!" Samuel pulled at him again. "You must see her!"

"Oh, verrae well." Brodie swigged down the remainder of his ale and allowed the young lad to pull him out of the inn into the chill of the November afternoon. "Is she so verrae hideous...with green skin

1

and a great wart on the end of her crooked nose?" His innate affability along with his Highland accent surfaced. He'd been in the British North American colony of New Brunswick for less than a year, and his speech, although he was struggling to change it, often reflected his Scottish roots.

"No, no!" The boy dragged Brodie out into the street, where a group had surrounded a pair of wagons, his one of them, in front of the town's mercantile. A snow-white mare was harnessed to the other. A woman emerged from the store, a sack thrown over one shoulder. Silence fell over the group as they backed away from her.

"Bloody hell!" Brodie stopped short.

If this was the witch, she was like no sorceress he could have imagined. An enchantress, more like. The description overwhelmed his mind as he gazed—her hair, an astonishing golden red or reddish gold, he couldn't say which, and her face—surely angels were blessed with none more fair. The boy's breeches, shirt, and coat she wore emphasized the fact that she was slim of body and comely in form.

Spellbound, he gaped.

"Uncle Brodie?" Samuel was looking up at him, a mixture of fear and surprise crinkling his countenance. "Uncle Brodie, you mustn't stare." He lowered his voice to a hiss. "She might put a spell on you."

"Whit? Oh, aye." He broke out of the trance as the woman, having deposited her burden in the wagon beside his own, turned back into the store. "Let us go and help the lass to load up, laddie."

"No, Uncle Brodie!" The boy clutched at his arm. "See? Everyone stays away from her! No one even dares speak! She'll put a curse on anyone who does!"

"Dunnae talk foolish, lad." Brodie broke free and headed for the wagons. "She's but a lass doin' a man's work."

Leaving Samuel and the semicircle of townspeople staring after him, he strode into the mercantile. At the counter with her back to him, that glorious hair tied back in a queue, the witch was accepting two more sacks from shopkeeper Angus Harper.

"Angus." Brodie went to stand at the counter beside her. "I see ye have a lady customer. Perhaps I can be of assistance...by helpin' to load her wagon."

The witch turned to face him. Further words froze in Brodie MacMillan's throat. A goddess with wide green eyes gazed back at him.

"Thank you, Mister...?" Her voice was soft yet strong as she queried him.

"Brodie...Brodie MacMillan." He stuttered out his name and wondered how he'd managed even that. Whatever this woman was, she had drawn him under her spell with three words and a single look.

"Abbott...Louisa Abbott." She held out a hand, startling him with the typically male gesture. "I'd be grateful, Brodie MacMillan."

Astonished, he paused. Finally, as she continued to hold out her hand, he rubbed his right palm on the seat of his breeches and took it into his. A shock raced up his arm.

"Your servant, ma'am." Bloody hell, he sounded like a damned Englishman, like his friend Harry Wallace when he was putting on his act as an aristocratic milord. She smiled up at him, making him think of sunrise on a perfect summer's morn.

When she released his hand, she took several gold coins from an inner pocket of her coat and pushed them across the counter toward the shopkeeper.

"I trust that covers my account, Mr. Harper?" She smiled at the man.

"Aye, yes, ma'am. More than sufficient." He looked down at the payment.

"Add any overpayment as a credit to my account for the next time I'm in need of your merchandise. Now, if you wouldn't mind…" She took up one of the sacks and, still with that amazing smile in place, indicated the second to Brodie.

He could only nod as he slung it over his shoulder.

Outside they were met by the silently staring crowd as they put the bags into the wagon hitched to the white mare.

"Do you know who owns the other wagon?" She indicated his conveyance.

"I…do." Again that half-witted stuttering.

"I believe it has a load of flour and oatmeal? Mr. Harper mentioned he was awaiting a delivery for his store. I should like to purchase several bags, if you're agreeable."

"Aye, aye." He willed his tongue back into control as he went to transport sacks to her wagon.

"What do I owe you, Mr. MacMillan?" She gazed into his eyes, and once again he was lost.

Later he realized he must have named a sum, because she placed a gold coin into his hand.

"No good will come of dealin' with a witch." A voice from the onlookers made Brodie whirl.

"And no good will come of castin' defamin' words at a visitor to our village." He snapped back to reality at the nasty remark. "You'd best stand aside and give the lady space to turn her horse. Or will I have to go about clearin' a path?" His hand fell to the hilt of the sword that hung in a scabbard at his side.

Muttering, they moved aside. Sometimes his reputation as a rogue, a man not to trifle with, especially when his sword was involved, served his purposes right down to the ground.

"Thank you." She looked up at him with those wonderful green eyes and locked onto something in his soul.

"A mere nothin', ma'am." He held out a hand to help her aboard her wagon. With all the grace of a lady, she accepted and climbed to the seat.

"You're a gentleman, sir. I shall not forget your kindness. My best wishes go with you, Brodie MacMillan." She gave him one last glance before flicking the reins over the horse's rump. "Walk on, Snow."

The mare strained into the harness and headed down the street, the load keeping her to a walk. He, with the crowd, watched them go. Just before they disappeared among the trees, she turned on the seat and, smiling a smile that shot a ray of brightness through the dull November day, raised a hand in farewell to him. A sudden urge to run after her gushed over him—to join her on that wagon seat, to go with her wherever her path might lead all but overwhelmed him.

Guid God, what's happenin' to me? Am I losin' my mind?

"So you've received the blessing of a witch. See where that will get you, Highwayman!"

The words of a man Brodie recognized as Michael

Kelly, who'd been the toady of Brodie's now-dead arch enemy Joseph Carmody, forced him back to the moment. Kelly had been injured in the same battle in which Brodie and his friends had put an end to Carmody's tyranny in the region. As a result, he bore a paralyzed arm and a bitter desire for revenge.

"You'd best be keepin' your great mouth shut, Kelly." Brodie's hands clenched into fists, but he managed to restrain himself.

Not in front of the lad. Michael Kelly is only one big-mouthed bit of horse manure in a town that respects me and Harry for freeing them from Carmody.

"Brodie, you took a great risk, man." One of the townsmen stepped forward. "Louisa Abbott is a sorceress, pure and simple. She has friends among the Indians and uses their heathen brews and potions."

"She burned her husband and a whole ship full of people! Burned them all to ashes, then walked back to her cabin, cool as a winter's frost!" Kelly wasn't about to cease his accusations.

"Whit!" Brodie swung to face the dirty, bearded man. Since Carmody's defeat, Kelly had taken to the bottle and had become a drunk about the village.

"Aye, it's true. Set the vessel *Blue Lady* ablaze with all aboard! Tell him, lads!"

"You're forgetting to mention that ship was flying a yellow flag to indicate there was disease aboard when it sailed up the river." Angus Harper came out of his store as he spoke. "The woman's husband, Dr. Abbott, was the only one brave enough to go out to see if he could help. The next morning when Mrs. Abbott rowed out in search of her man, she discovered all aboard, including the doctor, dead. She did the only thing she could to protect this village. She set the ship ablaze and rowed back to shore."

"A sound alternative to buryin' when there's fear of contagion." Brodie was familiar with the practice.

"A heathen alternative!" Kelly yelled. "A witch's alternative!"

"Argh!" Brodie swung back to his wagon. "You're the heathens, to go condemnin' an innocent woman."

"Then explain why she ran away." Kelly moved close in front of Brodie and thrust his raggedly bearded face up at him, his liquor-fouled breath all but taking Brodie's away. "She left the village a week later. She moved out somewhere into the bush...no one knows where or dares to find out."

"Aye," another chimed in. "We don't want to know. We're just glad she's gone and won't trouble us but twice a year when she comes in to buy supplies...and mail off packages of papers aboard Captain Joe Duffy's ship. It's been said she ships spells and incantations to witches across the ocean."

"You're all a superstitious bunch of old women." With a harsh guffaw, Brodie turned back to his wagon. "This is the year of our Lord eighteen-thirteen, not some deep, dark recess of the past. The French have declared enlightenment is burstin' over the world, and we'd best embrace it. Come on, lad, let's finish unloadin' this lot and purchase the supplies your mother needs. We'll gain nothing by listenin' to such nonsense. Witch, indeed!"

He pulled a sack from the wagon and deposited it over the young lad's shoulder. Although he managed to hide it, the villagers' accusations had left a disquietedness buzzing like a bee in his brain.

****

Soon the team of Clydesdales was pulling the wagon filled with casks of sugar and molasses, along with containers of salt, tea, and other necessities, back to the farm where he lived with his friend Harry Wallace, Harry's wife Margaret, and the couple's seven stepchildren. As he held the reins, Brodie found himself engulfed in thoughts of the beautiful woman the villagers had branded a witch. She'd stirred something deep within him, something he couldn't fathom. Of course there was the usual male reaction to a beautiful woman, but it was more. She'd left him with a restlessness of spirit that had him wondering if or when he might see her again…in fact, longing for such a meeting.

"Uncle Brodie, do you believe she's a witch?" The young lad seated beside him broke in on his thoughts. "She doesn't look like what I thought a witch would. I thought she'd be like you said—ugly as sin, with green skin and a great wart on her nose, and dressed in ragged black, and…"

"And ridin' on a broomstick?" Brodie forced himself out of his thoughts and turned to Samuel, who was staring up at him with wide, questioning eyes. "Aye, well, maybe witches in tales told by superstitious old women around a fireside on a winter's night might be as such, but that's the point. They're only in stories. Now"—he handed the reins over to Samuel—"I've a mind to take a wee nap. You take over."

Knowing how the boy loved to drive the team, Brodie relinquished control of Bonnie and Prince. It might distract Samuel from fanciful thoughts of sorceresses and leave Brodie time to mull over his memories of the beautiful, mysterious Louisa Abbott.

"Folks say she pays in gold, Uncle Brodie." The lad wasn't so easily letting go of his witch thoughts as he took over from his uncle. "Gold she conjured. She paid you in gold. I saw it."

"Folks can spin a tale much easier than the lass can make legal tender out of straw." Brodie pulled his cap down over his forehead and crossed his arms on his chest. He closed his eyes. Pretending to sleep might end Samuel's questions, but it wouldn't bring Brodie MacMillan rest. Visions of that beautiful, ethereal woman haunted his thoughts.

For a while they drove in silence. Then the boy spoke again, this time cautiously.

"Uncle Brodie?"

"Ummm?" He feigned drowsiness.

"Jonah Parsons told me a story before the witch—the woman with the white horse—came into town, when you went to the inn to wait for Mr. Harper to tally up our load."

"Oh, aye?" *Damn Jonah Parsons! Why did the man have to follow Harry and me here from the Old Country after he overheard our plan to escape to Riverhaven? We've warned him about spreading tales of our antics when we were rebels for the Scottish cause. What can he have been telling the lad now?*

"He said"—Samuel lowered his voice, although passing through the woods he was unlikely to have eavesdroppers—"he said that once, when a rebel was about to be hanged by the British, you and Father rode into the village where the condemned man stood on the scaffold. Father fired his pistol into the air while his mare Scotia kicked and bucked about, sending the onlookers scattering. Then you rode like a blessed fury toward the scaffold and flung your sword. It flew through the air as if it was enchanted and cut the rope. In the blink of an eye, the prisoner threw himself over your stallion's withers, you snatched up your sword from where it had landed on the boards, and the man, you, and Father escaped, yelling a victory cry for the Scots. That's how you got the name Brazen Brodie. Is it true, Uncle Brodie? Did you and Father do such a bold deed?"

Bloody hell! The boy is lookin' up at me, his eyes round as saucers, and, I fear, with more than a trace of wonder and hero-worship in them. The tale is half-assed true, but I don't want him to think such behavior is acceptable, not in this country, at least. Harry and me, we're done with being rebels.

"You mustn't go believin' everything Jonah Parsons tells you, laddie. Just because he knew us when your father and I rode for the Scottish cause doesn't mean everything he says is gospel."

"He said Father was known as Highland Harry and that you and him were the most notorious rebels of all. He said the British could never catch you, and he said…"

"All tales told around campfires and best forgotten." Brodie returned to his pretense of sleeping. "Harry Wallace and his wife were good enough to take on your family of seven after your birth parents passed. They're your father and mother now, and both fine people. That's all you have to know. Now urge these great beasts to a trot, or we'll not get home in time for supper."

He hoped his words had quelled the boy's curiosity

about the two men the lad respected most in his life. But as he cautiously peered from under a half-opened eyelid, he saw Samuel's face bright with excitement and knew he hadn't. He didn't want the lad to go spreading tales about Harry and himself or glorifying an outlaw way of life. He'd have to have Harry speak to the lad.

****

He was glad when they drove to the top of the rise above the valley that held the saw and grist mills that were integral to the family's business, glad to look across the dammed stream that offered power for both enterprises, to see the big log house and barn on the opposite hill. It was good to have a secure place to call home after so many years of running from the law, to be a millwright again and a partner with Harry Wallace, a man he regarded as his brother, if not in blood most definitely in spirit.

Samuel loosened his hold on the reins, and the team, sensing they were nearing home, food, and a comfortable stable, broke into a trot. Before they descended into the valley, Brodie glanced to the left at his own small homestead, at the log cabin and barn he'd built across from the family farm buildings on the opposite hilltop. He had hopes that someday he'd live there with a woman he loved, that he'd have children of his own, that he'd no longer have to go on sharing a family with the former companion of his outlaw days, the man once known as the notorious Highland Harry.

****

"Mother, Father, you should have seen Uncle Brodie!" Samuel burst into the log house. "He helped the witch load her wagon, sold her some of our flour and oats, and then made everyone move out of the way so she could leave town! He wasn't afeard or nothing!"

"Hold on, laddie, hold on." Harry Wallace raised a quieting hand from his place in a rocking chair by the fire while his wife turned from peeling potatoes at the counter. "Witch?" He looked questioningly at Brodie, who'd followed the boy into the room.

"Just a lass alone." Brodie removed his jacket, hung it on a peg by the door, and unbuckled his sword belt to place it beside it. "Some of the folks in the village were makin' a bit of a stir about her being some kind of unusual being."

He crossed the room and sank into the chair opposite his friend. He enjoyed coming back to the big log house that was home to Harry, Margaret, the children, and himself. Tonight, with the hearth giving off a welcome warmth in the chill November evening and the smell of supper wafting from pots hanging over the fire, he was especially pleased to be there. He looked over at his friend and again marveled at the change that had come over this former Highland rogue.

Harry Wallace, although changing his profession and settling down to be father to seven stepchildren and husband to former tavern worker Maggie, had lost none of his exceptional handsomeness or charismatic charm. At over six feet tall, broad of shoulder and chest, and narrow of waist, his hair a tangle of black curls, Harry Wallace was still a man who could capture a woman's eye and inspire admiration in men.

"Unusual being?" Maggie Wallace approached, rubbing her hands on her apron. "What do you mean 'unusual'?" Beginning to show signs of her pregnancy, Margaret, as Harry and Brodie called her, was a beautiful woman with her chestnut hair and lovely face.

"A witch, Mother!" Samuel cavorted around her. "Uncle Brodie helped her load her wagon and even sold her some of our flour and oatmeal! He made everyone move aside so she could drive out of the village! And then she put a blessing on him!"

"A blessin', was it?" The corners of Harry Wallace's mouth quirked with humor, his Highland inflection coming to the fore as it always did when he was angry or amused. "Hardly sounds like an evil bein' to me, does it, Mother?" He looked up at his wife.

"Don't tease the boy." Maggie Wallace put a calming arm around her youngest stepson's shoulders. "Samuel, what kind of a witch would bless your uncle?"

"Aye, your mother's right. A real witch would curse him right and sure." Harry chuckled.

"Stop encouraging the boy." Maggie frowned over at her husband. "Samuel, you know we've taught you there are no such things as witches and goblins and the like."

"But Father has told me how Highlanders plant rowan trees at their front gates to keep the fairies away and set out saucers of milk to keep them in good humor." Samuel gazed up at his mother, blue eyes wide.

"Harry, you didn't!" Maggie gave her husband an admonishing glare.

"Margaret, we agreed to teach the children about their Highland heritage…the place from which their blood parents came, not to mention their stepfather and uncle. Superstition and folklore are part of it."

"Harry, Harry." With an exasperated sigh, she

turned and went back to preparing vegetables.

"Now, lad, what did this supposed witch look like?" Harry put a hand on the boy's shoulder as he came to stand beside his father's chair. "Ugly as sin? Bone thin and green skinned?"

"Noooo." Samuel paused thoughtfully. "She had hair much the color of Uncle Brodie's stallion Fox. And she was like Mother, real pretty and not too fat or too thin."

Brodie caught the blush spreading up the side of Maggie's face he could see.

"Ah-ha!" Harry leaned back in his chair and grinned over at his friend. "A fair sorceress. Small wonder your uncle was so all-fired eager to help her out. I think you've no need to be concerned, laddie. Your uncle was only playin' the gallant to a fine figure of a woman. If she bestowed a blessin' on him, it just goes to show she has the rare taste to return the interest. Now run down to the barn and get your brothers to help you with unloading the wagon and stabling the team. I'm assuming neither chore has been done, since you two came into the house so soon after we heard you driving up."

"Yes, Father." The boy's lack of enthusiasm reflected in his words as he turned toward the door.

"And be smart about it, Sam. Your mother has a fine supper all but ready," he called after the young lad as he went out.

"Mother, I'm afeard." Three-year-old Eppie came out of the bedroom, the doll Harry had given her in the summer clutched in her arms, her pet dwarf pig Precious snuffling along beside her. "I heard Samuel talking about witches, and it scared me."

14

"Nothing to be afraid of, my darling." Margaret smiled at the child. "Samuel was only telling tales, like the ones in the books Father reads to you. Isn't that right, Father?" She frowned an admonition at Harry.

"Oh, aye," Harry replied, gathering his youngest stepdaughter into a hug. "You know your uncle and I will never let anything harm you. Now, you'd best run upstairs and put your baby to bed. She's looking right sleepy to me."

"All right." She wriggled out of his embrace and headed up the steps. "But I'll be down soon. I'm hungry."

"So you've met yourself a beautiful woman." After she'd gone, Harry stood and went to the shelves above the dresser to take down a flask. "I'd say a wee dram is in order to celebrate the event."

"Harry..." Maggie shot a brief frown in his direction.

"All right, all right, Margaret, I'll lay off the teasing." Her husband took a pair of tankards from the cupboard and poured a measure into each. "But you'll agree we both wish happiness for our brother."

"Yes, indeed we do." Maggie turned to face the two men as Harry returned to his place by the hearth and handed a drink to Brodie. "But I hardly think someone the villagers have branded a witch is an appropriate choice."

"Margaret, Margaret, it's but a bit of backwoods superstition. You know it as well as I do." Harry took a sip and bared his teeth before continuing. "A beautiful woman is a beautiful woman and not to be ignored...at least not until some devilish flaw in her character appears to blacken her charms."

"Lady Annabelle Spencer was a beautiful woman, was she not?" Maggie faced the pair of them, hands on her hips, her expression remonstrative. "If I recall correctly, she very nearly succeeded in getting the pair of you hanged in England before you escaped to New Brunswick."

"Dunnae go raking up old tales, Margaret love." Harry looked down into his mug and swirled the amber liquid about. "Long ago, far away, and best forgotten."

"Not as forgotten as we'd hoped, Hamish." Alone with Harry and his wife, Brodie dared to use the Christian name with which his friend had been christened in the Highlands. He proceeded to reveal what Jonah Parsons had told Samuel.

"Bloody hell!" The words came from Harry in a muttered curse. "Jonah Parsons is a good man, a man who helped us out of one of the closest calls of our lives, but he's got a blabbin' mouth."

"I have to admit I like the fanciful spin the old beggar put on the tale." Brodie shook his head, a corner of his mouth twitching. "That part about me flingin' my sword through the air as though it were enchanted, to cut the hangman's rope, then ridin' close enough to the scaffold to collect that ne'er-do-well brother of his who was about to be hanged was quite the yarn. I still wonder about the wisdom of our makin' that rescue. Jem Parsons was a dyed-in-the-wool poacher. I reckon he went right back to his trade the very next day."

"What actually happened?" Margaret's expression told him she couldn't refrain from asking even though she'd said she never wanted to know of their harrowing escapades back in the Old Country.

"Brodie rode into the square where they'd

constructed the scaffold, Fox running as if he had wings on his hooves." Harry chuckled. "He leaped onto the platform and, with a single swipe, cut the hangman's rope. I'd followed close behind, leading a pair of horses for him and the prisoner. They leaped onto them, and we escaped. Fox found us later."

"Thus the legend of Brazen Brodie was born." She heaved a sigh.

"Aye, aye, most of it." Harry Wallace drew himself up in his chair and looked over at his wife. "Apparently there's no easy rubbing it from our history. This incident has made it clear. Some day soon we'll have to call all the children together, tell them the truth, and swear them to silence on the matter. It's only fair they hear the facts...from us. What do you say, Margaret?"

"I suppose. I admit I'd be interested, as well. I only know you two were rebels in Scotland. A few details would be helpful."

"Aye, well, a few details." Harry dropped his gaze to the whisky in his mug.

"At any rate, Brodie"—Maggie returned to her supper preparations—"I thought you were going to ask Morag Green to the basket social at the church this coming Sabbath."

"Aye, well, I'll best be workin' up my courage before I do that." Brodie quaffed his drink, stood, and placed his mug on the table. "That mother of hers *is* a witch if ever there was one. She'll not easily allow her only child to go gallivantin' with the likes of me."

"Speak to her father." Harry offered words of advice. "Duncan Green is a reasonable man. I don't see him going against something Morag, the apple of his eye, seriously desires. If you're lucky, laddie, that might include you."

"Aye, well, we'll see." Brodie headed for the door. "I hear a deal of laughin' and teasin' goin' on in the yard, but not the sounds of unloadin'. I reckon Samuel is entertainin' his brothers with more witch tales. I'd best be puttin' a fire under those young lads."

He went into the yard, where Harry and Margaret's other three stepsons, eighteen-year-old James, George (Geordie), sixteen, and Robert, fourteen, were helping Samuel unload the wagon amid a barrage of teasing about the witch. He'd have to step in and warn them against spreading tales to their sisters Isabella (Bella), age twelve, and Elizabeth (Lizzie), age ten, and especially not to talk such nonsense to their baby sister Eppie.

****

As they sat at the supper table, Brodie glanced around at the group seated about its length. A wonderful family of four boys, three girls, and two amazing stepparents who'd taken on their care after the deaths of both their birth parents. Margaret, barely twenty years of age, was mothering this lot as if they were her own. Harry, the former outlaw, in his early thirties, was proving a steadfast father to the brood. Brodie hoped the one Harry and Margaret were to have in the spring would bring them all the joy they both deserved.

Much as he cared for this family, he wanted one of his own. Each night, after the children had gone to bed upstairs, a deep longing washed over him as he wished Harry and Margaret goodnight and watched them go into their room, softly closing the door after them. Sometimes he'd linger a while, watching the flames on the hearth, before banking the fire for the night and going into the cubicle off the kitchen that held his bed and belongings. Often, after he'd shucked his clothing and got between the blankets, he'd lie awake for hours. Hard work and weariness weren't enough to overcome the feeling of loneliness and need gnawing at his innards.

"Hey, Uncle Brodie, you look dazed." Geordie brought him out of his meanderings. "Not enchanted, are you?"

"That's enough." Margaret stopped the trend of conversation. "Lizzie, will you fetch the apple pies? They're from the last of the fresh apples we'll have this year."

****

Hands on his hips, Brodie watched the great wheels of the grist mill wind to a noisy halt. Outside, Duncan Green was loading the last of his flour and ground oats onto his wagon while his daughter Morag held the team quiet.

Come on, Brodie lad. It's now or never. Screw up your courage and approach the man.

He lifted his chaff-whitened cap to slap it against his dusty shirt and thighs. Sucking in a deep breath, he headed outside. As he passed the wagon, he touched his forelock and favored the pretty, dark-haired girl with what he hoped was his most affable grin. She smiled shyly before ducking her head and turning back to focus her attention on the team.

"Mr. Green, sir, might I have a private word?" He grasped the last bag of oats and swung it onto the man's wagon.

"I suppose." He straightened from his labor to

squint at Brodie in the declining rays of the cold November day. "But you'll have to make it snappy. It's late, and my wife will be expecting us home."

"I promise to be quick about it." Knowing what a harridan the man had married, Brodie understood. "If you'd mind just steppin' off a bit, sir." He inclined his head to indicate Morag.

"Very well."

Brodie caught the older man glancing at him warily as they walked side by side out of the young woman's earshot.

"It's about your daughter, sir." Brodie wet dry lips and fought the urge to fidget.

"Oh, aye?" This time outright suspicion tinged the two words.

"Well, you see, sir, there's a church social comin' up, and I'd be honored if you'd allow me to invite her."

This time it was the farmer who drew a deep breath. He looked off across the mill pond at the farm beyond. For the longest hiatus Brodie believed he'd ever experienced, the man didn't reply.

"Well, sir?" Finally Brodie couldn't wait any longer. "You said you had to get home, and I'd like your answer. That is, if you're prepared to give one," he finished more humbly.

"Well, you see, Brodie, it's like this." Shuffling his feet, Duncan Green avoided looking at the younger man. "I know you're a good man...a good man who together with Harry Wallace and his family rid this valley of the plague of Joseph Carmody. And we're all grateful. It's just that..."

"It's just that whit?"

"Well, there're stories going around—I'm sure you

know the ones I mean—stories about how you and Harry Wallace were outlaws back in the Old Country. Now..." He held up a hand as Brodie made to protest. "I know you've been upright since we've known you, but I'm not sure I want my girl associating with a man who might have been a bandit, who might some day be taken to task for offenses back across the sea."

"Guid God, man, I'm askin' to take her to a social, not marry her!" Brodie could restrain his annoyance no longer. "I'm not about to make her a bandit's bride!"

"Brodie, you are living with Harry Wallace—some say he was once Highland Harry—and his wife, who was a tavern girl. Now I know..." Duncan Green again silenced Brodie with an upheld hand as he attempted to protest. "Wallace has become our magistrate, and you and him did this valley a big favor in getting rid of Joseph Carmody, but be honest. If the pair of you hadn't had lots of experience as fighting men, you couldn't have done it. And don't get me started on your friends the minister and his wife. People are getting right suspicious about that pair. Their past would make an interesting tale, I've no doubt." Duncan Green turned to go back to his wagon.

"Just a minute!" Brodie's hand shot out to grab the older man by the arm. "You can defame me all you like, but I take right exception to you bad-mouthin' my friends."

"I'll thank you to take your hand off of me, Mr. MacMillan." Blanching as he faced the reputed outlaw, Duncan Green's jaw jerked in a frightened tick.

"Sorry." Brodie backed off.

"Aye, well, you should be." Regaining courage at Brodie's softened attitude, the man snapped at him.

21

"And if you ever dare come near my daughter, I'll see to it your magistrate friend claps you in his jail!"

The man strode back to his wagon, swung up beside his daughter, and took the reins. Snapping the leather lines over the team's rumps with a vehemence Brodie recognized as out of character for the generally mild-mannered farmer, Duncan Green urged the pair of horses away from the mill.

"Get on there, Peg! Move your great hooves, Brownie!" he yelled at the team. Lurching forward under the harshness of the commands, they broke into a shambling trot in spite of the loaded wagon behind them.

Brodie watched as they drove away from the mill. Sitting up straight and prim on the seat beside her father, her hands gripping the boards beneath her, Morag Green stared ahead. No backward glance, no day-brightening smile, no farewell wave such as he'd received from the woman the villagers had branded a witch. This one was too afraid of her father to do any such thing. Could he seriously consider such a spiritless creature as a wife? Maybe it was best he'd been rejected as a suitor. Nevertheless, Duncan Green's appraisal left him chaffed to the core.

"Old bastard." He rounded into the mill. "I'm good enough to grind his wheat and saw his lumber, but not good enough to take his daughter to a church social…or to even allow her to give me a backward glance."

"Look at yourself, laddie." Harry, who'd been finishing up tasks inside the structure, came to join him in time to catch his muttered reproof and chuckled. "Ye're coated from head to toe with chaff. You look like a bloody ghost. Maybe if you cleaned up and tried again…"

"Aye, and maybe if I learned to curb my temper…"

"Good God, man, what did you say?" Harry stared at him.

"Harry, he started talkin' about us…and your family…and Margaret…and even Lachlan and Iona, implyin' we weren't much better than a band of outlaws!"

"And you couldn't let that pass…even though most of it's true? You know the suspicions most people around here have of us. Although they're grateful for what we did for them in ridding them of Joe Carmody, they're not yet ready to forget the rumors."

"You can afford to be smug." Brodie went to attend to the great wheel that only minutes before had ceased its deafening grind. "You have Margaret and seven fine stepbairns, not to mention another of your own on the way."

"Man, you couldn't be more right. Margaret and the children have brought me happiness I never thought possible." He slapped Brodie on the shoulder. "Friend and boon companion, I can wish nothing less for you."

"My chances for such aren't great, Harry. You and I both know it. Much as I hate to admit it, Duncan Green was right. A respectable girl like Morag has no business gettin' tied up with a bandit."

"Brodie, that's behind us." Harry Wallace blocked his way and faced him. "We're respected and respectable members of this community. If you'll just be keeping your nose clean, that opinion will continue."

"You're still chaffin' about that wee foray I made on my first night stayin' on your farm." Brodie's mouth quirked at a corner. "Well, that old bastard Joseph

Carmody had sent his band of bastards to attack your family and home. He deserved to have his place raided."

"Aye, well, he's dead now, and I'm the local magistrate." Harry had to suppress a grin to look sternly at his affable friend. "Your breaking into his house and vandalizing his property on your first day in this country was hardly the way to start a new and lawful life. I don't want you being brought before me on charges of mischief or worse."

"Never fear, Hamish. I'm wantin' a home, a wife, and bairns in my future. Outlaws don't qualify for such."

"You need to get married again, laddie." Harry looked at his friend through the haze of dust lingering from the day's grinding. "Much as Margaret and I enjoy your sharing our home, you deserve a wife and bairns of your own. You must forget the past and move on."

"Aye, forget the past." The all-too-familiar sensation wrenched at his heart as the words brought back images of his wife…beautiful, full-of-life Annie, who'd died with the baby she'd been carrying in that god-awful fire that had destroyed their mill in Scotland, the mill she'd been desperately trying to save. Annie and their child, buried under the heather on a far distant hillside.

"I'm right sorry I used those words." Harry came to stand beside him and put a hand on his shoulder.

"Not your fault, Hamish." Brodie drew a deep breath as he struggled back to the moment.

"It was, and we both know it. If you and she hadn't taken pity on me when I was wounded, hadn't taken me in and hidden me until I was well, the redcoats never

24

would have come to your mill, never would have set it ablaze while you were away, and Annie wouldn't have died. Now the only way I can see to help you heal is to assist you to find love again. You're still in your prime, lad. Don't bury yourself just yet. Annie wouldn't want you to. We both know it."

"You're right. She loved life."

"Well, then." Harry slapped him on a shoulder. "Onward and upwards, eh? Right now that means up the hill to the house and supper."

"You go along, Harry. There are a few details I have to see to first. I'll follow directly."

Harry paused to look at his friend with narrowed eyes.

"Verrae well. But mind you do some thinking on what I've said. You're not my brother by blood, but I love you as such, Brodie MacMillan, and so does my family. Behave yourself, and everything will come out right. You'll see."

After his friend had gone, Brodie sat down on a battered stool and put his head in his hands.

"You need to get married." Harry's words echoed in his mind. Being allowed to share Harry and Margaret's lives and that of their growing family meant the world to him, but he was barely past thirty and, much as he tried to deny the fact, he had desires, desires that hadn't been satisfied for too long a time.

He was glad that with the help of Harry and his stepsons he'd been able to build a cabin and a stable on the hill above the mill, across the valley from his friend's home, over the past few weeks. Rudimentary though this small homestead was, it represented a beginning...a beginning of his making a life for himself in this new country. A respectable life. But he did have needs.

Morag Green had all the beauty a man could desire—blue-black curls piled in a mass on her head with a few errant bits escaping to touch a creamy cheek, big blue eyes demure and shy and more than a bit timid. Once, when he'd tried to steal a chaste kiss, she'd shied away like a frightened filly. She constantly looked to her parents when a decision had to be made, even in the smallest matters. He shook his head. No, Morag Green definitely wasn't what he needed in a wife.

He leaned back against the rough boards of the gristmill wall and heaved a sigh.

So what is it you'd want in the perfect wife, Brodie MacMillan? Well, I won't knock pretty off the list, but there are other requirements more to the point. Spirit, that's what she'd have to have, be a bit of a challenge with a mind of her own. She'd have to be clever, with a brain that can solve problems. Courageous and strong...ready to be my partner in all ways. And accepting. Not afraid to wed a man with a murky past. She'd have to want children, my children, and be a faithful wife and loving mother. Hell and damnation, I've just described Margaret!

He stopped short. *No, not someone exactly like Margaret. She'd have to be a bit of a rogue, someone who cared little for the conventions of society, who'd not be concerned with what the neighbor ladies thought. Someone who enjoys music as much as I do, someone who could ride like the wind beside me on a mount as spirited as my own stallion Fox.*

He paused a moment, reflecting. *Aw, what the hell. May as well finish this impossible wife wish list. It would be a right treat if she could cook and keep a decent house and enjoy a good roll in the hay.*

Above the mill a crow cawed. Its harsh cry brought Brodie out of his reverie.

As reality returned, he halted his fanciful ideas. *Stop dreaming, laddie. An outlaw such I once was has about as much chance of findin' that kind of lass, never mind gettin' her to agree to marry me, as I do of findin' a snowball in July!*

He stood, rolled weary shoulders, gave his shirt and breeches a few slaps in a vain attempt to rid himself of mill dust, and went out, barring the door behind him. As he started up the hill in the twilight, toward the log house, a thought struck him, and he stopped short. He'd felt nothing when Morag Green had failed to look back at him. Well, not nothing. A dash of repulsion that the young woman had not had sufficient courage to defy her father and wave a smiling farewell. Now, when Louisa Abbott had glanced back at him...

You're meanderin' again, laddie. The woman's gone, and accordin' to the villagers, there won't be another chance of seein' her until spring. Best put Louisa Abbott out of your mind.

He lengthened his strides up the hill, the cold November wind cutting like a knife. *Snow soon.* There'd be more than enough work to prepare for winter around the place to keep his thoughts occupied away from the woman the community of Riverhaven had branded a witch.

Nevertheless, that night, his dreams were haunted by the image of a woman with golden red hair and the face of an angel, a hint of mystery in green eyes that had the power to enchant him.

Chapter Two

After leaving the village of Riverhaven on the day she'd met Brodie MacMillan, Louisa Abbott drove her white mare back to her homestead deep in the woods. She'd allowed Snow to take her time. Although the day was damp and cold, she wouldn't rush the horse. The mare might be large for a saddle animal, but she was small by draft standards, and the load was heavy. Much as Louisa longed for home and the comforts of a fire and food, she had to be mindful of this willing, faithful creature.

The pace gave her time to think, to reflect on the tall, broad-shouldered, sandy-haired man with the handsome countenance and affable grin. For no other apparent reasons aside from what appeared to be kindness and concern, he'd taken her part in the village. She appreciated his effort. And no man had looked at her like that since Neil. Her husband's memory sent a shiver around her heart.

Neil, her husband, her lover, a fine-looking figure of a man, strong and brave, kind and clever. Neil, her partner in life. In the two years since he'd passed, he'd been so often in her thoughts she frequently had to fight to keep memories at bay, to stop them from driving her into despair, to avoid their keeping her from necessary work. And their child...but she couldn't bear to go further down that road.

The cold dampness in the air threatened a frosty night. She flapped the reins over Snow's back to urge her to a brisker walk. At her homestead, there'd be work to do, work that would take her mind off the past—and the near past, which included the man she'd encountered in Riverhaven.

****

When she drove into the clearing that surrounded her cabin and barn, a large white wolf leaped to his feet where she'd left him chained to the verandah and began to bark.

"Jasper." She halted Snow and jumped to the ground. "I trust you've done your usual fine job of guarding the place." She went up the steps to free him of his bond. She disliked restraining him, but if she hadn't he'd have followed her into the village. His chances there of being shot as a wolf or perhaps even a creature of the witch's creation were all too probable.

She knelt to hug the animal and receive his licking greeting. He'd been her loyal companion and protector for months. Shortly after she'd moved to the isolated farm, he'd arrived at her doorstep bleeding profusely from wounds that looked as if he'd been in a battle with wolves or a bear. She'd administered as heavy a dose of laudanum as she dared, sewed him up, and he'd survived to become her devoted companion. Now whenever she had to leave the homestead, he guarded it with a vehemence no reasonable creature would challenge.

"You must be hungry, Jasper." She went to her mare's drooping head and gave her a pat on the neck. "You, as well, Snow. As soon as I unload the wagon, I'll see to you both."

As she began to heave sacks of supplies up onto the cabin's verandah, she shook her head. Talking to her animals. Perhaps she was becoming weird, as weird as the witch the villagers had branded her.

She dropped a bag of flour onto the planks in front of the door. Did it matter? Her heart had died with Neil and the baby they planned to name Charlotte if a girl and Lachlan if a boy.

"Louisa." Startled, she whirled at the sound of her name, then relaxed into a smile as a woman dressed in buckskins, long black hair hanging in a plait over her shoulder, came out of the trees beside her cabin. On her back, she carried an infant.

"Marie, how nice to see you. I couldn't ask for a better homecoming. Go into the house, and we'll have tea as soon as I see to Snow." She threw the last of her provisions onto the verandah and reached to take the horse's bridle.

"I'd offer to assist you, but I've a feeling my best help can be having water on the boil by the time you've finished. You look as if you could use a hot drink."

"How well you know me, Marie," she called back over her shoulder as she began to lead the horse and wagon toward the log barn behind the cabin. "I've brought lots of sugar, so we can make it as sweet as we choose."

As she stabled her mare, she recalled the day she'd first met Marie. The young native woman had been wandering near Louisa's homestead in search of roots and herbs when she'd been overtaken by labor pains. She'd stumbled to Louisa's doorstep. It had been a breech birth, frightening and exhausting for both women, but somehow Louisa had managed to deliver

Marie of a fine, healthy boy. As a result, a deep and lasting friendship had been formed.

At first Louisa had been amazed at the young woman's fluency in English tinged with a Scottish accent. It had been explained after the child's birth when Marie had told her she'd had a Scottish father and a native mother. Her father had lived with her band for years, going west in search of furs in season, until one spring he didn't return. News had finally reached Marie and her mother that he'd died of a fever. Shortly afterwards, Marie's mother had passed, and the girl had gone to live with her grandmother, a woman reputed to make miraculous cures with her medicines.

When she was seventeen, Marie caught the interest of a young brave known as Runner because of his ability to travel long distances at amazing speeds. He carried messages between bands and sometimes for white settlers. He'd come to live with Marie and her grandmother. A year later the child Louisa had delivered had arrived. In gratitude for what he regarded as Louisa's saving the life of his wife and child, Runner had vowed to see that she would always be supplied with game and fish and that no harm would come to her.

He'd been as good as his word. Moose meat, venison, rabbits, partridge, wild geese, trout, and even salmon had consistently appeared on her doorstep and in her ice house at the back of her property. She paused in the stable doorway and looked out over her small homestead with a certain sense of pride.

Yes, Louisa Abbott, you're doing very well. You can take pride in surviving on your own.

She squared her shoulders and headed toward the

log cabin, eager for a chat with her native friend. Although she was comfortable with the solitude the isolated homestead provided, which facilitated the writing by which she made a living, she enjoyed Marie's visits. These generally included sharing tea steeped in a cherished china pot she'd brought across the Atlantic and bread toasted over the fire.

Remembering how their friendship had developed, she recalled the young native taking her to visit her grandmother. Seated on the ground in the old woman's dwelling, Louisa had listened as Marie translated the elder's wisdom concerning healing herbs and roots. While she appreciated this sharing of knowledge and carefully recorded the details in her husband's medical journal when she returned to her cabin, Louisa was too astute to believe the medicine woman was telling her everything. Some secrets weren't for sharing with this white woman. At least, not yet.

Entering the cabin, Louisa found Marie carefully pouring steaming water from a kettle into the treasured teapot. It occupied a safe place in the middle of the table, which had been set with a pair of mugs, a small jug of sugar, and a plate of sliced, buttered bread.

"Ah, just what I need after a long, cold drive. Thank you, Marie." Louisa hastened to pull off her outerwear and hang it on a peg by the door.

"I do enjoy tea." Marie put the cover on the pot. "What our band serves as such is made from roots and leaves, not nearly as lovely and satisfying as this." She breathed in the aroma rising from the spout.

"Your father introduced you to different tastes." Louisa smiled over at the baby sleeping on his cradle board on a bed of spruce boughs covered with a blanket in the corner. "How is Runner?"

"He's off on a mission from our band to one many miles to the south. I hope he'll be home soon. Our child needs his father."

"I'm so happy for you." Turning away from the child, Louisa struggled to suppress a small dash of jealousy that tingled in her heart. She missed Neil so very much, she missed having a man of her very own, a father for children…

"You do know that Runner was our first friend among your people." She tried to change the course of her thoughts. "It was Runner who introduced Neil to your band, who convinced them to share some of their medicines and healing ways with him. It was Runner who helped me fill the ice house with frozen blocks from the stream last winter. It was Runner who has provided game to stock it even back then, even before he was trying to repay me for delivering his son."

"Runner said he can never do enough for the man who gave his grandmother medicine that eased her pain as she was leaving this life, medicine that made her passing peaceful. He will always owe a debt to the man…and now his woman."

"Yes, I remember," Louisa said, her voice soft with remembrance as she recalled Neil taking doses of laudanum to the elderly lady suffering from a terrible tumor. "He wanted to do more, but it was too late."

She stood and went to the cupboard. "My larder is well stocked, and I have stores enough to see me through the winter. That calls for a small celebration. I have a jar of honey left from the summer. I think we should make this day special by putting some on our bread."

Chapter Three

"Brodie, I need a wee favor." Harry approached his friend, rubbing cold hands together. The late November wind chafed at the six men working in the barnyard. Brodie had been helping three of Harry's stepsons to load saws, peaveys, and other paraphernalia needed for the coming winter's cutting into the farm wagon. At a grindstone nearby, sixteen-year-old Geordie sharpened axes. Preparations were at fever pitch. They'd all be leaving for the lumber camp back in the hinterland to start cutting timber in three days.

"Aye?" Brodie paused in checking the heavy harness the team would need to skid logs out of the bush and down to the edge of the stream. In spring, when warming temperatures freed the brook from ice and flushed it with the freshet of melting snow, the boys would dump the piles of logs into the fast-running water to send them rushing downstream.

"Margaret has a mighty craving for salted herring." He drew a deep breath and grinned. "This being with child has given her some rare desires. She says she'll be washing it down with buttermilk, if you can imagine such a mixture." He grimaced before continuing, "I'm needed here to help the boys—and to learn about this part of the operation, what with it being my first time involved. Would you ride into the village and get some for her? Also…" He paused.

"Whit?"

"Though I'm loathe to admit it, your stallion Fox is faster than my Scotia. The beast has been acting finicky of late, and Margaret says she feels she must have those fish right soon."

"Finally, you admit my animal is swifter than yours." Slapping his friend on the back, Brodie chuckled. "Verrae well, I'll be more than happy to go."

He headed into the barn, whistling.

****

"So what's all the cheer?" Brodie's vibrant stride as he entered Angus Harper's store reflected his mood. He liked the shopkeeper, and he'd just had a great run on Fox. He was in fine fettle.

"Not good, I'm afraid, Brodie." The big man placed his large, hirsute hands, palms down, on his scarred plank counter and leaned toward the newcomer. Even though the store was empty save for the two men, Angus lowered his voice when he continued, "Joe Carmody's daughter has arrived."

"Whit! No, no, man. You must be haverin'. The man wasn't married…"

His thoughts raced backwards. Joseph Carmody had been the bane of the area, forcing his will over residents, seizing mortgages on their homes, businesses, and farms, and indenturing everything and everyone in the small community. That summer Brodie, Harry, and Harry's family and friends had defeated Carmody in an all-out battle for supremacy. As a result, Joseph Carmody had died. Riverhaven and the surrounding district had believed itself forever free of the tyrant. This revelation sent a shock wave coursing over Brodie.

"That's what we all thought." Angus straightened

up and sucked in a deep breath. "But it turns out he had a wife in England who handled his business affairs over there but had no desire to come out to the wilds of New Brunswick...and at least one child, a daughter. She arrived three days ago with a cook, a maid servant, and two roughnecks dressed as gentlemen. I'd lay money that pair is nothing more than a couple of nasty blokes off the back streets of London, ready to do anything she asks of them for a price. She's taken up residence in Joe's mansion. Surely you must have noticed smoke coming from the chimneys as you rode in?"

"No, no. I was ridin' hard, hell-bent on gettin' back to the farm as soon as possible." Brodie squared his shoulders as he let this information settle in his mind. "How old might this lady be? I'm guessin' she's not a wee bairn."

"I've seen her only once, but I'd be betting she'd not be much beyond one and twenty. And haughty as a queen. She rode through the village yesterday on a fine horse—something she must have brought with her—with those two mean-faced bastards riding behind her like a guard of honor. She spoke to no one, just kept casting belittling looks left and right and holding up her head with such an appearance of disgust you'd think we all stank."

"Hell and damnation!" Brodie pulled off his cap and ran a hand through his sandy curls. *Harry and his family don't need this. Not after the summer they've just been through.*

"She can't do nothing, can she, Brodie?" Angus Harper's broad, red face furrowed. "Harry said what was ours is ours again, now that old Joe is dead."

"Dunnae greet, Angus. Harry and I took care of

everything. All will be well." Brodie forced himself to sound confident and unconcerned, but a bilious feeling had slithered into his gut. "Now, Margaret has a great cravin' for some of your salted herrin'. If you'll fetch me a few, I'll be on my way back to the farm."

"Of course, Brodie. For Maggie, only my best."

Reassured, the shopkeeper headed to the room at the rear of his establishment where barrels of salted meat and fish were kept. Apparently struck by another thought, he stopped and turned back.

"Do you know, that woman sent her two great louts in here, demanding a crate of my best oysters? When I told them I had but one left and was saving it for Christmas—I was planning to give it to you and Harry as a way of showing my gratitude for what you'd done—they pushed past me into the storeroom and took it. Laughing, they said to put it on Mistress Carmody's account and went out carrying it between them."

"Not to worry." Brodie forced a grin. "Although I've no doubt Harry and I would have enjoyed those shellfish, we'll be happy just to have a peaceful Christmas."

"We can but hope." With a sigh that raised his wide shoulders, Angus Harper continued on into his storeroom.

Drumming his fingers on its planks, Brodie leaned on the counter, unsettling thoughts filling his mind. He might have managed to quell Angus Harper's worries, but not his own. After Joseph Carmody's death, he and Harry had destroyed all the indenture and mortgage papers the despotic entrepreneur had held over residents. They'd freed the citizens from fear of seizure of their lands and the attempted collection of impossible debts by the man. Now, here was this woman declaring to be his daughter, with God only knew what thoughts for revenge in mind. He had to get back to the farm and Harry with this news.

****

Sack in hand, Brodie stepped out of the mercantile to face a group of villagers, worried frowns creasing their weathered faces.

"We heard you were in town, Brodie," one of them addressed him. "We need to know what you and Harry make of this woman's coming."

"Not to worry." He feigned nonchalance. "Harry Wallace told you all will be well, and so shall it be. Harry's word is his bond. Don't forget he's now magistrate of this area. He's the law. Go about your day. You're safe from any and all Carmody claims." He gathered up Fox's reins and stuck his foot into a stirrup. "Now, I'd best be gettin' on with my errand. I've promised to be back at the farm as fast as this beast can run. Come on, Fox, my lad." He swung into the saddle. "It's home and supper for both of us."

As he rode down the street and out onto the trail leading to the farm, he wished he felt as confident as his words to the shopkeeper and villagers had been. His thoughts traveled back to the night following Joseph Carmody's death in their mill pond, a drowning facilitated by Harry's eldest stepson James. He recalled how, under cover of darkness, he and Harry had ridden to the Carmody house on the edge of the village. Using skills acquired during their outlaw days, they'd gained entry and set to work to destroy all of the man's documents.

Harry and I burned everything in the way of old

Joe's papers. We destroyed anything of value, anything that could give his heirs claim over any of the people and property in this area. Harry doubted that Joe had filed copies of deeds or indenture papers with the government in Fredericton. The old bastard probably felt confident in the fact that his claims were safe in that strongbox in his office, Harry said. All it took was a few blows with an ax to open it. A right good fire on his hearth put an end to them.

As he passed the Carmody mansion on a rise at the edge of the village, Brodie looked for signs of residency. No one had lived there since the despot's death. Now columns of smoke rose from two of the chimneys.

The cold stillness of the day wrapped around him. He drew up the collar of his woolen coat and urged Fox into a lope. It would be dark soon. Night came early in November in this country.

****

He was several miles from the village when Fox skidded to a halt, shaking his head and dancing sideways.

"Aye, laddie, whit is it?" Brodie leaned over the horse's neck and spoke softly. "You've not behaved like this since there were redcoats in the vicinity." He glanced about apprehensively. The dusk of the autumn evening was casting long shadows out of the surrounding dark woods.

Then he saw her. By the side of the trail lay a woman in a black riding habit, dark curls spilling out among the frost-killed fern. Her eyes were closed.

"Guid God!" Brodie leaped from the saddle and ran to kneel beside her. "Lass, can you hear me?" He bent over her. "Lass!" He picked up a hand encased in an ebony leather glove and chafed her wrist.

Slowly she opened her eyes and gazed up at him. For a moment she stared blankly, then apparently coming back to her senses, she fought to sit up, brown eyes wide with what he saw as fear.

"Dunnae be afeard." Brodie's Highland brogue came out softly. "I'll no' do you harm. Lie still a minute while you catch your breath. Then we'll see about gettin' you on your feet."

"My-my horse…" she stammered. "Something scared my horse. He reared. I fell off."

"You're safe now." Brodie put an arm under her shoulders to raise her to a sitting position. "Do you think you might get up if I help you?"

"Perhaps." She grimaced.

"Nothing broken, I trust." Brodie remained down on one knee beside her. "If you can get to your feet, I'll put you on my horse and take you down to the village."

With his arm about her, she staggered upright, but once standing, collapsed against his chest.

"I can't…can't."

He swept her up into his arms, causing her to gasp. With the ease born of strong muscles, he placed her onto Fox, sidesaddle style. Once he felt confident she was balanced, he swung up behind her.

"Now, lass, we'll head into the village." He nudged Fox to a walk, his arms around her. "Where might you be staying?"

"In Joseph Carmody's house. I'm his daughter."

Sweet Jesus! Joe Carmody's daughter!

Shock made him all but release his arms from about her.

With a soft moan, she sank back against his chest. He caught a whiff of something seductively alluring. An impulse to bury his face in those soft, dark curls wafted over him.

Guid God, have I become as needy as that? She's just confessed to being the daughter of our bitterest enemy, deceased though he is.

Nevertheless he was not such a fool as to fail to recognize his desires, desires that grew stronger the longer he remained celibate. Morag Green had been a long way, a very long way from satisfying them. Now this sweet-smelling lass was leaning against his chest, her long dark hair falling against him...and who was to say she in any way resembled her father in character?

Use your brain, think! Don't go letting your urges overcome common sense.

Shortly, something in the manner in which the woman rested against him, in the way her hand caught at his thigh as Fox broke into a trot, began to erase reason from his mind.

****

As darkness enveloped the countryside, they arrived at the Carmody house. Brodie swung to the ground, then reached up to take his companion about her slim waist and lower her to the ground.

"Thank you, kind sir. You're a gentleman." She started to walk toward the verandah steps but swayed. Pausing, she pressed the back of a gloved hand to her forehead.

"You're not yet recovered, lassie." Brodie reached to steady her.

"I don't believe I am. Will you help me inside?" Looking up at him, beguiling dark eyes soft with appeal, she clutched at his arm while she leaned against his chest.

His body flinched at the contact, and he issued himself a stern rebuke. *Hold steady, laddie. Remember who she is.*

"Aye, aye." He started to assist her up the steps, but she buckled against him. Instinctively he once again gathered her into his arms. He paused when he reached the door.

"It's not locked," she breathed against his neck, and somehow he managed to open it without putting her down, although his senses were whirling, tightening his body from head to toe.

"In there." She indicated a doorway where the shadows cast by a hearth fire suggested warmth and light.

Once in the room, he placed her on a sofa. When he and Harry had made an inventory of the place several weeks previous, he recalled being impressed by the house's elegant furnishings and decoration. A drawing room he believed this place was called.

"Are you alone here, lassie?" he asked. "Is there no one to see to you?"

"I have a maid and a cook." Her voice in the shadows was soft and seductive, her dark eyes gazing up at him with something he was astonished to see as...God help him...desire? "But I should like you to stay. I must thank you for rescuing me."

"No need, lass. I should be goin'...I'm on an errand to the village..." His resolve melting with each syllable, he mouthed the words. "Is there anything I can fetch for you before I leave? A blanket, water, perhaps call for your maid?"

"In my father's office, near the rear of the house, there's a bookcase. Behind the volumes in the right hand corner of the second shelf there is a supply of my father's best brandy. He wrote to my mother and me that he kept it hidden away from his servants. Will you fetch it? Take a candle if you think you might need light." She indicated an unlit pair on the mantel.

"No need. I'm right good at seein' in the dark." The moment the words were out of his mouth, he realized his mistake. The admission hinted of his former midnight forays as a bandit.

Harry was right in warnin' me to keep out of trouble, and that includes watchin' what comes out of my big mouth.

Silently cursing himself, he strode off to do her bidding. After Joe Carmody's death, Harry Wallace had decreed that nothing in the house was to be touched. The villagers, happy to be freed from Carmody's control, had readily agreed. Now Brodie's perusal as he walked toward the office told him they'd obeyed.

While his hand searched behind the books, he remembered Harry's plans to make the house into a school. If his friend succeeded in carrying out his plan, these volumes would come in handy.

His fingers closed over a bottle. He pulled it out and yanked the cork free with his teeth. He inhaled and sighed. Brandy, and fine stuff at that. He wouldn't mind a wee drop before he left the house for the long, cold ride back to the farm in darkness.

Put such thoughts aside, laddie. Even a wee drop might break the last of your resistance to that beautiful woman. With the heel of his hand, he jammed the stopper back in place.

At the drawing room door he paused, startled by the changes. Casting out seductive shadows, candles flickered in holders along the wall. Reclining on a sofa near the fire, she'd removed her spencer to reveal a low-cut, lacy chemise. Round breasts swelled against the scant covering. Brodie wet his lips and swallowed hard.

"You're recovering nicely, ma'am." He advanced into the room. A virulent mix of suspicion and sexual attraction roiled in his gut. *Bloody hell, she's beautiful. And those dark eyes are…what?…inviting, taunting, daring? She must be up to something, but…*

"I'm a Carmody." She cocked her head to one side to cast him a sly glance, sugar-coated with a coy smile. "We're hardy stock."

"Aye, well, good." He advanced across the room to place the bottle on the table in front of her. He saw two brandy snifters already there. *My, my, the woman works fast.* "I'd best be going."

"Surely you can stay long enough to share a small libation with me? A reward for your gallant rescue?"

She was looking up at him, dark-eyed gaze weakening his resolve, eating away at what he knew he should do. Reaching up, she ran a finger down the lower part of his chest and hooked it into his belt. There her hand paused to spread out against his belly.

Dear God, how much temptation is a man supposed to bear, a man who hasn't been with a woman in…

Abruptly she pulled away and turned her attention to the bottle, removing the stopper and pouring a generous measure into each snifter.

"Perhaps this will strengthen your desire to

remain." She held one up to him.

"Well, maybe just a wee drop…"

Chapter Four

Brodie awoke as a sunbeam hit his eyes. He rubbed them, squinting up into the brightness.

Where in hell am I? The softness beneath him told him he wasn't on the straw tick in his cubicle in Harry's house. And the sheets, satin… He struggled up on one elbow and squinted around the room.

Guid God! Joseph Carmody's bedroom! He recognized it from the day following the man's death, when he and Harry had made a tour of the place. *And I'm stark naked!*

As his thoughts began to clear, he forced his eyes into focus. Two brandy snifters sat on the bedside table. His clothing lay scattered about the floor, mixed with a woman's riding habit and undergarments.

In an effort to clear his thoughts, he sat up and shook his head. Crashing pain made him moan and catch at his temples. His gut roiled.

What in the name of heaven have I done?

Stumbling to his feet, he staggered as he tried to right himself. A ewer and basin on the washstand in a corner caught his attention. He jolted over to pour water into the bowl and splash it across his face, then his chest. Grabbing a length of toweling linen from a nearby peg, he made an attempt to rub himself dry. A surge of nausea gushed to the back of his throat.

Guid God, let there be a chamber pot!

He lurched across the room to wrench a decorative china vessel from beneath a corner of the bed.

When he'd finished retching up what he thought had to be his last several meals, he went back to the basin, splashed more water over his face, and dried himself. Grimacing, he began to gather up his scattered clothing. When he glanced into a mirror above a dressing table, he saw a purple lump the size of a hen's egg over his left eye. Somewhere in his confused thoughts he recalled smashing forward, and blinding pain. Then nothing. *Bloody hell, what have I been up to?* He dressed, then sucked in a deep breath as he paused to try to decide what to do next.

If only my blessed head and gut weren't whirling like a windmill in a gale...

He looked at the disheveled bed. A dreadful possibility shot through his tousled brain. He threw back the covers. *Sweet Jesus! A virgin! Brodie MacMillan, whit have you done?* Before remembrance could invade his thoughts, he was sick again. Wiping his mouth with a corner of the sheet as he straightened up from the chamber pot, he battled to become sensible.

I have to get the hell out of here. I have to find Harry. He'll know what to do even as he'll think I've been the right idiot, the worst bastard he's ever met. And after he warned me never to get into any more scrapes!

He went to the window that overlooked the side verandah of the house and eased it open. Glinting so brightly in morning sunlight it hurt the eyes in his pounding head, frost covered its roof. From somewhere around the front of the building, he heard voices. Among them he recognized Harry's. Of course. When he, Brodie, hadn't returned to the farm the previous evening, Harry would have set out to look for him at first light. He'd probably seen Fox near the Carmody manor and come to investigate.

Old instincts from his rebel days burst to the fore. He couldn't risk being seen by anyone, his best friend included. He'd slither down the verandah roof, slip around to the back of the house, and disappear into the trees. A shrill whistle would bring Fox from where he'd left the stallion ground tied the previous night. He trusted that the animal would have strayed no more than a short distance and would still be within calling distance.

He eased up the window and moved out onto the frost-slick shingles. *Like old times, stealing around the rich folks' houses.* The thought dashed across his thoughts, and he almost grinned, but then the memory of those stained sheets returned. *No, definitely not like old times. Even dead drunk, I'd never do anything so dastardly.*

His boots slipped on the ice crystals. With a cry he fought to stifle, he plunged across the shingles and over the edge of the verandah roof. Cat-like from experience, he landed on his feet, staggered to right himself—to face Harry Wallace and Cassandra Carmody's two burly henchmen as they bolted around the corner of the manor to confront him.

"There he is," one of them yelled. "There's the bastard who seduced our mistress!"

"Brodie, ya daft bastard, whit have ye done now?" Harry's expression would have made a thundercloud look friendly.

****

"Harry, I was drugged!" In the village magistrate's office, Brodie, hands tied behind him, faced his friend, who sat glaring at him from behind the desk. "I had to have been! I had only a couple sips of the brandy she gave me." He jerked his head to indicate Cassandra Carmody huddling in a chair to Harry's right, sniveling into a lace handkerchief. Her two hired guards stood blocking the door, arms crossed on their broad chests. "The last thing I remember is pitching face forward onto the hearth. Look at my face, man! There's the evidence."

"She's saying you promised to marry her, begged her on bended knee in front of these two witnesses." Harry pointed a finger at the pair by the door. "After you'd had your way with her in the night, you reneged."

"Harry, you know I wouldn't..." Brodie stared at the man he'd regarded as his best friend for years and saw a cold, questioning stranger. Something inside Brazen Brodie shriveled.

"These two *gentlemen*," Harry put emphasis on the last word, "are swearing they heard you in the parlor of the manor house, saw you on bended knee begging for her hand in marriage before you took her upstairs. This very morn I myself witnessed you escaping from the house in a right suspicious manner. A charge of seduction has been laid. I must do my duty as magistrate and hold you in custody until the circuit judge arrives to hear your case." He held out an arm to indicate the barred door that led to the pair of jail cells attached to the office.

"Bloody hell, Harry!" Brodie couldn't believe what was happening. Harry, the man he considered like a brother, was actually going along with the woman and her hired witnesses, was going to imprison him. "It's all a lie, concocted by this woman and those two bastards in her employ!"

"Ah, well, if that's to be your defense, that we're prejudiced," one of the men bellowed, "well, then, Clem, bring in the old bugger who has no such claim!" He turned to his companion.

The one referred to as Clem strode outside. A moment later he dragged Jonah Parsons into the room.

"Tell these people what you saw this morning, Clem," the first speaker ordered, while Parsons shrank back against the wall near the door.

"Right you are, Tom. I saw this old blighter trying to catch up a red horse in front of Mistress Carmody's house. When he failed to capture the creature, he attempted to chase it away, but it turned on him and near trampled him. I'm guessing it wasn't willing to leave its master. Stories about that beast from hell and the man who owns it have become famous around here."

"Is this true?" Harry asked, turning to the old man.

"I was only trying to capture a runaway before it did mischief," he muttered. "The creature is a stallion, and them can be awful unruly...run women and children down in the street, they can."

"With the evidence given by this eyewitness and your own friend, the magistrate, having seen you escaping the scene with his own eyes, there can be no doubt as to your guilt." The man referred to as Tom glared at Brodie. He swung on Harry. "Magistrate, I order you to do you duty."

"Given such evidence, I can see no alternative." Harry heaved a sigh, shaking his head sadly.

"Harry!" Brodie couldn't believe what he was hearing. His best friend, his boon companion of years, was condemning him to prison.

"Get along with you." The one called Clem prodded him in the back with the pistol he held. "Into the cell."

As Brodie passed Cassandra, she shrank away from his path with a pathetic little gasp, pressing the handkerchief to her face. It took all his will power to keep from yelling "lying bitch" in her face.

As Harry slammed the barred door after him, Brodie caught his conspiratorial wink. A trickle of relief slid into his whirling reality. Highland Harry wasn't deserting him. He was up to something, one of his old tricks. He, Brodie, had only to play along.

"You should be ashamed of yourself, laddie." Harry fixed an angry glare on him as the two accusers moved where they could see his countenance. "I took you into my home, made you a part of my family and its business, and this is how you repay me. Bastard of the first water, that's what I call you. Come along, gentlemen." He spoke to the pair at his elbow. "Let us leave this miserable excuse for a human being to reflect on his infamous deed."

The three men left the cell area and went back into the office, closing the door with a heavy bang. If he hadn't caught that wink, if he didn't know from experience Highland Harry's ability to get himself and others out of the tightest spots, Brodie MacMillan would have despaired.

Chapter Five

"They've gone, and I'll be heading home in an hour or two." Harry stepped into the cell area and closed the door to the office behind him. "Jonah Parsons will take over. He had no work and no place to sleep, so in return for allowing him to spend his nights here, I hired him to clean the place and do guard duty when required." He glanced ruefully around at the dirt. "As you can see, he's not proven a dab hand at the first of his duties, never mind we've had few prisoners aside from a few overnight drunks who got out of hand and his workload has been light. Right now, he's feeling mighty guilty about what those two bastards made him confess, but I've warned him not to consider letting you go. That would be putting his own neck into a noose. I don't think he's ready to be that loyal to us."

Crossing his arms on his chest, Harry Wallace planted his feet shoulder-width apart and faced Brodie. "Now tell me the truth. How did you get yourself into this god-awful mess? Didn't I warn you to keep your nose clean? Didn't…"

"Harry, I never did what that woman has accused me of." Brodie went on to describe how he'd found her on the road, how he'd taken her home, how she'd offered him a drink.

"Once I got out into the fresh air and my head cleared, as you and her two great oafs were bringing me here, I knew I hadn't done the thing she accused me of. And I understood what had happened. She drugged me."

"Good God, man, are you telling me you let a woman get the better of you so easy? Have you lost all your Highland clever slyness?"

"Harry, you know how lonely I've been of late."

"Still…"

"Aye, aye, still I made one hell of a mistake."

"Too late now for regrets and recriminations. Go on. Tell me your tale."

"I remember her giving me a snifter of brandy, and my taking a big swallow." Brodie began to pace the cell as he talked. "Quick as a heartbeat it seemed, a queerness no liquor ever produced rushed over me. My last memory of the night is of pitching headfirst into the hearth, with a crash of pain." Hoping to see belief in his friend's expression, Brodie paused to look over at him.

"Go on." The two words were flat, without either condemnation or sympathy.

"The next thing I knew, I was waking up in her father's bed, sick as a dog, naked as the day I was born, with a raging headache and a roiling gut." Knowing he had no choice, Brodie continued his account. "There were stains on the sheets that suggested an even greater infamy, but they could have been faked. It wouldn't have been difficult."

"That great lump on your forehead bears witness to the truth of what you're sayin'." Harry relaxed his stance to move closer to the bars and speak in sotto voce. "I believe you. I know you can be a reckless fool but never blackhearted. Now we must begin to work on a plan to get you out of this latest pickle."

"I was assumin' you had one, Harry, seein' how easy you let me be put into this cage." Brodie came to grip the bars and hiss the words. His spirits rose.

"Aye, I've a strategy. You'll have to remain in custody for a few days. If you escaped within hours of being incarcerated, it would look right suspicious. You'll be safe from prosecution for a while. The circuit judge isn't due for a month."

"But what's the plan?" Brodie struggled to keep desperation from his voice. For all the times he'd been a fugitive, this was the first time he'd been imprisoned. It tore at his nerves to be confined.

"I'll let you know when I've got all the details in place." Harry turned and headed back to the office. "In the meantime, keep the faith. I'll send one of the boys down with blankets and a bit of supper." He glanced back at his friend, the corner of his mouth quirking. "They can slide it through that space between the bars in the corner. You have to keep your strength, and there's nothing better than a bit of my wife's good cooking."

****

"I only did what every decent resident in this valley has been longing to do!" Brodie heard Maggie Wallace's voice raised in anger coming from the magistrate's office. "That woman, she called me a tavern wench and Brodie a fornicating bastard...in front of our sons!"

"Aye, aye." Her husband's reply was placating with its soft Highland inflection. "But brawlin' with her in the public street, especially in your condition..."

"In my condition! Do you think I want our child born with this huge injustice hanging over his uncle and

54

his mother branded as a tavern wench? Cassandra Carmody has to be stopped, Harry Wallace, and if you can't, I will!"

"Hush, hush, lass. Dunnae distress yourself. You must calm down, or I'll not let you see Brodie and present him with that basket of food."

Guid God, what have I done? Margaret getting mocked in the street, causing her, with a child on the way, to fight for me in public, taking away her family's respectability that she's fought so hard to obtain... Brodie MacMillan, you are a miserable piece of work, and that's for sure.

"Very well." Maggie's voice dropped to a lower if slightly tremulous tone. "I'm calm. Only you're never, never again to pick me up under your arm and cart me off in front of people as you did just now. I'll fight whatever battles whenever and wherever I believe just and necessary, and you won't stop me! Now open that door, Magistrate Wallace. I wish to visit your prisoner."

The door to the office creaked open. Maggie Wallace strode into the cell block, head held high, shoulders back, a basket on her arm. Even with her hair straggling from its queue, her dress torn and streaked with dust, evidence no doubt of her recent scuffle with the Carmody woman, she walked like a queen, proud and unbowed. Brodie had to admire her. James, Geordie, and Robert, her three eldest stepsons, followed. But once inside, her haughty reserve broke as she saw Brodie behind bars.

"Brodie, oh, my dear man!" She rushed to the cell to look in at him, her lovely face furrowed in distress, tears glistening in her green eyes. "Oh, Brodie, this is so very, very wrong! Harry!" She swung on her husband, who'd followed her. "You must do something. You are the representative of the law in this district."

"Yes, and as such, I must carry out my duty." He came to stand close beside her. "Otherwise, no one will respect it, or me...or our family."

Harry was treading on his wife's Achilles' heel. She'd fought so hard to make her family respectable in the eyes of the community. Her husband's appointment as magistrate had been the crowning achievement.

"Respectability be damned," she snapped. "All that matters is clearing Brodie of this ridiculous charge."

"Margaret..." Harry tried to speak, but she ignored him and went to the opening at the end of the cell. Removing the cloth that covered the basket she carried, she began to hand wrapped dishes through to Brodie.

"Bread, a dish of stew, and some applesauce." She described each as she passed them to him. "Harry will brew you some tea on that bit of a hearth he has in the office...won't you, Harry?" She gave her husband such a dark look Brodie knew his friend dared not refuse.

"Of course, my love. Now you'd best be getting back home. It's a cold day, and in your condition..."

"Harry Wallace, I swear if you mention my condition once more..."

"Verrae well, verrae well. Come into the office. Let the lads have a moment alone with their uncle. Man talk."

She hesitated to look at the three young men standing behind her, their faces mirrors of her concern for this man they'd come to regard as their uncle.

"Of course." Drawing herself to all of her five-foot-six-inch height, she adjusted her empty basket on her arm. "Brodie, know that we love you. No one aside from that awful woman and her two ugly louts puts any stock in her lies."

"Thank you, Margaret, love." A lump formed in his throat as he looked at the proud little woman standing outside the bars, a woman who was willing to sacrifice the respectability she held most dear, aside from her family, to see him freed. "Go now, and take care."

"Uncle Brodie, how?" As the office door closed behind his parents, Geordie came close to the bars and asked the question in a soft, astounded whisper. "That woman…"

"I should have known better. She tricked me." He clutched the bars in both hands in front of them. "Ye must be right vigilant, lads. She and her two henchmen are out to take revenge on our family. Promise me you'll watch out for them while I'm in this fix."

"We will." James's blue eyes had become hard and cold as sapphires in winter. "You can trust us, Uncle Brodie."

"Good lads." Brodie relaxed his grip on the bars and heaved a sigh. "Now, you'd best be going. This isn't a place for your family to be seen hobnobbing with a prisoner."

"I don't care!" Geordie exploded. "I don't care who sees us here! You're innocent, and we won't let that witch destroy you!"

"Hush, laddie, hush." A special bond had grown up between the once-hostile teenaged boy and himself over their shared love of music. The thought sent trepidations washing over him. He knew only too well what these passionate Fowler lads were capable of, once aroused by any perceived grievance against their family. "I'll be fine. Her lies will soon become apparent, and I'll be free and ready to go into the woods with you to start cutting timber for next summer's milling." He turned away to the containers of food on the floor of the dirty cell. "Go along with you now. From what she's brought to me, I'd say your mother has a fine meal waitin' for you at home."

"Come along, lads." James took charge. "We can't help Uncle Brodie standing here gaping at him. We've plans to make."

"Now, hold on there just a minute, my fine lads." Catching the conspiratorial look the eldest cast at his younger brothers, Brodie was quick to sense trouble. "I'll not have you gettin' yourselves into this pickle with me."

"Don't worry." James paused, his hand on the door to his father's office. "We've learned a few things from Father and you. We know what we're about."

"James…" Brodie tried to protest, but the young man led his siblings out of the cell area without a backward glance.

Bloody hell! Those lads are going to get themselves into a mess, and it's all because of me. I can only hope Harry comes up with a plan and lets them in on it. At least that way they'll have a clever hand and head in charge.

He stared after them. *Guid God in heaven, what a mess! Bad enough for me to be in this fix, but I've dragged Harry and his family into it. Brodie MacMillan, you deserve whatever punishment that's handed out to you.*

He looked down at the food on the floor and thought of Margaret, feisty, brave, pregnant little Margaret, taking on the Carmody woman at fisticuffs.

A wry grin twisted his mouth. Aye, the Fowler-Wallace clan would be more than willing to fight his battles. He couldn't let that happen. When he got out of this prison, he'd distance himself from them. It was the kindest thing he could do.

Keeping up his strength to be ready to make a run for it, to put miles and miles between him and the family at the first opportunity, that was the answer. He picked up the dish of stew and dug into it with the wooden spoon Margaret had thoughtfully stuck in among the meat and vegetables.

****

"Uncle Brodie, Uncle Brodie!" The hissed summons came midmorning the next day. He looked up from where he was sitting, hands on his bent knees, to the barred window a couple of feet above his head. Samuel's freckled face peered in at him.

"Lad, whit in the name of time are ya doin' here?" Scottish accent spilling into his astonished words, Brodie stumbled to his feet and stared up at the boy. "And how are ya able to see in through that window?"

"I'm standing on Prince's back."

"Whit? You're standin' on the back of one of your father's Clydesdales? Laddie, laddie, the great beast might move. You could take a huge tumble."

"No, I won't." The boy sounded confident. "Papa"—Brodie knew he referred to his birth father, now deceased—"taught Prince to stand still as long as he told him to. I had to come. Father and Mother wouldn't let me visit you with the other boys. They said I was too young to be in such a place, but I had to see you. There's someone else who had to come, too."

He vanished from view. A moment later Brodie

59

caught his breath as Eppie's cherubic face and golden curls appeared in the opening.

"Uncle Brodie, I love you." Tears began to run down her face. "Tell Father to let you out of this awful place at once. If he doesn't, I'll...I'll..." Her words stumbled as she searched for a suitable threat. "I'll run away."

"No, no, darlin'." Fear burst over him as he looked up at her. "No, that won't help at all. If you did something like that, it would only make your father spend time lookin' for you and not workin' on gettin' me free. Promise me you won't do anything so bad that it will make it harder for me to get free."

She hesitated.

"Promise, Eppie. You're getting heavy on my shoulders." Samuel's voice stirred the child to a decision.

"If that's what you want, Uncle Brodie." The sentence was given on a defeated sigh. "But you must promise *me* you'll come home soon. Mother and Father are angry at each other all the time. Nothing is right without you there."

"I promise I'll be home soon, little love. Now you must go."

The child's face disappeared amid a muffled, scrambling sound. Brodie's breath caught in his throat. Had she fallen? Had both children fallen? Had the big, gentle horse moved? Would he accidentally step on one or both of them?

"Samuel! Eppie!" he yelled. "What happened? Are ya both all right?"

After what Brodie felt was one of the longest pauses in his life, Samuel's voice replied, "We're fine,

Uncle Brodie. Eppie got too heavy for my shoulders. She slipped down onto Prince's back behind me. Prince was a good horse. He didn't move at all."

"Verrae well." Relief washed over him. "Now both of you get on home before your parents go mad with worry."

"Aye, Uncle Brodie." Samuel used his father and uncle's favorite word of agreement, good-natured acquiescence in his tone. "Walk on, Prince."

"I love you, Uncle Brodie." The little girl's parting words came back to him.

"I love you, too, lassie." His head dropped forward onto his chest as he listened to the sound of the horse's big hooves moving away.

Guid God, what a mess I've made of that family's lives!

****

"Listen up, laddie. Here's the plan."

Harry Wallace's tone was low, conspiratorial, as he closed the door to his office behind him and approached Brodie's cell.

"It's about time." Brodie got up from the dirty bit of straw on the floor that was his bed and went to confront his friend through the bars. "A week in this dungeon is more than enough. It's getting right ripe, and using that bucket as a privy…"

"I had to wait until the time was right." Harry crossed his arms on his broad chest. "I couldn't risk that Carmody woman accusing me of conspiracy with you and bringing in the militia to arrest me as well."

"No, no, I see your reasonin'. Now to the plan."

"Verrae well. Tonight my lads and I are going to a meeting at the church to discuss with the Reverend Mr.

Morgan the replacing of parts of its floor with good Fowler Mill planks. All four boys will accompany me. I've also asked Duncan Green and Ezra Gardiner to attend. None too fond of us, they'll make irrefutable witnesses to our whereabouts." Harry moved closer to the bars and spoke softly. "At that time Jonah Parsons will release you. He's more than willing to help, seeing as how we once saved his brother from the noose. Furthermore, he served as a witness, albeit a reluctant one, against you in this miserable affair. He'll later tell the story that you feigned sickness and when he went into the cell to check on you, you overpowered him. I'll see to it that Fox, with your belongings and a fair deal of provisions, will be waiting a short distance back in the trees beyond this building. Ride like the wind. Head over the American border. Here's a map Angus Harper drew up for me." He shoved a folded bit of paper through the bars. "He's been to Maine a few times over the years to purchase merchandise. He knows the way. If what's on the paper isn't enough, I'm reckoning you're still as clever as you were in the Highlands at taking your bearings from the sun and stars."

"Wasn't Angus suspicious that you should be asking for such directions now?"

"I told him I might be heading down that way sometime soon to check on a milling operation I've heard about that uses finer equipment than we do in ours. I don't think he entirely bought the story, but if he suspects, he's not about to tell anyone. Remember we rescued his business and house from Joe Carmody not all that long ago."

"Aye, aye." Brodie stared down at the rough drawing. "God help me, this isn't much to go on. I could end up in the Arctic in a blizzard."

"Aye, well, it's the best I can do. The British authorities won't dare to send troops down into the States after you, for fear of provoking another war. Hide out in Portland, Maine, until I send word that it's safe for you to return. Give yourself the name of Charles Bonnie. That way I'll be able to locate you when the coast is clear."

"Harry, you're taking one hell of a risk…"

"Small recompense for what I owe you, laddie." Harry's voice became soft for a moment before reviving and continuing, "Dunnae greet. I've thought it all through carefully. No one can suspect the boys and me; we'll be safe with the minister and two upstanding members of the community as witnesses. Fortunately no one aside from our family in this country knows of Jonah's conspiracy with us in the Old Country when he helped us escape the trap Lady Annabelle Spencer had laid for us. He won't be suspect. I warned him to keep his mouth shut after he told Margaret about our exploits and all but got me divorced." A sardonic grin quirked his lips. "Now." He sobered. "It has to be tonight. With snow not far off, you have to get away before tracking becomes easy."

"I'm right glad you're keepin' the boys with you. I was afeard they'd do something rash, trying to get me free."

"You don't have to worry on that score. They'll be within my sight at all times."

"Aye, aye." Brodie turned away, his tone reflecting his suddenly downcast feelings.

"'Whit now?" Harry's words and gusty sigh reflected his exasperation. "Tonight you'll be free."

"Free to run again, to be a blessed outlaw once more." Brodie put his hands on his hips and threw back his head with a heaved-out breath. "Harry"—he swung back to his friend—"I thought those days were over, that I could think about settlin' down and havin' a family…again."

"I know, I know, brother." His friend's words were filled with compassion. "I realize this mess wasn't entirely your fault."

"Entirely? Bloody hell, Harry, she snookered me!"

"Agreed, but you should have known better than to take even a single drop of anything from her hands. You should have been clever enough not to trust a Carmody, beautiful or otherwise."

"You're right." Brodie hung his head. "I've gotten soft and trustin'."

"And more than a tad too needy in the female department." Harry stopped his friend as he opened his mouth to retort. "I have to be gettin' home. There's still a bugger-all lot of work to do to get ready for lumbering, and now we're a hand short." He held his right hand through the bars. "Good luck, Brodie MacMillan. Until we meet again."

Brodie clasped it in a grip so strong his friend flinched. "Blessin's on you and yours, Hamish Wallace. God willin', I'll see you some time this side of heaven."

****

"Bloody hell, you don't have to truss me up like a pig for the slaughter!" Jonah Parsons squirmed as Brodie tied his hands behind his back. "I won't be going anywhere or raising an alarm. Do you think I want to give folks an inkling that I helped you escape? I don't want my neck stretched!"

"If I tie you too loose, don't you think that will cast suspicion on you?" Brodie gave the ropes a final jerk and stood. "Thoughtful of Harry to leave these bonds in his office. Tied up, you've no way of moving about and yelling for help out of that high window over there." He jerked his head in the direction of the small, barred opening far up on the wall. "Just be thankful Harry didn't think you should be gagged. He's willing to trust to your keeping quiet for a couple of hours at least."

"Aye, well, give me a swallow out of my flask before you go." Parsons jerked his chin downward at his shabby coat. "It's in the pocket."

"Verrae well." Although knowing every minute counted, Brodie paused to find the flask, pull out the stopper, and hold it to the man's mouth.

He gulped down a great swallow, then choked as Brodie drew it away and helped himself to a drink.

"Here now!" Parsons cried. "I'm risking my neck for you! Don't go taking all my best tipple!"

"Best?" Brodie bared his teeth and grimaced. "Guid God, man, what are you in the habit of drinkin'? This is swill." He rammed the cork back in place and returned the flask to the man's coat pocket. "Now I must be off. My most sincere thanks, Mr. Parsons. Till we meet again."

"May the good Lord ride with you, Brodie MacMillan."

****

Once outside in the frosty night, Brodie paused behind the jail to suck in a deep breath. *Damn, but it's good to be out of that dirty, stinking cell and free...free at last.* But there was no time to waste. Pulling himself back to the moment, he stuck two fingers in his mouth and emitted a shrill whistle.

A snort and the sound of prancing hooves not far off replied. A moment later the stallion trotted out of the trees, reins tied to his saddle, burdened with Brodie's belongings and supplies, even his fiddle case. The animal blew a greeting as he approached.

Although he was grateful for his friend's obviously thoughtful and thorough preparation, Brodie felt hope sink. Harry must not believe he would be able to clear his name any time soon.

As he swung into the saddle and slapped his mount a greeting on the neck, he came to a decision. He pulled out the map Harry had given to him, the one intended to direct him to the United States. Barely able to see the pencil marks on the crumpled paper, he stared at it in the moonlight. Finally, with a muttered oath, he crumpled it and flung it into the bushes.

Turning the animal away from the village of Riverhaven and the farm and mills he'd come to think of as home, he made a decision. He *was* a loose cannon. He would never return. An outlaw to the core, he would go back to Scotland and once again fight for the cause Harry had said they'd best leave to younger men. And die there.

Chapter Six

"What in bloody hell are you doing here?" His face distorted with outrage, Harry Wallace yanked out a chair at the table and sat down opposite him. "I told you to head for Portland, Maine, ya daft bastard. When Captain Duffy arrived at Riverhaven and told me he'd seen you still in New Brunswick, here in Richibucto, I couldn't believe it."

"And I can't believe you've followed me." Brodie looked over at him. "Fox and I are about to head back to Scotland today on the last ship to leave this port before it freezes over. I won't be causin' you and your family any more grief. I'm a condemned man on both sides of the Atlantic. I plan to die fightin' for Scottish independence. But you, you great fool, you should be with Margaret. She's carryin' your child, for God's sake."

"Aye, and you're drunk. You look like hell, and you smell worse. When was the last time you shaved or washed or changed your clothes?"

"Sweet Jesus, Hamish, can't you get it through your thick head? I don't care any more. What's left for me, aside from the bottle and the grave?"

"How do you expect me to tell Eppie that the uncle she fair dotes upon is dead?" Harry met his stare head on. "She watches the road over the hilltop every day, convinced you're coming home to us, because you promised."

"Eppie…" An image of the golden-haired cherub wafted across his alcohol-muddled brain.

"Yes, Eppie, your niece who loves you more than you deserve, you stubborn Highlander. She sent you a kiss when she thought I was going to see you in the jail…which I'll not be giving you." A shadow of humor quirked a corner of Harry Wallace's mouth. "Furthermore, if Geordie plays that damned sorrowful lament 'Banks of Loch Lomond' one more time on that fiddle, I swear I'll take it from the lad. They're not the only ones. The entire family is pining for you."

"Now you're hitting well below the belt with your arguments, Hamish…usin' the bairns and Margaret. You know if I come back you'll have to whack me back into that stinkin' cell."

"I know you can't come back immediately, but dunnae greet. I'll find a way to clear you of that daft charge. Just be patient. Go to Maine. I'll send for you as soon as I get this mess straightened away. If you head off to Scotland and go back to outlawing, God only knows how I'll find you."

"That will be for the best, Harry…if you can't find me. I've done enough harm to you and your family's reputation. I'll not chance another blunder at your expense."

"Where's Fox?" Harry's eyes suddenly narrowed as he looked over Brodie's shoulder.

"Out back with all my worldly possessions tied to his saddle. We're due to board the ship at midnight. Why?"

"Because an officer and three armed soldiers just entered. Although I thought I'd covered my tracks, they must have followed me. I'm surmising they're after your hide, my fine laddie."

"Jesus…"

"Upset the table, punch me in the jaw, and run like hell!"

"Hamish…"

"Just do it!"

"You there! Brodie MacMillan? Hold!" The officer's orders threw him into action. He upset the table. As Harry made a move as if to stop him, he swung out at his best friend. His fist caught Harry squarely in the jaw. As Harry toppled to the floor, his body blocking the soldiers' pursuit, Brodie dashed for the rear door.

Outside, he vaulted into the saddle. With years of experience in such situations, Fox snorted and leaped into a full gallop.

"There he goes!"

A door slammed, a musket blasted, and hot lead ripped through Brodie's left thigh.

"Run, lad, run!" He leaned over the horse's neck, shock momentarily blinding the pain.

****

Snowing. It had begun to snow. Brodie clung to the saddle as Fox walked steadily forward. He was cold. So bloody cold he couldn't feel his fingers. Or his toes. Only the searing pain in his thigh. The stallion's sweat had soaked his breeches and, in the bitter cold, frozen. Where was the daft beast taking him? Surely not over the vast miles to the Fowler farm. Weakness had forced him to abandon any attempt to guide the animal.

As the storm thickened, consciousness deserted him, and he hung limp over his horse's neck.

Chapter Seven

The blizzard had begun at sunset. By dawn, Louisa Abbott estimated, she'd be well and truly snowbound.

Looking out her cabin window, she shivered not from fear but with anticipation. Cut off from civilization, she'd be free to write. If the snow kept up, by spring she'd have a collection of tales and a novel ready to ship off to England on the first outward-bound vessel. By autumn, she'd receive payment in more of the gold coins she'd requested, hopefully more than enough to buy supplies that would carry her through the following winter in the wilderness of northern New Brunswick.

Supplies. Her thoughts abruptly returned to her last trip to Riverhaven for provisions and the tall, broad-shouldered, sandy-haired man who'd sold her flour and oatmeal and assisted in loading her wagon. There'd been such warmth in his affable outlook, such roguish disregard for what the other villagers thought in his handsome face, that he'd returned to her mind time and time again. She smiled. He was a man with whom she might well have enjoyed becoming better acquainted. The thought surprised her. After Neil, she'd never considered another man would catch her interest.

Drawing in a deep breath, she forced the memory aside. It would be spring if she ever had an opportunity to see Brodie MacMillan again. And what was to say he wasn't married or at least betrothed? Certainly he had the looks and charm to attract a woman.

Stop it, Louisa. She reprimanded herself. *You were fortunate to have found a deep and abiding love once in your life already. You have no right to go hoping you'll ever meet with such again. Furthermore, what man in his right mind would want to go sharing his life with a woman condemned as a witch?*

She carried a lamp to the small secretary near the window and sat down on the chair in front of it. The desk's top held a neat stack of papers and the pen and ink stand that had belonged to her husband. She laid a fresh sheet in front of her, took up the pen, but paused before dipping it into the small pot of black liquid.

Neil. His memory caused her to finger the implement gently. His pen, his old desk and chair, his inkwell. She squeezed her eyes shut. She had to move him to the back of her mind, at least while she worked. Haunted by his memory, she'd discovered she was incapable of doing anything constructive.

Neil, my darling. You'll always be in my heart, but now I have to envision a new hero for this book. You've been my main character in too many.

Opening her eyes, she drew a deep breath. With a sigh, she wetted her nib and began to write. A small smile curled the ends of her lips as her new hero emerged. Tall, broad of shoulder, with sandy hair curling about his ears, he was blessed with both an affable grin and a manner that caught the eye and could charm any woman of his choosing. She paused thoughtfully for a moment. Her smile broadening, she began to sketch his character. As pleasant and amiable as Mr. Bingley in the new novel she'd just finished reading, entitled *Pride and Prejudice*, this man would also possess the strength of character of Mr. Darcy and the adaptability of the frontiersman. Better still, he'd be open to new people and ideas, not bound by Old Country manners, rules, and mores.

With her hero firmly in mind, she began to conjure up a heroine. She'd have to be as unusual as the hero, with similar beliefs and daring ways. And beautiful. She'd have to be beautiful to attract his attention initially, because he was a man who liked women and would be passionate about having a lovely, unique one for his own. After a series of adversities, they'd come together to fit their lives together in a hand-in-glove comfort and companionship.

She wrote intently, too engrossed in her story to notice the worsening of the blizzard raging around her cabin. A half whine, half yawn drew her attention to the hearth, where Jasper lay stretched before its warmth.

"Big ninny." She chuckled. "You have little to complain about. You could be out in the barn with Snow." At this time of year, aside from a daily romp in the snow in the paddock behind the barn, the white mare grew fat and lazy in her stall.

A growl issued from the animal's throat. He stood and slunk toward the door.

Something hit the plank panel with a dull thump. Whirling, she jumped to her feet. Another sound that could have been a moan followed.

Reaching for the pistol she kept primed on the sideboard, she signaled the wolf to silence. Stealthily she moved toward the door. A clawing grated against its planks. She sucked in a deep breath, leveled the gun, and yanked the panel open.

A crumpled bundle fell in at her feet. A snow-crusted hand and raggedly bearded countenance raised up to her with what was apparently the last of his strength. With a groan, he collapsed face down on her floor, unconscious.

"Good God, Jasper!" She replaced the weapon on the sideboard and knelt beside the newcomer. "It's a man…a half-frozen man."

Grasping him under what she found to be his armpits, she reefed with all her strength. A big man, he seemed a dead weight. With dogged determination, she managed to drag him far enough into the cabin to be able to shut the door against the storm.

She rested for a moment before going back to her task of moving him, this time to bring him closer to the fire on the hearth. Once she'd gotten him in front of the flames, she paused to catch her breath and peruse him. Jasper, hackles raised, circled the newcomer, sniffing, a growl rumbling in his throat.

"Hush," she admonished. "This man is no threat to us. He's barely alive."

Bearded face crusted with ice and snow, his body encased in frozen garments, he presented a grotesque appearance. She knelt beside him. What was the man's ailment? Did he perhaps carry the seeds of the same illness that had devastated her family?

Then she saw his left leg twisted askew. Relief washed over her. No, he'd been injured. Bending closer, she recognized the ragged tear, surrounded by frozen blood, that marred his trousers.

"Shot, I'd say. I think we've got a fugitive of some kind on our hands, Jasper. But he needs help, and Neil would not have denied him."

She went to the sideboard to gather up medical supplies. When she returned to the man, she dropped back onto her knees. As she pulled the cap from his head and wiped snow and ice crystals from his face, she received a shock. She lurched back and stared.

It can't be! But it is. The man from the village who helped to load my wagon. Surely, possibly...even fate couldn't behave in such an outrageous manner.

Reminding her of the necessity of getting him out of his frozen clothing, he moved and moaned. It was no easy task. She began with his ice-crusted jacket and shirt. A big, muscular man, he was heavy to move about in his comatose state.

When she'd managed to remove all of his clothing, she covered him with quilts and blankets and placed a feather pillow under his head. Stripping the man naked had not been a concern. In her years as a doctor's wife, she'd done it not infrequently as she assisted her husband in tending injured or sick male patients.

She bent to examine his wound. A bloody hole in his leg, halfway between knee and hip, was definitely a gunshot wound. Since she could find no exit point, she suspected a musketball was lodged inside. She'd have to remove it. Her husband's surgical equipment was in a black bag in the bedroom. Her heart pounding, she willed herself to be calm as she went to fetch it. While she'd assisted Neil in performing such an operation on two occasions, she'd never done one on her own.

She drew a deep breath and closed her eyes. What would Neil have done? Where would he begin?

First, of course, he'd place the patient on a firm, waist-high surface. She opened her eyes and looked at the table in the center of the room. There was no way she could lift this powerful man onto it. Therefore, she'd have to make the best of where he lay.

Next? The patient must be rendered as far beyond the pain of the operation as possible. She stood and went to the cupboard. On a top shelf were several small bottles filled with a reddish-brown liquid. Laudanum. It would render the man unconscious beyond what he was presently experiencing. Hopefully, it would prevent him from awakening during the procedure. How much could she safely give him? She forced her thoughts back to operations in which she'd assisted Neil.

She returned to the man, knelt, raised his head, and held the bottle to his lips to allow a trickle to slip into his mouth. He muttered and choked, but she managed to force what she thought was a proper amount into him. When she replaced his head on the pillow, he appeared to go limp, relaxed in the effects of the drug.

Is he dying? Have I administered too much?

She bolted to her feet and rushed to her desk. Rolling a sheet of paper into a tube, she knelt again by the man. Thrusting it against his bare chest, she listened intently at the other end.

Yes! There it is! A regular if somewhat weak heartbeat.

Relief flooded through her with the force of a mountain freshet. She sank back on her heels, allowing herself a silent prayer of thanks.

The next step? Neil, be with me now. Immobilize the patient. Of course. You'd secure them to the table in the event of them returning to consciousness before you'd finished the procedure and causing themselves harm. But how?

Toweling linen. She'd have to fetch some to bind

up the wound. She'd use some to bind his hands and feet. It was the best she could do under the circumstances. She stood and set about the remaining preparations for the surgery. When she knelt beside him again, she was ready.

He flinched in his unconsciousness as she slowly inserted a probe into the wound. It touched something hard and foreign to the sensation of human flesh. Willing her hands to be steady, she worked the surgical instrument around the object and gently pulled. When a musketball emerged, bloody but complete, she heaved a sigh and allowed herself a moment as relief washed over her. But not for long.

The wound was gushing blood. No time to lose courage or weaken. Grasping a pot, she rushed to the door, opened it, and filled it with snow. Shortly she had a cold compress against his leg. The bleeding slowed.

****

There! It was done. She leaned back, away from where she'd been kneeling over the man, and pushed damp hair off her forehead. A wide, neat bandage covered his leg from knee to upper thigh. Beneath it she'd used honey from the jar in the cupboard to stanch the bleeding. A bloody basin beside her held the musketball she'd pried from his wound. Mercifully, he was still breathing, albeit in a labored fashion. She pulled a blanket over him and staggered to her feet.

Bending to gather up the remains of her operation, she was suddenly overcome by such a wave of weakness she all but pitched forward.

Not now, Louisa, not now. The worst is over. This isn't the time to drop into a swoon. What would Neil think?

She set about tidying the room. As she placed the materials she'd used on the plank table, her knees weakened, and she sat down hard on a chair beside it. What now? She stared down at the man's bearded, blanched face. His breathing was ragged. She dared not try to move him. Wrenching him across the floor could restart bleeding. Her thoughts returned to his identity.

Yes, this definitely is the same man who helped me in the village. But what act of fate has brought him here to me in his need? Has this been an opportunity for me to repay his kindness?

Jasper whined at the door.

"You have to go out?" Cautiously she stood. When she discovered her legs would once more support her, she turned to the wolf, hands on her hips. "That's not like you. On a night such as this, usually nothing can draw you from the cozy warmth of this place."

The animal jumped up on the door, this time barking.

"Hush, hush!" she admonished as the man at her feet stirred and moaned. "What is it?" The wolf's actions bespoke of something…or someone…outside.

Picking up her pistol, she moved cautiously to the door. The man she'd been tending had been shot. As she'd already speculated, he could be a pursued fugitive, a renegade. Hadn't his treatment of her in the village last fall branded him as one with little or no regard for the status quo? Although it seemed unlikely even the most vehement of pursuers would be chasing after him on such a night, she had to be careful.

With Jasper close beside her, she eased the door open. Nothing. With a roaring bark, Jasper broke past her and raced toward the barn on the edge of the forest.

In that strange illumination that a snowy night affords, through gusts she saw the animal—a horse, she reckoned—at the shelter's door. It rocked back and forth as if in pain or desperation.

Good God! The poor creature.

She glanced at the man on the floor. He was beyond pain and the need of any more immediate assistance. If this was his horse, he'd want it tended. Past experience had told her that he had a caring heart. She pulled on knee-high, fur-lined moccasins and the patched woolen coat that hung to below her thighs. Drawing a woolen cap over her hair, she stepped outside.

Moving cautiously forward, she came abreast of the creature.

Yes, definitely a horse. A snow-crusted horse, saddled and bridled, with provisions tied to its back as well as an elongated case of some sort.

"Whoa, whoa." She spoke softly, moving slowly closer to the creature. The animal snorted as he shook snow and ice crystals from his head and neck. A bit of mane appeared. Red. And from its restlessness, a stallion, she guessed. Quite possibly, scenting her mare, he'd brought his master here. She couldn't leave him out in the elements, sweat and snow frozen to his body, but she'd have to be extremely careful.

Perhaps a handful of grain could entice him inside. Easing her way past the creature, she opened the door just enough to allow her to slide into the barn. The stallion, possibly catching a stronger scent of the mare, revived to bolt toward her. With a snarl, Jasper hurled himself between the horse and his mistress. The horse snorted and veered away long enough for Louisa to get inside, slam the door shut, and put a bar in place.

Inside, she fell back, her shoulders against the panel, and looked around. She needed no lantern. Illumination from the wild, snowy night flooded the stable from windows high in the walls. Even if it hadn't she knew her way around it as well as the back of her hand.

What to do. She had to get the animal inside, out of the blizzard, unsaddled, and dried. Across the barn, Snow stuck her snout through the bars of the top half of her box stall and muttered a greeting. The enclosure was sturdy. The stallion couldn't get at the mare, but she still had the problem of getting him inside as peacefully as possible.

At the far end of the barn was another box stall, one heavily reinforced with stout poles at the top. She'd assumed the former owner had used it for a bull…or maybe a stallion. Either way, she judged it would be strong enough to hold this newcomer. All she had to do was lure him into it.

All! The word brought a sardonic quirk to her lips. As if that would be an easy task. She paused to think.

Food and drink. The creature had to be hungry and thirsty. She went into the empty stall and set to work. She placed hay in the manger and carried a bucket of water she'd left for emergencies outside Snow's stall into the enclosure. Finally she went to a sack against a wall and scooped into it with a metal dipper that she kept on its top.

"You keep very quiet, Miss Snow," she cautioned the mare as she made her way past her to the door. "I'm about to try to calm a savage beast." The mare blew and tossed her ivory-colored head, looking like a ghost horse in the weird night.

She'd barely begun to ease the door open when the stallion burst inside, slamming her back against a support beam.

"Whoa, whoa." Fighting to ignore the pain the blow had sent racing through her shoulder, she staggered upright and managed to speak softly, soothingly, to the creature cavorting about the barn. As Jasper attempted to follow, she slammed the door shut against him. Protective of her, the wolf would only cause more chaos in his efforts to get the better of the stallion.

Against the closed door, the animal clawed the boards and howled.

"Easy, easy." As the horse slowed slightly, Louisa moved away from the wall, holding out the dipper, speaking softly, gently. "You're safe now. You and your master will be fine. Whoa, whoa."

The stallion slowly came to a halt and stood, head drooping, blowing heavily, pawing the floor.

"You're tired, aren't you?" People had always said she had a special way with animals. Now she used it to the best of her ability. She approached carefully until she was able to place a hand on his neck. He wriggled his skin, but made no move to attack or jump away.

"Good boy." She put the pot holding the grain beneath his mouth, his frozen whiskers rubbing over her hand. Slowly, then more rapidly, he took the food.

"That's enough for now. Mustn't sicken you." She eased her hand to his ice-coated bridle. "Come along," she continued, her voice so soft it carried a musical quality. "There's a nice comfortable stall waiting for you."

He snorted, and for a moment she thought he'd resist, but finally, with a soft wheeze, he followed her lead.

Only once she had him inside the stall, his saddle and bridle removed and as much as possible of the ice and snow rubbed from his coat, did she feel she'd done all she could for the creature. She threw the bridle and reins over her shoulder, dragged the saddle with its attached supplies from the stall, and shut the door after her. With a weary sigh, she leaned against the barred panel. For a moment she closed her eyes as she listened to the horse munching the fodder, the blizzard howling around the stable.

What a night this has been. And the storm appears in no way ready to let up.

Another thought struck her. *If my patient truly is a fugitive, if he's being pursued, trackers will be foiled, his trail obscured by the snow.* The idea sent a spurt of happiness through her.

Don't go courting foolish ideas. Simply because the man once played the gallant to you, Louisa, you're thinking he's like one of the wonderful rogues who are characters in your novels. This is hard, cold reality. The man, in spite of his charming ways, might be any kind of outlaw.

From behind the closed door, Jasper's whining brought her back to the moment.

I have to return to my patient. She roused herself and headed for the door. *Patient. I haven't used that word in some time. Strange how one wounded man...*

Chapter Eight

In the cabin, she found him much as she'd left him, ensconced amid blankets and quilts, his head supported on the pillow. He appeared to have moved only slightly. She knelt and put the backs of her fingers to his forehead.

Fevered. Definitely not a good sign. Snow. I need more snow.

Grasping a cooking pot, she headed back into the blizzard. Filling it was easy. Snowbanks were everywhere and growing rapidly higher. She was thankful she had supplies sufficient to see her through the brutal months ahead.

Back inside, she found a length of linen, filled it with snow, and knelt to apply the compress to the man's hot forehead. At first touch, he tossed away from it, but she spoke softly, soothingly, and shortly he lay still while she held it in place.

"Annie." The name rattling from the man's swollen lips startled her. "Annie."

That was all. All the air in his lungs seemed to come out in a slow, ragged wheeze. He dropped back into silence.

Annie. So there is a woman in his life. Someone so important to him she's deep in his unconscious thoughts.

The realization sent a strange feeling washing over

her…a feeling of what? Surprise? Curiosity? Disappointment?

The last thought gave her a jolt. Disappointment? For heaven's sake, why should it? She'd only met the man once while he was lucid, a chance encounter of a few minutes. Why had she assumed he was unattached? He was a fine specimen.

"Annie!" This time the name was an anguished cry. "Annie, no! No, not you and our babe! Sweet Jesus…no, no, no! Gone…burned to ashes! No, no, no!" His voice rose to a roar as he thrashed about in his improvised bed, flinging her hand away with a violence amazing in his present physical state. "I'll kill the bastards…every last one of them!"

"Rest, rest," she soothed, even as her heart raced from his words. Annie. And a baby. Dead in a terrible fire that appeared to have been the product of those he was threatening to kill, perhaps had already killed. Memories, fueled by fever, were rushing back into his brain, driving him mad. He'd suffered…as much as she had.

She moved the compress to his temple and slowly down his face to his neck, where she knew blood coursed through an artery. He flinched at the movement and tried to raise a hand.

"Rest, Mr. MacMillan," she soothed in the same gentle tones she'd used to quiet his stallion. "All is well. You're safe, and so is your horse."

Although she doubted he understood her words, he sighed and dropped into quietude. Relieved, she stood and went to bank the fire for the night. A yawning whine from Jasper made her turn. The wolf, who'd followed her back inside, was settling across the entrance. He seemed to have an uncanny sense of what was needed, what was expected of him. Louisa smiled. Neither man nor beast would enter the cabin with the animal on guard.

She resumed her place by her patient and would continue to bathe his face and body with snow until the storm had abated and the first rays of a bright winter's day slanted in through the cabin windows above the snowbanks half obscuring them.

****

She dropped the cloth she'd been using into the pot of melting snow, the last of many she'd fetched from outside during the night, and got to her feet. Looking down at her patient, she heaved a sigh. The fever had broken at dawn. Now he was resting peacefully. She glanced at the bed of spruce boughs in a corner of the room, covered with linen sheets, quilts, and blankets. She'd constructed it as an emergency bed when Marie had had her child at the cabin. Although she hadn't greatly expected more patients, she'd decided to be ready if and when another arrived at her door seeking help or shelter.

She was weary, so weary. She'd lie down on it for a few minutes before she went out to the stable to tend the horses. With a sigh, she sank onto the bed, pulled a quilt over her, and fell into an exhausted sleep.

Chapter Nine

Louisa awoke to a glare of sunlight striking her eyes. For a moment she didn't recall how she came to be sleeping in a corner of the cabin. Then she saw the blanket-wrapped form beside the hearth. Memories of the wounded, nearly frozen man arriving in the night, and the ice-crusted stallion that had waited outside her stable flashed into her mind.

Jerking up on one elbow, she groaned. Every bit of her body seemed to ache. *Ignore it. You have a wounded man who needs you.* Shoving back the bed covers, she struggled to her feet and crossed the room to her patient. Kneeling beside him, she reached out a hand to once again touch his forehead with the backs of her fingers.

Warm but with no indication of the return of fever. Her breath came out in a sigh of relief. Still, she knew the battle for his life was far from over.

With a groan, she forced herself to her feet and headed for the hearth. The previous night had taken a toll on her both physically and mentally. Sunlight streaming in at the windows told her the blizzard of the night had passed, but the cabin had grown cold, the hearth glinting with only a few remaining embers. Moving stiffly, she restored it to flames and placed a kettle of water to boil.

Tea. I need tea, strong and sweet and hot.

The idea brought other thoughts to her mind. Thoughts of the man who'd helped her heft containers of tea leaves and a sack of sugar onto her wagon weeks before. Thoughts of twinkling blue eyes and a charming grin that she felt sure could melt the coldest heart. Now this man lay before her, with her rudimentary skills as a doctor all that kept him from death.

She measured tea leaves into the kettle, removed it from the flames, and sat down in a rocking chair before the fire to wait for it to steep. Only then did she realize her dress was dirty, stained with blood, and her hair hung raggedly about her face. A right sight, Neil would have teasingly described her, his wonderful smile belying any meanness in his words after they'd finished a difficult medical procedure together. It had been his way of lightening the moment. Then he'd kiss her gently on the cheek before, together, they'd set the surgery to rights.

"Neil." She breathed his name aloud as she so often did, unable to repress it.

Jasper, still lying across the cabin's entrance, cocked his head to one side and barked.

"Hush!" Louisa admonished. Best the man remained oblivious for the time being, until the worst of the pain had subsided or... She pulled her mind away from the other possibility.

"Louisa." The voice that came from beyond the door was familiar and welcome. "It's Marie and Runner."

"Marie." She hurried to raise the bar and let her friends inside.

"We snowshoed over to see how you'd weathered the storm," the native woman began. She saw Brodie and stopped short.

"He arrived at my door in the height of the storm," Louisa explained. "He was wounded…a musketball in his leg. I removed it, but now I fear infection may set in. Come, sit. I've just made tea. How is your son?" She indicated the baby warmly bundled on her friend's back. "Here, let me take him."

When they were settled with steaming cups of tea before the fire, the baby cooing softly in his bundling on the bough bed, Marie looked over at Louisa.

"Why do I feel there is more to this story than the fact that this man arrived here wounded in the night? Are you in the practice of taking in injured strangers?"

"As a doctor's wife, I could do no less, but yes, you are correct. There is more to the story. When I went to the village this autumn for supplies, a man kindly helped me load my wagon, then ordered the people who were calling me a witch to allow me to leave peacefully. This is that man."

"An omen." Marie sipped her tea and looked over the cup's rim at her friend, dark eyes bright with innuendo.

"Now don't start with prophetic ideas. It was simply coincidence that he ended up here. That and the fact that he was riding a randy stallion intent on finding my mare." A corner of her mouth curled. "So not as serendipitous as you're supposing."

"As you wish." Marie stood and went to the sideboard. "You look exhausted. I'll make breakfast. Have you treated your patient's wound to avoid infection?"

"I've done my best. I've cleaned it and stanched the bleeding with honey."

"My grandmother once treated a man for a musketball wound with the liquid obtained by boiling the root of a certain plant. He survived. Runner." She turned to her companion. "You must fetch some for Louisa."

"That would be wonderful. Thank you. But first, a favor." Louisa stood. "Will you and Runner help me get him into the bed in the other room? He can't remain lying on the floor."

"The bed in the other room…your bed?" Marie looked at her, dark eyes keen and questioning. "Where will you sleep?"

"Where I slept last night…on the bough bed in the corner." She indicated the quilts and linens.

"Louisa, be careful. You don't know anything about him."

"I appreciate your concern, but what I suggest is best. Be assured my moving him to my bed is not entirely altruistic. It will simply make it easier to tend him if he's not on the floor."

"Very well." Marie drew a deep breath and looked down at the man. "You saved my life and that of my child. We'll do as you wish."

"Carrying him is not a chore for a pair of women." Runner hunkered down beside the man and paused for a moment to peruse his countenance.

"I know this man," he said. "He came not long ago from across the sea." He looked up at Louisa.

"Yes?" She knew there was more to come.

"It's been said that he was an outlaw, that he and his friend Harry Wallace, the village magistrate, were highwaymen in the country from which they came."

"I suspected he was some kind of fugitive." The

revelation didn't take Louisa by surprise. "Seeing as how he was wounded and on his own in the blizzard."

"Yet you took him in and are planning to give him your bed?" Marie asked. "Louisa…"

"Do not question your friend, woman." Runner glanced at his wife, his expression stern. "She took you in, saved your life and that of our child. It is her way." He put one arm under Brodie's and slid the other beneath his knees. With strength that astonished Louisa, Runner lifted her patient and carried him into the bedroom.

She hurried ahead to draw back the bedclothes. As Runner placed Brodie between the sheets, the wounded man moved and moaned.

"Rest easy, Brodie." Louisa spoke in the same soothing tone she'd used with the stallion. She deliberately used his Christian name, hoping it would reassure him. "You're among friends."

Either comforted by her words or sinking beyond the realm of caring, he gave up the battle and settled back into his previous state. Louisa drew covers over him and stepped back, hands on her hips, to gaze into his face.

"Now, Runner, you must go swiftly." Marie spoke to her companion. "Louisa will need Grandmother's healing ointment as soon as possible. I'll stay here to prepare food, and return with you later with our child."

Chapter Ten

Brodie opened his eyes. Somewhere in his clouded mind he recognized a woman's voice singing softly. The scent of freshly baked bread tantalized his nose. His surroundings were dim, too dim for him to make out. Tangled thoughts rambled around in his head.

Annie's voice. Annie was near. He must have died and was with her again. The possibility began to thin the frost from the window in his mind. He, Brodie MacMillan, bandit, was in heaven with his beloved Annie.

No, no, no! Improbability wiped a small clear space in his thoughts. No, somehow he'd survived something…something that had almost cost him his life. He tried to move. Excruciating pain shot up his leg and through his thigh. He cried out.

And suddenly there was a woman standing over him, then kneeling beside him, putting the backs of cool fingers to his forehead.

"Awake at last." Her words were soft, gentle, soothing.

He struggled to focus. Golden-red hair, a delicately beautiful heart-shaped face, that voice… He knew them from somewhere, somewhere.

She stood and moved away. Again his thoughts reeled incoherently. Cold, so cold, and pain, so much pain. Memories straggled back…

She returned, kneeling beside him, a cup in one hand, raising his head with the other.

"Drink." She held it to his lips.

The liquid trickled into his mouth. He tried to swallow but was overcome by a fit of coughing. She put the cup aside and drew him more upright until the spasm subsided. As she lowered him gently back into his former position, he realized that he was in a bed. Somewhere nearby a wood fire crackled out warmth and light.

"Where...am...I?" he croaked. "What...?"

"You arrived at my door during a blizzard." Entrancing green eyes looked down at him. The thought again staggered across his mind that he'd died and gone to heaven. Surely no angel could be lovelier than this mysterious stranger. But why did she look familiar—why?

"You were wounded." She was speaking again. "You're in my cabin...and safe."

"Wounded." His thoughts were clearing, lining up with a bit of remembrance and logic. "Aye, I'm beginning to ken. Fox!" Gritting his teeth against pain, he tried to jolt upright. Her hand, surprisingly strong on his shoulder, restrained him.

"If you're referring to that great, unmannerly red stallion that brought you here, he's well. He's penned in my barn behind a barrier suitable to keep him from my mare."

"Ah." Brodie allowed himself to relax. *Fox is well.*

"You...appear familiar." He looked up at her, reality coming more strongly to him. "Do...I know you?"

"You sold me flour and oatmeal and helped me

load my wagon last autumn in Riverhaven," she said. "I'm Louisa Abbott, the woman your villagers have branded a witch."

"Witch?" He willed his thoughts to come to order but, like a half-made picture puzzle, only bits and pieces fell into place. *The village. Riverhaven. Wagons. A cold autumn day, a woman with golden-red hair… this woman?*

"Just so." She stood and went out of the room toward a hearth he could see through the doorway. The sight of its warming flames made him relax. He watched as she took a mug from a sideboard and filled it from the contents of a pot she swung out from over the fire.

"Soup." She placed it on the sideboard and turned back to him. "Once it's cooled, you must drink its broth. It will help you regain your strength. Now rest. I have work to do."

As she returned to preparing vegetables, Brodie became aware of a hot breath near his face. Seeing its source, he started. A great white dog—or wolf, he couldn't determine which—stood close beside him. Eyes that suggested a savagery of roots gazed steadily into his.

Sweet Jesus! Where have I ended up? With a woman declared to be a witch, and a wolf to watch over me. I have to…

Wondering if there had been a sleeping potion in that drink the woman had given him, he felt himself drifting back into oblivion, the blessed oblivion beyond the pain raging in his leg. He'd been drugged before by a woman…hadn't he? What did this one have planned for him? Thoughts whirled around in his mind as he dropped back into darkness.

Remember, remember…

****

The next time he awoke, his thoughts were beginning to clear. The tangle of memories and fantasies that had been impaling his mind was retreating. Through the bedroom doorway he could see the woman sitting at the table, mending a garment and humming softly an old folk tune he recognized, albeit an English song. From the sunlight slanting in through windows, he judged it to be a clear day.

"Good morning, mistress." The words sounded harsh and gravelly from a dry mouth and throat.

"Ah, good morning, sir." She turned to him, and he saw a small smile twitch her lips. "You've decided to come back to the land of the living, I see."

"Aye." He moved and flinched. "I…" He gave up trying to speak. His bone-dry mouth denied him access to words.

She stood and went to a sideboard which held a hand pump beside a sink. She worked the handle several times before she thrust a mug under its flow.

"Drink." She came into the room to kneel beside him, raising his head with her free hand and putting the container to his mouth with the other.

He caught at her hand, holding the mug greedily to gulp its reviving contents. The cold water tasted better than the best ale or whisky he'd ever consumed.

"Enough." She pulled it from him with a gentle determination that his weakness wouldn't allow him to countermand. "You'll cramp yourself."

"Aye, aye." From dealing with parched animals, he knew she spoke the truth. Without further protest, he sank back on his pillow. As she returned to the sideboard, he wet his lips. The ache in his thigh reminded him that he had questions, many questions. And he was coming to realize that beneath the quilts and blankets he was naked.

"How did I come here?" he asked as she busied herself with food and dishes. "From the pain in my leg, I know…and a bit remembered…I've been shot. After that, I rode into a blizzard…and then nothing…until now." He suppressed a grunt as he tried to turn more in her direction.

"Your horse…that great pain in the rear…brought you here." Wiping her hands on the apron that protected her dress, she went to sit in a rocking chair by the fire. "And before you go giving him any medals, I believe it was as much the scent of my mare as a desire to save your life that prompted him."

Her lips curled at the corners. When he tried to return the friendliness, his frostbitten face produced a grimace.

"Is he…the lad…well?" He had to know. No matter how lacking in altruism this woman saw Fox's actions, Brodie knew better. While the stallion might have at least partly been lured by the mare's scent, he'd saved his master too many times in the past for Brodie not to attribute a goodly part of his rescue to him.

"Fit as a fiddle, as the saying goes. He's gobbling up my hay and oats at an alarming rate. When I turn him out into the pasture at the back of the barn, he paws up more fodder."

"Aye." This time Brodie did manage a cautious grin. "He's got an appetite, he has. But"—the idea suddenly dawned on him—"you've stabled him and even managed to turn him out to pasture?"

"You sound amazed."

"Fox is one magnificent beast, but he's never been much manageable by anyone aside from myself."

"Well, Brodie MacMillan, as you'll recall from your villagers monikering of me that day last autumn in your fine community of Riverhaven, I'm a witch. I have powers that can calm the most savage of beasts." She indicated the great wolf lying by her side. "Case in point, Jasper. As near as I can determine, he's a wolf. He dragged himself to my door one day, bloody from an ugly wound. After a bit of persuasion, he let me mend it. He's been my devoted companion ever since."

"So I'm to take that to mean he's your protector and I'd last about as long as a snowball in hell if I tried to harm you?"

She inclined her head in acknowledgement.

"I've a deal of bandages about my thigh, lass." He shifted to make himself more comfortable and flinched again. "I recall being shot. In most such cases I've known, a man's leg would have to come off or he'd die." He looked up at her, hoping the question didn't show fear in his countenance.

"Perhaps that has been the result in other such incidents." She straightened and put her hands on her hips as she looked down at him. "But amputation need not be the only remedy. There are others."

"Such as?" He caught himself wondering if her methods included sorcery.

"Removal of the musketball, then cleansing with whisky, stanching the bleeding with honey, and finally applying an ointment made from herbs, provided by my native friends."

"And you did all that…on your own?" Amazed, he stared up at her.

"My husband was a doctor. I learned from him…and the local native people. Don't be concerned." He caught a hint of humor in her tone. "I've not bewitched you nor cast a heathen spell over you."

She stood and went to check the pot of food bubbling on the hearth.

****

She was standing on a hilltop, golden-red hair blowing in a summer's breeze, her diaphanous gown wafting about her body to reveal every curve. Beside her stood the white wolf, alert and rigid. Looking downward, she gave a soft call. A magnificent horse, his shining coat the color of her hair, raced up the slope to join the pair on its zenith. Fox. Gentle as a lamb, he thrust his head against her shoulder. Standing together the three were a magnificent tribute to wild beauty.

"Mr. MacMillan." Her soft voice stirred him away from his dream. The woman herself stood silhouetted in the door of the room, the candle in her hand turning her hair to the colors of sunset.

"Aye."

"Are you comfortable? I can offer you a potion to relieve your pain and help you sleep." She crossed the shadowy room to place the candle in its stand on a table by his bed.

"No…no, thank you. I've done quite enough sleeping of late." He tried to move, but once again pain stilled his movement. He grimaced. "But perhaps a wee bit of that fine bread I smell."

"Very well." She turned to leave.

"If you wouldn't mind, lass, will you leave the

candle? I feel I've been in darkness long enough."

"As you wish." She placed the candle on the bedside table, and turned away, her gray gown swishing over the plank floor. "I've left a bucket near the bed for your…needs. If you want assistance…"

"No!" The word snapped out more sharply than he intended. "No, no, no, I'll manage," he continued more softly. Good God, he couldn't leave himself open to more embarrassment before this woman than he'd already experienced, either consciously or unconsciously. He had to get back some of his male dignity.

Later he returned to sleep, a peaceful sleep. He wondered the next morning if it had been natural or induced by the drink she'd given him with the bread. He awoke feeling rested, the pain in his leg bearable if he didn't try to move about.

"You're looking better this morning, Mr. MacMillan." She entered the room carrying a basin of steaming water, a length of drying linen, a bit of soap, and a razor on a tray. "I think it's time you became a bit more civilized in appearance. Let me raise you on your pillows."

She placed the items on a table and moved to put an arm beneath his shoulders.

"Whit are you plannin' to do, lassie?" He held back.

"Shave you."

"Ah, now, lass, I don't know…"

"I've shaved a number of my husband's patients and…even my husband, on occasion." The last brought a mischievous twinkle to her green eyes. "All survived my ministrations. Now sit up."

"Verrae well, verrae well." He tried to help as she drew him to a sitting position against the cabin wall behind his pillows. "But mind you go careful."

"Mr. MacMillan, I've already removed a musketball from your leg. I think I can be trusted to take a few whiskers off your face."

"Put that way, I must believe you can." He waited while she made a lather from the soap between her hands, but when she began to rub it over his face, a sensation tingled through him. It had been a long time since he'd been touched intimately by a woman, and now this goddess, this beautiful creature, was gently, sensuously moving her hands over his face. His jaw twitched.

"You must stay quiet, Mr. MacMillan," she said as she took up the razor and began to scrape away lather and stubble. "You don't need any more wounds."

"Aye, aye." He closed his lips and willed himself to remain inert. But as she leaned close, green eyes mere inches from his, breasts all but touching his chest, it took all of his inner fortitude to obey.

Chapter Eleven

Days and nights came and went. Brodie's bodily strength returned with the passage of each. He became able to manage some of his intimate bodily needs, but her care never faltered. From medication to food, from (the thought shamed him) emptying his bucket to changing the blankets around him, shaving him, and easing him into a man's nightshirt which he assumed had belonged to her deceased husband, she never failed to do all that could be expected of a caregiver. If she was a witch—and with her amazing ability to heal, he could think her no less—then she was a white sorceress, one whose powers were used only for good.

The thought eased his mind until late one night, in a bout of pain, his Highland superstition kicked in. What if she was a succubus, a creature who drew men's souls from their bodies while they slept and brought them forever under her control?

Bloody hell, Brodie MacMillan. What manner of fool are you? You're as bad as the villagers ready to persecute the woman simply because she knows a few remedies from the native people. The woman saved your life. This is 1813, man! Let common sense be your guide, not old wives' tales told around fires in the Highlands.

He became able to sit up in bed. As his strength returned, so did his desire to be back on his feet and to see Fox. Drawing himself as high on his pillows as he could, grimacing with the effort, he determined to tell her of his resolve and not let her thwart it with any argument against it. Furthermore, he had to begin shaving himself. That act, with its physical intimacy, was becoming more than he could bear.

She'd gone down to the barn to care for the horses. When she returned, he'd confront her with his plans.

As he heard her reenter the cabin, he pulled himself up against the log wall at the head of the bed. He bit his lip against the pain. Although each day his thigh gave him less misery, its injury was still a force to be reckoned with. He squared his shoulders in the clean nightshirt she'd helped him put on that morning and prepared for confrontation.

You're a hell of a man, Brodie MacMillan, when a woman not only takes care of your every need but tends to farm chores as well. It has to stop. You have to start pullin' your weight.

"Here." Holding out a pair of crutches, she paused in the bedroom doorway. She was dressed in the knee high moccasins, coat, trousers, and woolen cap she wore for working in the stable. "I had stored these in the barn. I think it's time you tried taking a short walk…to the other room."

"I was thinking along the same lines, lass." He gestured to the implements she carried. "Those will come in right handy."

"Let me help you to your feet." She laid the crutches aside and moved to assist him.

"No, no." Grimacing, he struggled to swing his legs over the edge of the bed. "You've done more than your share. It's time I helped myself."

She hesitated, then shrugged. "Very well." She pulled open a drawer in a chest by the wall. "Your own clothing was pretty much ruined. In here you'll find items you can wear. They belonged to my late husband."

"Lass, are you sure?"

"It's all right." She swung back to face him, her smile a little too bright. "Neil was a Scotsman to the core. He wouldn't want them to waste away." Leaving the room, she swept closed the curtain that served as a door.

Hell and damnation. I didn't expect her to give in so easy. What's that old expression about bitin' off more than you can chew? To top it off, she offers me her husband's clothing...

Grasping the crutches, he sucked in a deep breath. His first attempt at standing upright resulted in his sitting back down on the edge of the bed harder than he'd planned. He stifled a yelp of pain. On the second attempt, he managed to stagger to his feet and grasp the crutches. For a few moments, he stood clutching the hand grips, chest heaving, dampness dewing his forehead.

Who would ever have thought, Brodie lad, you'd be struggling to stand between two sticks, sweating in the depth of winter like it was midsummer. But if it weren't for that beautiful, unusual lass humming softly in the next room, I'd most likely be lying dead under the snow, chewed to bits by animals or ready to rot in the spring thaw.

Gripping his supports and steeling himself against anticipated pain, he made an effort to move forward.

Bloody hell, it hurts. And I'm weak as a newborn

lamb. But I'm alive and will recover...with two legs, thanks to the lass.

Gritting his teeth, he hobbled to the chest and began to search for clothing among the clean, neatly folded assortment inside the drawer. Dressing proved to be a long, awkward, frustrating task, but he persisted. When he finally succeeded in getting into underwear, trousers, and shirt, sweat sheening his body and face, he paused to look into the cracked mirror above the chest of drawers. He was amazed at how well the garments fit. Apparently Neil Abbott had been much the same height and build as himself. A thought flashed across his mind about trying to fill another man's shoes...or trousers.

No, no, no. It's clear as glass. No other man can take the place of her beloved Neil, any more than any woman can take Annie's spot in my heart.

"Come, sit at the table, Mr. MacMillan." Her voice interrupted his thoughts.

When he made his way into the kitchen, the crutches thumping over the board floor, she turned from the hearth with a smile that made rainbows dull by comparison. With a steaming bowl in her hands, she indicated a chair. "More oatmeal. Although I've fed you the same for breakfast for days, you still seem to enjoy it. I've never met a Scotsman who didn't."

"Aye, aye." The effort to get out of bed, dressed, and to the table had left him weaker than he'd reckoned. He dropped into the chair.

"The clothing fits you well." She paused to look him up and down. "I'm glad."

"It does." He searched her face for signs that his appearance pained her but saw only a flash of something he guessed was a fleeting memory.

"There's sugar in the bowl." She moved it toward him. "I'll fetch tea. But first…" She took a pair of woolen socks from a drying rack by the fireplace and knelt in front of him. "You can't go about barefoot. Give me your foot, right first, then the left."

"Whit! No, no, no, lass." He shrugged back as if burned. "You've already done more than enough for me. I'll not have you tendin' me like a servant."

"Mr. MacMillan, I'm tending you as a medical person who knows what it will take to bring you to full recovery. Catching a chill won't facilitate that goal. Now your right foot…please."

She looked up at him with such determination he couldn't refuse.

"Very well." The words came out as a resigned sigh, but when she set to her task, his fingers flexed in a desire to reach out and stroke the golden-red hair bending over his knee. He was further startled to discover that even in his weakened state he was capable of feeling a surge of desire.

"There." She stood and put her hands on her hips as she surveyed her handiwork. "Surely you must appreciate the warmth."

"Aye, aye." He had to admit he did as he looked down at the stockings. "My mother used to knit such stockings…from the wool of our own sheep, before…" His words trailed off. He couldn't continue the memory.

"Eat your oatmeal before it gets cold." She turned away without questioning. "I'll fetch your tea."

As she moved toward the pot on the stones in front of the hearth, he noticed his fiddle case hanging on the wall near the door. It gave him a small rush of pleasure to see it intact and not so near heat that its contents would be warped. He turned his attention to the porridge in front of him.

With sugar spread over it, the oatmeal fresh from the pot on the hearth warmed his insides and brought back pleasant memories...memories not only of his youth but also of his days in Harry's log house with Harry and Margaret and their family. Why in the name of all that was holy had he allowed himself into the clutches of that Carmody woman? Why had he given her the opportunity to ruin his life and quite probably those of the people he loved?

But deep down he knew. He'd been enticed by a beautiful woman, a woman whose dark eyes had tempted him with suggestions of what might be. Harry had been right. He'd behaved like a randy bastard and now was forced to pay the price.

As he finished his oatmeal and his second cup of tea, he looked around the neat, clean little cabin and marveled at his good fortune in ending up in such a place. He could have died, frozen, in the bush if not for Fox...and the minor miracle that had brought him here to this beautiful, astonishing woman. He looked at the back of her slim form at the counter and knew he had to distract himself from where his thoughts kept heading. In an effort to succeed, he glanced around the cabin.

"Whit's all this?" He indicated the desk beneath a window on the far side of the room. Its surface held neat stacks of papers, an inkwell, and in a stand, a metal pen the likes of which he'd never before seen. "Do you keep records of your cures?"

"Sometimes, but..." She turned to him, began to

speak, and hesitated.

"But?"

"You may as well know." She advanced to the table and began to gather up his breakfast dishes. "I write stories for a publisher in London."

"An author?" Surprise enhanced the two words.

"Yes."

"And you make a fair livin' at such?" The words were out before he realized they were inappropriate. *Damn Scotsman!* "I'm sorry," he hastened on. "None of my business."

"Your query probably came from wondering how I managed to pay Angus Harper last fall when I have no visible means of income." She paused, the stacked dishes in her hands, to look down at him. "Were you thinking that perhaps I had the ability to weave straw into gold?"

"No, no." He lowered his head to look down at his hands. "I shouldn't have asked."

"I was teasing you, Mr. MacMillan." He caught the humor in her tone. When he looked up, he saw she was grinning at him.

"Oh, aye? Well, you had me fair ashamed there for a minute." He regained his composure. "What is it you write about? Are you willing to tell me?"

She paused before sitting down opposite him at the table and placing the dishes on its surface in front of her.

"I'm willing." She met his gaze squarely. "Only you must promise not to scoff or denigrate."

"I would never do either."

"No, I believe you wouldn't. Very well, then. I write love stories... Well, more than that. Situation stories, stories of the conflicts in people's lives that prevent their finding true and lasting happiness. Have you heard of a book called *Pride and Prejudice*?"

He shook his head.

"Well, a lady has written several such stories set in England. I've just read her latest, which is, according to what I've read in newspapers I received this past autumn, a huge success. I ordered copies of her latest publications and was delighted to find it among the supplies I received from London in the spring. Mine run along the same lines, but are set here in British North America."

"Then I'll be wishing you all the success of this lady authoress."

"That would be an amazing feat, Mr. MacMillan." She smiled. "But I appreciate your good wishes...and your nonjudgmental outlook. Writing has allowed me sufficient financial security to continue with my husband's work with native remedies—not with the skill or knowledge he would have brought to the study, but nevertheless, his efforts won't fall entirely by the wayside."

"You're one amazing woman, Louisa Abbott." Brodie shifted in his chair and flinched as a pain from his leg made itself known. "I'm right astonished. But this place...how did you come by it? The villagers said you and your husband lived in Riverhaven until..."

"Until my husband's death. Yes, we did." She gazed down at the table and paused a moment before continuing. "After Neil died and people seemed bent on condemning me as a witch, I knew I had to leave...at least until they came to their senses. I'm sure you've heard the story of my burning that fever ship. I'd heard about this place, abandoned the previous year by a family who'd set up farming here. The husband had died, leaving a wife with three young children. When her brother, who lives in the United States, heard of her plight, he came for her, secretly in the dead of night, because of the difficulty of crossing the border with the war raging at the time. She and her children left with only their most cherished and personal items."

"But why did no one take it over? If this cabin is any indication of the state of the rest of the place, it would make a fine homestead."

"Again, the war." She looked up at him. "Setting up and maintaining a farm isn't easy anywhere, but especially in this rugged land. It's definitely not a way to become rapidly wealthy. With the war and England's supply of timber from the Baltic areas cut off, the British were turning to their North American colonies for badly needed lumber and spars. The tall white pines from this province are excellent for the latter purpose. Consequently, most people took to lumbering as a much more expedient way of making their fortunes. Few would want to get involved in reviving a small farm such as this. Thus, this place had lain fallow for several months."

She stood, gathered up the dishes, and headed for the sideboard.

"You're one amazing woman, Louisa Abbott. And pretty as a picture as well."

"Best be careful, Mr. MacMillan. Don't be too charming, or you might become a hero in one of my stories."

"Don't talk daft, Mistress. Who'd read a book with a Highland rogue as a hero?"

I wouldn't mind being your hero in real life, but with this damned leg... The thought dashed across his mind.

Chapter Twelve

It had been a week since his first tentative steps using the crutches had gotten him into the kitchen. Lost in thought, Brodie sat at the table. Louisa had gone out to do the barn chores. Clean, warm, well fed, and each day growing stronger, he decided it was time he expanded his horizons.

Clenching his teeth, he clutched the crutches beneath his arms and levered to his feet. The agony of the effort made him curse, but once he was upright, it subsided. He sucked in a deep breath, adjusted the crutches beneath his armpits, and stumped carefully across the room to where his own boots sat by the door.

The lass has dried and oiled them. Thank God. I wouldn't want to fit into any more of her husband's belongings, especially not his footwear. It would be way too much like stepping into another man's shoes. I'd understand her resenting that right down to the ground.

It took a good deal of effort and his entire vocabulary of curse words, but he struggled into them. He lurched to his feet and reached for his coat. Balancing on first one crutch, then the other, he got his arms into the sleeves. Finally, fully dressed for the first time in weeks, he grunted in satisfaction.

Must take care not to fall. He pulled open the door and hobbled out onto the snowy verandah. *If I hurt my leg again, that lovely lady won't think twice about stripping me to take care of it, just when I'm starting to regain a small drop of my manly dignity.*

Amusement curling the corners of his mouth, he started down the steps.

****

A sharp whinny from the red stallion made Louisa swing from her task of lifting manure into a wheelbarrow. Silhouetted against sunlight flooding into the barn, her patient, fully dressed, stood in its entrance.

"Good mornin', lass." His words carried the inflection of what she'd come to recognize as an indication of his good-natured grin. "A fine winter's day, is it not?"

"Aye." She mocked his usual response. "Good to see you out and about. There's someone here who is most anxious to renew your acquaintance." She indicated the stallion that, at the sound of Brodie's voice, had begun to cavort about in his stall.

She refrained from rebuking him for his rashness in making his first outdoor trek alone across the ice and snow of the dooryard. She'd learned that, in most cases, it was best to allow a patient to gauge his own abilities as he recovered.

"Fox." He hobbled toward the cavorting animal at such a pace Louisa feared he'd fall. Still she remained as she was. He wouldn't appreciate her interference... not at that moment.

"How are you, laddie?" He thrust his hand through the bars to rub the whiskered nose. His voice, soft with its Scottish lilt, delighted her. Brodie MacMillan exuded an earthy, virile charm that made her heartbeat quicken. A feeling suffused her that she hadn't experienced since she'd had a husband.

Endeavoring to shake off the sensation, she recognized his wisdom in not going into the stall with the excited horse. The animal, in his joy to see his master, might injure him.

"Easy, easy, laddie." Again the soothing voice that sent a tingle dancing over Louisa. "Give me a few more days, and we'll go for a wee run, shall we? I see the lass has been takin' good care of you." He turned to smile at Louisa. "He's lookin' right fit."

"He doesn't appear to have suffered from your unfortunate foray through the blizzard." She went into her mare's stall and rubbed the arched neck as the horse nuzzled her. "But his feet need tending. That will have to wait until you're fully recovered. I'm not about to attempt that task."

"Aye, well, once I can bend, I'll get right to it." He continued to rub the horse's nose and spoke without turning back to her. "Soon, I promise, I'll be doin' my share of the work around here. I've no desire to be a layabout."

"Not to worry." Recognizing his embarrassment, she spoke lightly. "There's little enough to do in winter."

"Perhaps." He turned to face her. "But looking after a house and a barn..." His gaze stopped on the white mare whose arched neck she was rubbing. "A fine beast." He hobbled over to stand outside the horse's stall. Fox snorted his disapproval. "That will be quite enough, laddie." He swung from the waist to speak to the stallion, and the animal quieted.

"You've trained him well," Louisa said.

"It was essential. May I?" He looked the question as he prepared to go into Snow's stall.

111

"Of course. She's not a fractious creature."

"My, my, she is one fine lady." With what Louisa recognized as the tone and appreciation of a knowledgeable horseman, he perused her mare. "Big enough to pull a wagon and yet a fine ridin' animal, I'll venture to guess."

"Yes, she is. That's why my husband chose her. We could afford but one horse. Therefore, our choice had to be strong and broken to harness as well as saddle, able to carry both of us when the need arose."

"Your husband..." He let the two words hang in the cold air as he looked at her.

"Dead, as you know. That's enough for now." She swung away and picked up her pitchfork. "Now, you must excuse me, Mr. MacMillan. I've barn work to do."

"Aye, aye." His words held weary defeat as he went out of the stall and headed back to the cabin.

She paused long enough in scooping up her mare's droppings to watch him hobble toward the house. He carried a deep-seated regret somewhere inside, she sensed, something that had little to do with his inability to help her with barn chores. She must find a way to distract him from such musings. Dark thoughts never helped a patient heal.

****

When she returned to the cabin, she discovered he'd spread the covers over the bed in the room he'd been occupying. He'd also moved his belongings, which she'd brought in from the stable, out into a corner of the kitchen by the bough bed.

"What is all this?" She spread her hands to indicate his handiwork.

"High time you had your sleeping quarters back.

High time I started sleeping nearer the hearth and being responsible for the fire in the night."

"Very well." She began to remove her outerwear. The thought of having a man to tend to a few of the chores around the homestead made her suddenly feel lighter.

"Lass, I have to ask." He turned to face her. "How have you managed to have a loft full of hay, bags of oats for your horse, vegetables in your root cellar, and split wood for the fire in the lean-to beside this cabin? I know you're one amazing woman. Still, I find it difficult to believe you managed all of that alone."

"Gold. Poor farmers and even woodsmen will supply even a supposed witch with her needs, for gold."

"Ah." He drew in a deep breath. "Of course."

"You weren't thinking I conjured up all those supplies?" She cast him a sly smirk before turning away.

"No, no, of course not! Lass…" Then he saw she was teasing.

****

Two weeks later he sat on a chair and pulled on his boots. Getting to his feet, he took his coat and cap from their peg by the door. She looked up from where she was seated at her desk, writing.

"You're going out?"

"Aye. You need solitude to work. Furthermore, now that I'm managing without crutches, I'm going to start to pull my weight around here. I've noticed more than a few things around this place that can do with mending."

"Such as?"

"Well, your stable needs a rare bit of work, not to

mention this cabin. The previous owners must have been planning to start repairs. There's a fair amount of building materials in the corner of the barn…planks, tools, and the like."

"You're convinced you're up to it?" The moment the question was out of her mouth, she regretted it. She and Neil had agreed a patient should, as long as it seemed reasonable in their medical opinion, be allowed to advance toward wellness at their own chosen pace.

"Aye, aye." He slapped on his cap. "I'm not so foolish as to get injured again. I can't have you nursing me back to health a second time. I'll leave the roof mending for a week or two…"

"A sensible thing to do."

"I have to say I'm sorry about that last bit." She caught a glimmer of amusement in his tone as he continued. "I'd fair like to get at the privy's roof. Snow and rain comin' inside is right distractin'."

After she'd heard the door open and close as he went out, she returned to her writing, a chuckle brimming in her throat. He was one enjoyable rogue, and no doubt about it. She also believed his was a totally unconscious charm, that he had no idea of the effect his good looks and personality had on women.

****

He released Fox into the pasture and set about chores, whistling. Working again for over a week, being useful. Damn, but it felt good. And with two legs, thanks to the woman in the cabin.

He carried a pair of planks out of the stable and paused to look toward the log house. Louisa Abbott was one amazing lass. He'd been blessed the day he'd offered his help to her in the village, having no inkling of what an important role she'd later play in his life.

He leaned the boards up against the side of the barn, put his hands on his hips, and threw back his head to savor the sunshine glinting off the snow and to breathe in the crisp winter air. Life had taken on a very different tone since that dark November afternoon when Harry had found him drunk and despondent in that tavern. Now he was filled with the desire to get back at it, to make a future for himself…and Louisa?

Enough foolish speculatin', laddie. Don't go forgettin' you're a fugitive, a bandit with no right to ask a fine woman to be part of your life. As soon as you finish the mendin' that has to be done around this place, you'll have to be on your way. Forcing thoughts of Louisa from his mind, he picked up the planks and headed for the privy. *Now to fix that god-awful hole in the roof.*

Whistling, he rounded the corner of the barn. A tall, broad-shouldered native man confronted him. Brodie stopped so abruptly he nearly dropped the boards he was carrying.

"You look well." The man spoke. "The last time I saw you, you did not appear long for this world."

"Runner. You must be Runner." Brodie leaned the planks against the shed and held out his right hand. "Louisa tells me you carried me in to the bed. Thank you, lad. I'm right pleased to meet you."

Looking down at Brodie's extended hand, Runner hesitated, then grasped it in a strong response.

"Your woman has sent me to tell you your meal is ready," he said. "She has asked my woman and me to join you."

"Well, then we'd best be gettin' on up there,"

Brodie said. "Mustn't disappoint the ladies." He gave the native man a friendly clasp on a shoulder before starting toward the log house. Louisa had told him how much she liked and trusted the couple. That was enough to recommend them to him.

Chapter Thirteen

"I was thinking we might go for a wee ride." A week later as they were finishing their breakfast, he surprised her with the idea. "Our horses could do with a bit of exercise, to say nothing of reminding them of their training and manners. It's a lovely day, snow has drifted off the meadow enough to allow us a fair canter. What do you say?"

Tea cup halfway to her mouth, she hesitated. Although he'd been working steadily at chores around the place, even mending the privy roof, she wondered if he had the stamina needed to handle a horse as fractious as that red stallion.

"I can guess what you're thinking, lassie." He stood and gathered up his cup, bowl, and spoon to carry them to the sideboard. Appealing grin in place, he turned back to her. "It's a right daft idea."

"Not at all. Since you've allowed me freedom to write while you do the chores about the place, I've been spending too much time bent over my desk. I'm only adverse to the plan on one score. Snow hasn't been under either harness or saddle most of the winter. Before I attempt to ride her, perhaps all that saved-up energy needs a good airing in the pasture."

"Louisa, in the short time I've known you, I've never heard a lie cross your lips…until now." He used her Christian name. Days ago they'd agreed to abandon formality of address. He headed for the door to snatch up his coat from its peg. "You're not apprehensive for yourself but for me. Trust me when I tell you Fox knows his master and how to behave with him in the saddle. We've been together these many years, and he's only once thrown me onto my backside. And that was an accident. The lad would never do it a-purpose."

"Very well, then, we'll go." She stood and began to clear the table. "You saddle the horses while I give Jasper what's left of our breakfast. If he's to run beside us, he'll need food in his belly."

"You'll not be leaving him to guard the place?"

"We'll be able to see the cabin from the meadow. Furthermore, the road to the village is a long one, still blocked in more than a few places by snowdrifts. We've had no visitors all winter aside from Marie and Runner and their child. I also believe I'm safe in assuming that whoever was pursuing you has given up by this time, convinced you either died of the cold and your wound or managed to get far, far away."

"Pursuin' me?" He looked over at her sharply.

"Brodie MacMillan, I know a fugitive when I see one." She headed for the sideboard with the dishes. "And a good man. You're both."

"You're one astonishin' woman, Louisa Abbott." His words, soft with the accent that made small quivers rush over her body, came back to her as he headed for the door. "I'll saddle the horses."

From a window, she watched him walking toward the barn. He was handsome, he was affable, he had natural charm. It would be a rare woman who didn't find Brodie MacMillan desirable.

Stop it, Louisa Abbott. The man has to be in

trouble with the law. Runner has heard of his past life. Probably everyone in the village of Riverhaven has, as well. Perhaps all of his crimes didn't occur across the sea. Quite possibly he's returned to his old way of life here in New Brunswick and is currently a fugitive in this country. Why else should he have turned up on your doorstep in the thick of a blizzard, wounded and alone? He's helping you out now, but be prepared. Some morning, no doubt, you'll wake up to find him either gone or packing to be so. Don't get involved with the man any more than you already are.

****

As he waited for her, the white mare's reins in his hand, he wondered at the wisdom of his suggestion. The animal was prancing and shaking her head. He recognized the signs. She was ready to take off at full gallop the moment she was released.

"Ready to go?" Louisa came toward him from the direction of the house, clad in trousers, boots, cap, and jacket, a smile brightening her face.

Hell and damnation but she's lovely…inside and out.

"More than ready, if your mare's antics are to be taken as an indication." He handed her the reins. "Are you sure you want to do this? The beast is feeling a tad frisky."

Their breaths formed a soft, white cloud in the frosty air between them.

"Of course." She swung into the saddle. The horse quieted to pawing and blowing a frost of vapor out into the cold air. "Where is that great nuisance of yours?"

"I left Fox saddled in his stall." Brodie, confident that she was in control, turned to head back into the barn. "Two rambunctious beasts might have been more than a handful for this recent invalid."

"Wise thinking."

He quieted the cavorting stallion before leading him out of the barn and swinging into the saddle. Once mounted, he brought the animal under control as easily as Louisa had calmed her mount.

"We seem to have the situation well in hand." She smiled over at him. All the sunshine of the winter morning couldn't have brightened the day more for him.

"Aye, aye. You lead."

"Very well." She swung the white mare about. In the blink of an eye, she was racing across the meadow beyond the barn.

"Hell and damnation, Fox, the lass is out to give us a run for our money." He clucked to the stallion. With a snort, Fox leaped forward in pursuit.

As they raced around the wide meadow after the woman and her mare, Brodie's heart filled with a delight he hadn't experienced in months, possibly years. Riding flat out in the company of the most amazing woman he'd ever met, he let happiness engulf him.

When finally she reined to a walk, Brodie urged Fox into position beside her. Her face bright from the nip of cold air and the excitement of the run, she smiled over at him.

"Louisa Abbott, you're the most beautiful thing on this earth."

"Brodie MacMillan, you've a smooth tongue and no doubt about it. A woman could be quite taken in by your flattery." Green eyes sparkling, she glanced over at him.

"Not flattery, lass." Although his words had startled him in their spontaneity, now that they were out, now that he saw her reaction, he was glad he had spewed them forth. "The God's own truth."

As their horses moved close together, their legs touched. Louisa Abbott leaned toward him and he toward her. For a moment their lips touched.

Then Brodie jerked away.

"Lass, I have no right…"

"Why? We're both unmarried people…aren't we?" Her voice hesitated over the last two words. Only then did he realize he'd never mentioned his marital status.

"Oh, aye, unmarried people. Adultery is not a sin that will be added to my list of…misadventures." This time it was Brodie who stumbled over the last word of his sentence. Beneath him, Fox snorted and moved restlessly. The mare was too close to be ignored.

"Misadventures? So whatever it is you are running from, it is not of a criminal nature?" Emerald eyes gazed intently into his.

"Louisa…"

"Ah, I see." She swung the white mare around, heading her back toward the homestead. "You're not yet ready to confide in me. Very well. Now…" She cast him a taunting grin. "Snow and I will race you and that great beast back to the barn. Go!"

As she put her heels to the mare's sides, the animal leaped forward and off across the long field. Brodie paused a moment, giving her a head start, holding a snorting, prancing Fox in check before letting him loose in pursuit. The stallion jumped forward with a smoothness that reminded Brodie of his days with

Harry in Scotland, when only the stallion's swiftness had saved him from capture.

But as he rode after her, he realized a cold, hard fact. He would have to be very careful around Louisa from now on. That kiss, innocent and tender as it had been, had told him he had strong feelings for her, feelings that must be kept in check, feelings that Brodie the bandit had no right to visit on her.

Chapter Fourteen

"You did a fine job mending the privy." Pausing in kneading bread dough, Louisa turned to face him as he came into the cabin and stopped at the basin and ewer on a stand by the door. "It was about to fall down."

"Aye, well, a bit of a temporary job." He stripped off his coat, hung it on the peg, and rolled up his shirtsleeves. "When the frost comes out of the ground, I plan to dig a huge hole thirty feet to the left and have your mare pull it over to it. She's a fine beast, broke to both harness and saddle. If I tried to put Fox to the task, he'd fair go mad."

"You've done such a task before?" She plunked the mound of dough into the bowl and covered it with a cloth.

"Aye. You sound surprised." He rubbed soap over his hands and up his forearms.

Somehow I wouldn't have imagined an outlaw doing such a chore."

"I wasn't born an outlaw." He dried his arms and hands as he faced her. "Nor do I consider myself truly one. I'm willing to admit I've had a few misadventures. Anything I am reputed to have done was always, at least in my humble opinion, for the greater good."

"Like Robin Hood? A laudable rogue?"

"Ah, now that's high praise." He changed the subject. "I see you managed to salvage my fiddle. I've noticed it hanging on the wall for some time now."

"I assume you can play it?" She'd rescued it from among his gear in the stable the morning after his arrival at her farm, brought it into the cabin, and hung it to dry.

"Once upon a time." He went to the sideboard, took up a cup, and headed for the teapot on the hearth.

"While you were recovering, I opened the case." She cast him a sideways glance with a hint of a smile in it. "The instrument inside appears fit as a fiddle can be. Would you be willing to attempt a tune...for me? I enjoy music. It would please me."

"Well, now, lass..." He wet his lips and stared out the window across the room into the gray winter's morning.

"It would brighten the day."

"Ah, well, then." He stood and went to retrieve it. With the case in hand, he returned to the table and placed it on the surface before him. He paused, looking down at it. She allowed him his moment. It held memories.

Finally, slowly, he lifted the lid to gaze inside. Glancing at him from the corner of her eye, Louisa watched him. Gingerly he lifted the instrument out and ran his fingers carefully, lovingly (she thought) over it.

"You've done a fine job of keepin' it from ruin, lass," he said, a catch in his voice. "You dinnae set it near the fire to dry."

"I know very little about the care of musical instruments, only to understand too much heat can bend and crack fine wood. Now, in recompense for my foresight, I request a tune." She swung to face him, cocking her head to one side and smiling. "Anything you fancy will be acceptable."

"Lass, I don't know…" He hesitated, eyes focused on the fiddle.

"Consider it payment for my dragging you from the storm, for giving your fractious stallion food and shelter," she teased. Then, softly, "Please."

"Verrae well." He wet his lips, drew a deep breath, and lifted the bow from the container. Pausing he stared at the instrument beneath. Louisa allowed him to take his time. She sensed this was an emotional moment.

Finally he heaved a sigh and set about adjusting the bow and the tension on the strings. When he appeared satisfied, he searched further into the case until he found a small container of rosin in a corner. With careful hands he applied some to the bow's horsehair.

"Are you ready for this?" He hefted the fiddle to beneath his chin. "I'll be more than a tad rusty."

"Ready." Louisa seated herself at the table and waited.

And suddenly there was magic. Into the dull winter day the haunting strains of "Greensleeves" broke gently, beautifully into the still air. A thrill passed over her. Louisa Abbott was enchanted by the man and his magic.

****

As Brodie played, warmth and joy began to seep into his heart. He loved music; it gave him a pleasure he couldn't describe…at least not to one who didn't share his feelings. He closed his eyes and let his hands move as gently over bow and fiddle as a lover over his adored one's body.

Then it happened. From near the window, a voice, pure and sweet, began to sing the words.

His eyes jolted open to see her silhouetted against the light as she gazed outside, her voice sending waves of pure delight coursing through him.

A sunbeam slipped through the clouds and into the cabin to touch her hair, turning it to a golden-red glow. Brodie MacMillan, inspired as never before, drew his bow across the strings to conjure beauty into sound that would match the image and the enchantment of the moment.

When the song ended, he let the fiddle and bow rest on his knees. His head dropped forward onto his chest, his eyes closed. Those moments had been magic, mystical, beyond compare. He wanted to hold them inside forever.

"Brodie?" She came to stand before him. He sucked in a deep breath, opened his eyes, and looked up at her. His name fell from her lips as softly as a benediction.

"Ah, lass." The words, issued from his soul, were all he could manage.

She bent and put her lips to his forehead. When he didn't react, she dropped to her knees before him, took fiddle and bow from his hands, and drew him down and forward to place her mouth over his in a soft kiss, a questioning kiss.

The answer came in a flash. He jolted to his feet, drawing her up into his arms.

When she finally pulled away from him, her smile greeted him with warmth and—dared he think it?—love.

"Louisa, Louisa." He pulled her back to him, burying his face in the cloud of her soft hair.

"Is that all you've got to say, Mr. Brodie

MacMillan?" Her tone teased gently. "After a woman makes so bold as to come to you as I have?" She looked up into his face.

"The wonder of it leaves this Highland laddie speechless. That the likes of you can see anything in the likes of me to find worth kissin'…"

He lowered his head to do it again, but she stepped out of his arms and stood away from him, arms crossed on her chest.

"Now that we've discovered that we, neither of us, finds the other unattractive"—she cocked her head to one side, a sly satisfied smile on her lips—"we must put boundaries on our attraction."

"Oh, aye? And just what might these boundaries consist of?"

"Simply because I initiated a change in our relationship, that does not mean I'm about to become your mistress or at any time warm your bed…at least not until certain matters are settled."

"Such as?" The words snapped out sharper than he'd intended. That kiss had awakened every ounce of male interest in his body. Now her putting conditions on how far he might take his desire chafed. It made him speak more abruptly than he'd intended.

"I've already told you I was married." She went to sit in one of the rocking chairs by the fire and indicated he was to take the other. Once he was seated, she continued, "I enjoyed being married…in every way." She paused, as he took the meaning from her words. Again desire washed over him in nearly consuming waves, but he stifled it sufficiently to listen as she continued.

"Doctor Neil Abbott was the only man I've ever

had." She looked over at him, her gaze unfaltering in its blatant honesty. "I am not about to take another easily or thoughtlessly. Therefore…"

"Therefore?" *Good God, what are her conditions? At the moment, I'll grant her anything.*

"My first condition is that we get to know and trust each other to the point of confiding all of our past lives between us before we make any serious commitments."

"Aye." Although he felt far from being in agreement, he saw the wisdom of her words. "And the others?"

"That once we're fully acquainted, that if we wish to enhance our relationship, we're willing to accept each other exactly as we are."

"Agreed. And next?"

"That if we then see ourselves as having a future together, that we marry before we share a bed. I'm not about to be any man's mistress…or whore."

"Lass, lass, no decent man would expect to do less by you." He leaned toward her, hoping she saw the sincerity of his words registered in his voice and countenance.

"Then you agree?"

"Aye. But…" He let a roguish grin quirk his mouth. "I'm assumin' that until we've bared our souls to each other, I may continue to court the beautiful Louisa?"

"I'd expect you to do no less, Mr. MacMillan." She stood and with a swirl of her skirts went to the cupboard and took down a flask. "Now, I think I should seal our bargain with a wee dram."

Chapter Fifteen

As Brodie opened the cabin door after finishing the morning chores at the barn, the smell of something cooking stopped him short. It made his mouth water. He'd learned Louisa was a fine cook, but this, whatever it was, had to be special. Then he saw it. On a spit over the fire, a large bird was roasting.

She stood from where she'd been stirring something in a pot on the stone ledge in front of the hearth and smiled at him. Another wave of astonishment, this time even greater, swept over him. She was wearing a cream-colored dress trimmed with matching lace and made of some sort of fine material, cut low to reveal the rounded tops of her breasts. She'd piled her shining hair on her head in an amazing style, allowing a few alluring curls to trim her lovely face.

"Lass." He pulled his woolen cap from his head and clutched it in both hands as he breathed the word. "Whit have ya done ta yerself?"

"Aren't you aware, Mr. MacMillan?" She bobbed him a neat curtsey. "It's Christmas. I thought a little dressing up was in order."

"A little!" Astonished, he sat down harder than he'd intended on the chair by the door, where they usually removed their boots. "Lass, you look like a blessed angel."

"Come, come, now." He thought he caught a slight

129

blush as she returned her attention to the pot. "You're simply surprised to see me in anything aside from trousers or a gray work dress."

"Aye, aye, that as well, but I will continue to declare you look like an angel." Still in a state of amazement, he managed to remove his boots and go to stand beside her. "What's that heavenly aroma? I swear it's fair makin' my mouth water."

"A goose that will be served with a sauce I learned to make back in England." She straightened to face him. "Runner brought it to me in the early autumn when I happened to mention it was a traditional meal in England at Christmas. It's been keeping in the ice house ever since, awaiting this special day. Now." She indicated the table he noticed had been carefully laid on a snow-white cloth, sprigs of pine in a container at its center. "Sit yourself down, good sir, and enjoy."

****

"If the old saying is true, Mrs. Abbott, that the way to a man's heart is through his stomach, I'm verrae much afeard I'm yours forever." Brodie leaned back in his chair and patted his belly. "That bird was as good as it smelled, maybe even better. And then nuts and raisins to top off the meal—where in heaven's name did you get them?"

"I purchased them at Angus Harper's store last autumn and was saving them, along with the goose, for this special day. I'm glad you enjoyed them."

"So much so, I'll clean up from this lovely feast." He stood and reached to gather up dishes.

"Much as I appreciate your kind offer, I'd be even more grateful if you'd see to the horses. I'd say there's another blizzard brewing, much like the one we had on the night you arrived here. It could be morning before it's fit to go outside again."

"Aye, aye, you're right. I'll be off, then. Come along, Jasper. After all the Christmas food you've enjoyed, a romp will do you good."

As he walked through the rising wind and swirling snowflakes, the wolf capering along beside him, Brodie MacMillan smiled. He couldn't have imagined a better Christmas.

****

Snow-coated, he and Jasper returned to the cabin. Inside the door, he paused to stamp his boots and remove them. Taking off his coat and cap, he took notice of the neat, clean room and the fire crackling out warmth and light from the hearth. Before it, in bewitching shadows, Louisa, still looking like a heavenly being, sat in one of two chairs, a cup in hand. She turned to smile at him, and his heart seemed to lurch in his chest.

"I'm enjoying some of the brandy I've been saving for a special occasion, as well." She indicated the bottle and another cup on the table cleared of the meal. "Help yourself."

"You're a right little squirrel when it comes to hidin' treats away." He moved to do as she invited.

"Are you complaining, Mr. MacMillan?" When he turned back to her, brandy flask in hand, he saw she was teasing.

"No, no, lass." He turned his attention to splashing liquor into a mug. "I would niver, niver complain about anything you did."

****

"I was a Highland rebel in Scotland. Now I'm an

131

outlaw in this country."

That night, with fine brandy relaxing him both in body and mind, while the blizzard raged about the cabin, Brodie decided it was time to tell his story. Only the dancing flames on the hearth lighted the room. There was a warm, close intimacy between them that, for Brodie, invited revelations.

"I suspected as much." She looked over at him, and he saw calm acceptance in her expression. "Any man who arrives on my doorstep in the heart of a blizzard, with a musketball in his leg and a horse coated with icy sweat, could be little else."

"Yet you took me in."

"You were injured and half frozen. What manner of human being would turn away another under those circumstances?"

"Perhaps one who feared for her safety. Perhaps a woman living alone in the wilderness."

"Perhaps, but not this woman. Will you go on with your story?"

He paused, drew a deep breath, then nodded. "Aye."

He'd thought it would be difficult to tell her about his grist mill on the edge of the Highlands in Scotland, about his father's death, about his loneliness until he'd met Annie, but the words, eased by the brandy, came easier than he'd imagined as she sat silently, mostly gazing into the dancing flames, sometimes glancing up at him. It was only when he came to the story of how the rebel known as Highland Harry had arrived at his home, a great bayonet wound in his side, that he began to falter.

When he fell silent and lowered his head to look at

his hands holding the mug of brandy clasped between his spread knees, she went to the table and picked up the bottle. Without speaking, she replenished his cup.

"Thank you, lass." He looked up at her. "It is a difficult tale."

He took a drink as she regained her seat across from him.

"Annie and I took Harry in, mended his wound, and tended him as best we could," he continued. "We weren't deceived. We knew who he was. He rode a mare everyone could recognize...a magnificent creature, charcoal gray with a silver mane and tail. Sympathizers with the Highlanders' plight, we were more than willing to help him. We wanted him to stay longer, until he was stronger, but he insisted on leaving, saying each moment he stayed he was putting us in mortal danger. And so he rode away. The next day I went off to the village on business, leaving Annie alone. She was six months pregnant with our first child."

He swallowed hard. A great lump had formed in his throat. She stood and went to stand beside him, her arm going about his shoulders, fingers gently massaging the tense muscles. Memory overriding his self control, he buried his face against her, sobbing great wrenching sobs. It was as if he hadn't been able to vent his grief until that moment.

She didn't speak. She let him have his grieving, holding him about his shoulders, standing beside his chair. Later he'd wonder how this remarkable woman knew that was exactly what he needed in those moments, how she'd silently waited until he was able to speak again and continue his tale...his tale of how the redcoats had come seeking Highland Harry, how they'd threatened to burn their home and mill if she didn't tell them where he was. When she refused, they did exactly as they'd said. Annie, in what Brodie could only guess had been a desperate attempt to save what she could, must have rushed back into their house and died there. She and the child she carried. It was his outrage at the atrocity that had driven him to join Highland Harry and become an outlaw against the British.

By the time he finished his story, she'd sunk down at his feet, her head bowed, the golden cloud of her hair spread out over his knee. He stroked it gently, the catharsis of those moments giving him an inner peace. They remained silent, the storm raging about the cabin the only sound aside from the occasional snapping of a log in the fire.

"Thank you, lass," he muttered finally.

"For what?" She looked up at him.

"For soothing my soul."

"You only needed someone to listen with their heart." She kissed his calloused hand and stood. "Now." She returned to the chair opposite him, took up her mug of brandy which she'd placed on the floor, and smoothed her skirts. "You must hear my tale."

"Aye." He wiped his face with his shirtsleeve, his word filled with soft Scottish inflection.

"The villagers say I burned my husband's corpse without shedding a single tear." She drew a deep breath. "What they don't talk about is the fact that my husband died saving their community from a deadly fever."

She paused, looking down at the mug in her hands. Brodie waited.

"My husband, Neil Abbott, was a doctor, a brilliant man, a graduate from the University of Edinburgh," she continued finally. "He was also a scientist, a man constantly in search of new and better medicines. He'd heard about native cures here in British North America and was determined to learn of their validity. Shortly after we were married, we sailed for this colony, Riverhaven in particular."

She stood and, fingering her mug, walked across the room to gaze out into the storm.

"For a time all was well. People were only too glad to have a doctor in their village. But when Neil began visiting the native settlements and investigating their remedies, residents became suspicious of him and his methods. They began to avoid us.

"Then a ship arrived and anchored off the village. No one came ashore. When one of the men rowed out to find a reason, he discovered the vessel was infested with a raging fever, that most of the passengers and crew were dead, a few left dying in horrible agony. The captain and crew had apparently been too ill to hoist the yellow flag that would indicate there was sickness aboard. Neil knew he had an obligation to help those still alive."

Again she paused, staring out into the storm, and Brodie waited.

"Although I offered to accompany him aboard, he ordered me to stay ashore…I was carrying our child."

A sharp intake of breath all but made Brodie choke. *Sweet Jesus, a child…and none now in evidence.*

"After he boarded that dreadful ship, I watched and waited." She held her head up proudly, dry-eyed, but Brodie saw her throat move as she swallowed. "It was the longest day of my life. As evening drew on, I could stand it no more. With the villagers watching, I took a boat and rowed out to the vessel."

This time when she paused, she turned away and went to the table. She picked up the brandy bottle and replenished her cup. Brodie watched and ached but knew he mustn't interfere. She'd listened to his story without interrupting. He owed her the same courtesy.

"I found all dead but Neil, who lay barely alive against the mainmast. He could scarcely speak but managed to order me ashore, to get away before I was seized by the sickness...to get away not only for myself but for our unborn child. He said I was to set the ship afire to prevent the fever spreading to the village."

She took a swallow from the mug, coughed, and closed her eyes for a moment before continuing.

"I couldn't do it. I couldn't leave him." Her words trembled. "I held him in my arms until he died."

"You loved him, lass." Brodie spoke softly. "You could do no less."

"After he'd passed, I did as he'd ordered. I set the ship afire and left in the boat that had brought me."

She wet her lips, hesitated, then continued. "When I reached shore, I could only stand mesmerized as I watched the vessel go up in flames. It was as if my heart was in the fire as well."

"You did what was right."

"Yes, I know." Her countenance reflected her pain. "But the villagers didn't see it that way. They branded me a witch. Who else, they said, could stand dry-eyed and watch her husband being burned...perhaps still alive."

"No, they couldnae be so ignorant!" Brodie came

to his feet and went to take her into his arms. She shrugged away. "Didnae they know some sorrow is too deep for tears?"

"If they did, they chose to ignore it. I went back to our cabin on the edge of the village with their mutterings following me." She swung away from him to stare back out the window into the blizzard. "The following morning I lost our child."

"Sweet Jesus!" This time it was Brodie who knelt in front of her, taking her hands in his as he dropped his head against her thigh.

Only the howling of the wind filled the cabin as the couple—who'd confided losses that had been, until that Christmas night, locked too deeply inside for release—took comfort from each other.

Chapter Sixteen

A week later, as they finished their evening meal, Brodie stood and began to help her clear the dishes.

"What in the world do you think you're doing?" On her feet at the opposite side of the table, she faced him, looking astonished.

"Clearing away." He paused to meet her stare. "That will leave you free to get back to your writing. I don't want you falling behind because of work I can do near as well."

"Brodie MacMillan, you are one remarkable man." She put her hands on her hips and grinned across at him.

"Why?" He went back to stacking dishes.

"Because you've been a warrior." She startled him with her response, and he let a bowl clatter from the pile as he looked at her again. "Definitely not a domestic kind of man."

"Aye, well, those days are in the past. Last night I told you about how I came to this country to live with Harry and Margaret and their children. I've not been blind to how Margaret and her girls clear away a meal. Don't doubt I know what I'm about. Now, let me get to the washing up and you, woman, to your desk."

"Are you certain? This is hardly your province. When I dragged you inside out of the blizzard, you had a sword in a scabbard at your side and the pistol in your belt. And your body." Lowering her gaze to her task, she gathered up her bowl and cup and headed for the sideboard.

"My body? Lass, I know you've seen it all...more than I'd like a decent woman such as yourself to see, but what do you mean? That how I...look brands me a warrior?"

"You've the hard, lean body of a fighting man." She spoke without turning back to him, and he was amused to see a slight blush moving up her neck. "And, unless my medical knowledge is entirely askew, that scar on your arm is from a knife or bayonet wound. Such men do not lower themselves to domestic chores."

"Aye, well, this lad owes his healer a debt of gratitude such as he'll not be able to repay simply by clearin' a table and washin' up a few dishes." His Highland accent broke through as he spoke.

"Very well. I'll leave you to it and get back to the next chapter."

She seated herself at the secretary, where she picked up her pen and dabbed it into the inkwell. Shortly she was bent over her papers, absorbed in her writing.

Quite a woman, quite a woman. Now if I could just figure out how to wash the blessed things to her satisfaction...

****

"Brodie?" As he rubbed at food on a plate, she turned on her chair at her desk.

"Aye." The word came out with a trace of annoyance. This dishwashing wasn't as simple as he'd thought.

"What crime were you accused of in this country

that forced you to become a fugitive?"

"Whit?" He swung to face her, wet hands dripping water onto the floor.

"What crime were you accused of…"

"I heard, I heard." Lowering his head, he shook it slowly. "Lass, if I tell you…"

"Brodie, you must know by now I'm an accepting woman. Furthermore, after living with you this long, I'm confident you're not the marauding type of outlaw. Your crime cannot be so very heinous."

"Aye, well, perhaps." He drew a deep breath as he met her gaze. "Seduction."

"Seduction?" Her calm demeanor never faltered.

"Aye. Need I say I was falsely accused, that I never seduced the lady or promised her marriage? Need I say that she leveled the charge simply to ruin Harry, his family, and myself because she blames us for her father's death?"

"It's good information. Of course, you don't have to tell the woman you've been living with for weeks that you were falsely accused of such a crime. Experience assures me of your innocence." She returned to her writing more calmly than when he'd told her he was going to wash their dishes.

You're one amazing lass, Louisa Abbott. Aye, one amazing lass.

He went back to rubbing at the plate.

****

"Brodie, you must see this!" As he put the last mug into the cupboard, Louisa burst into the cabin, her face glowing with excitement. "It's positively magnificent!" She pulled his coat from its peg by the door and held it out to him. While he was finishing with the dishes, she'd taken a break from her writing and stepped out onto the verandah.

"'Whit in heaven's name..."

"Hurry, hurry!"

"Verrae well." He shoved his arms into the sleeves and followed her out onto the verandah.

"Look!" She waved her arms upward.

Brodie looked. And words deserted him.

Sprouting higher and higher up among the stars, Northern Lights undulated into the night sky. Like mystic spirits gowned in green and white, they wreathed across the darkness, then doubled back to rise again. Alive with their essence, the heavens danced. Brodie MacMillan, outlaw and highwayman, was speechless.

"Magnificent, isn't it?" Her voice close beside him was so soft, so enchanting, it matched the magic of this display of natural beauty. "I've never seen them so bright, so perfect. Perhaps..."

When she didn't continue, he looked down at her, into those wonderful green eyes that seemed to glow with reflection from above, and saw all that he desired to know. She moved in front of him to meet his kiss as he lowered his head.

Her body, even through the layers of winter clothing, seemed to meld into his, to touch every bit from shoulder to thigh. Desire overwhelmed him as never before.

Sweet Jesus, how can I be expected to face such temptation and yet respect this woman as she deserves?

"Brodie MacMillan." She said his full name when he finally let her come up for breath, when she looked up at him, eyes mirroring what he recognized as desire matching his own.

"Aye, lass." He could barely breathe the words as she touched a hand to his cheek.

"Brodie MacMillan, I desire you with all my body, heart, and soul." Her blatant confession dumbfounded him.

"Lass…" His thoughts tangled, he couldn't find words to reply.

"Have I shocked you, my love? For such you are, or I'd not speak so boldly."

Enchanted, that's what I am. Enchanted. Or bewitched. This woman is sayin' I'm her love…

"Louisa…" Her name stumbled from his lips with all the reverence he'd ever used in prayer…when he'd still prayed.

"I've taken your breath away." She took a step back from him, but not so far as to be out of his arms. "Still, I would like to hear your response."

"Lass, of course I desire you." The revelation burst over him like a great epiphany. "How could I do less?"

"And love me?"

"Of course, of course."

"Then you'd be willing to consider my proposal of marriage?"

"Marriage?" A wave of lightheadedness swept over him.

Is this moment happenin'? Or have those cavortin' lights bewitched my brain?

When he failed to reply, she slipped from his embrace and turned away to stare up at the sky, into those erotically dancing heavens. In the ensuing silence, he fancied he heard them crackling, snapping out into the night.

"I take it your answer is no." She spoke, her back still toward him, rigid and straight.

"Then you take it wrong." He moved to stand close behind her and put his hand on her shoulder. "I was only speechless for a moment that such as you would have the likes of me. I'd be honored to marry you, Louisa Abbott."

He was relieved at the soft smile that turned up the corners of her lips, at the welcoming desire he saw coming into her eyes as her arms went back about his neck. When she kissed him, it was with a passion that staggered him, that made him swell with need. But when his hand slid down her back, she moved away from him.

"I meant what I said about our relationship, Brodie." She looked up at him. "I want marriage, nothing less. While it is apparent we desire each other, I will not be your doxy or your whore."

"Lass, I'd never expect that of you." He let his hand fall to his side, his words startled with surprise. "Forgive me. I've been celibate a very long time, and…"

"As have I." She met his gaze directly, no faltering in her outlook. "But we must be married first."

"Aye, aye." His acquiescence came out as a weary sigh. "But how can we marry with no minister, no man of the cloth of any persuasion? We'll have to wait for spring, when the snow melts, to find one. And, my darlin' girl, I have to tell you I'm a whole lot too eager to wait months."

"We'll say our vows here tonight, with our hands on the Bible." She astonished him with her reply. "God is just as much in this place as in any church."

"I don't know..." He sucked in a deep breath. "Louisa, darlin', the last thing I want to do is involve you in any kind of mock marriage, anything that isn't right. Much as I want it..."

"Brodie MacMillan, you've made your feelings clear to me, and I'm not prepared to wait." She turned to go back into the cabin. "We'll marry this very night, here, with our hands on the Bible and Jasper as our witness."

"Verrae well." His affability kicked in. "But since you've chosen the time, I'll choose the place. I choose the stable, with Fox and Snow as witnesses. Jasper can be my attendant."

"Verrae well." She swung back to face him, imitating his Highland brogue, a devilish twinkle in her eyes. "The stable it is. Go down there and wait for me. As I recall, one other important event took place in such a location. Perhaps stables have remained holy places."

Chapter Seventeen

After she'd gone back inside, Brodie stood gazing up into the large, soft flakes that had begun to fall. The Northern Lights were fading. They'd worked their magic and were slipping away. Stars sparkled from around the scattering of clouds that were bringing the light snowfall. A beautiful night, gentle and kind. Peace settled over the anticipation in his spirit.

Beside him, Jasper whined.

"All right, all right, let us make our way to the stable." He picked up the lantern she'd passed out to him and started down the steps, realizing he barely limped anymore. The lass had done a fine job of patching him up.

Together he and the wolf made their way to the barn. Snow nickered softly at their entrance, but Fox, true to form, began to stamp and paw and snort his restlessness.

"Take it easy, my lad." Brodie went to the wooden bars of the stallion's stall and stuck a hand through to calm him. "You can't be any more eager than I am."

He was rubbing the horse's nose when a slight sound made him turn. And catch his breath.

Holding a lantern, swathed in an emerald green hooded cloak trimmed with white fur, she stood smiling at him from just inside the door. Snowflakes glinted like diamonds on the garment and on the soft curls of her hair peeking from beneath her hood in the shadowy half-light. She carried a black book he recognized as a Bible. No witch, this vision. An angel, most surely.

"Louisa." Her name fell from his lips, reverent as a prayer.

More words failed him. The bandit Brodie MacMillan was utterly and entirely enchanted by his bride.

****

"I, Louisa Abbott, take you, Brodie MacMillan, as my husband in the eyes of God and the laws of this land." They were kneeling before a scarred old bench, her hand over his on the Bible. "I promise to love, honor, and respect you. I will care for you in sickness and health. Only death will take me from your side."

She paused and looked over at him, emerald eyes capturing his body, heart, and soul forever.

"I have no fine words, my darlin' Louisa." He had to battle to speak over the hard lump of emotion in his throat. "I can only promise, as there is breath in my body, I will love and respect and honor you with every ounce of my body, mind, and spirit. Please, God…" He looked up into the rafters, his tone breaking with emotion. "Grant us a long and happy life together." He coughed, lowering his gaze to their clasped hands on the Bible. He hadn't prayed since before Annie and his child had died. "Amen."

"Amen." She pronounced the benediction softly as their gazes met in the reverent hush of the stable.

Fox snorted.

They chuckled as Brodie got to his feet and held down a hand to help his bride to hers.

"Nothing like the lad to break up a moment."

"Perhaps he's jealous."

"Aye, and why wouldn't he be? I've just married the most beautiful creature in the world." He spoke softly as he reached out with both hands to lower the hood to her shoulders, to take her into his arms and kiss his bride.

When they walked back to the house in a night enchanted with the combined glitter of stars and snowflakes, Brodie held his arm about her shoulders. Halfway to the house, he couldn't help himself. He had to stop, turn her to him, and kiss her again.

"I am one happy man, lass."

"And I am a happy woman, Brodie MacMillan. And by morning"—she slanted him a sly, coquettish glance—"even happier and much more content."

"You are a minx." He chuckled as they continued on their way. "But tell me. Where did you get such a fine garment?" He touched the velvet cape.

"My parents gave it to me when Neil and I were leaving Scotland." She smiled a little wistfully. "I think they fancied, as a doctor's wife, I'd be invited to balls and such. Their concept of this new country was sadly incorrect."

"You must miss them." They'd reached the verandah of the cabin and paused before the door.

"After Neil and our child had passed, for a time I missed them very much." She avoided looking at him, and he heard the catch in her throat. "But"—her tone brightened, and she raised her gaze to his face—"I learned to cope with my loneliness. I had to struggle to survive on my own. For comfort I had my writing, and Snow, and then Jasper. Now I won't have to feel lost and empty anymore…will I?"

****

Brodie awoke, a sense of euphoria such as he'd never before experienced flooding through every fiber of his body. What had happened to him? Then, as memory of the night he'd had with Louisa returned, an involuntary grin widened his mouth. A sense of utter satisfaction flooded through flesh and soul. He stretched, enjoying his nakedness and the sense of complete relaxation.

"Good morning." She entered the bedroom with only a shawl thrown over her body. "Are you hungry for breakfast, or..." She dropped the garment, and he knew it wasn't food he longed for.

Was he in heaven, or was he enchanted? At the moment he wasn't thinking about either. He simply knew he was happy, absolutely happy.

****

The winter months that followed were no less euphoric for Brodie. Each day he awoke to marvel at the great good fortune that had given him this wonderful woman with whom to share his life. Isolated as they were by snow, he had few apprehensions of their being found out.

As he worked about the homestead, as he carried in wood, fed the horses, shoveled snow, and cleared away dishes after their meal, he caught himself whistling from the pure joy of what life had given him. When he watched Louisa bent over her desk, intent on her writing, he never could suppress the smile that involuntarily curled his lips.

Brodie MacMillan was a happy man, and so he would remain while the snow lasted. He tried to push away the thought of what he would be forced to do when the farm once more became accessible to the outside world. The prospect of leaving the woman he loved more than life itself, of going back on the run, of possibly never seeing her again, made his gut knot so violently he had to struggle not to double over in agony. He knew he had no choice. If he were found here, if it became known she'd harbored a fugitive, she'd be as much an outlaw as he was. He couldn't risk that happening.

He fought thoughts of the future aside. For now, he'd simply live in the paradise that was his marriage to the most amazing woman he'd ever known.

****

The following morning, he eased out of Louisa's arms as dawn peeked through the window. She moved and reached for him in her sleep, but he avoided her and slipped out of bed. Shortly he was dressed and heading for the stable. He felt a great need to go for a run on Fox. His night with Louisa had left him feeling full of youthful exuberance and the desire to act wild and free. It had been a night of enchantment, a magnificent fulfillment for body and soul. Now he had to wear off the euphoria or burst.

At the stable, he bridled the stallion and led him outside.

"Now, my fine lad, let us act like a couple of creatures wild with happiness," he said. He grasped the stallion's mane and vaulted onto its bare back as he'd done so often in the Highlands, as he'd done when pursued, when the joy of the chase had coursed through him like a heady wine. As if remembering those days, Fox leaped forward, driven by his master's heels and hands to race across the meadow.

At a breakneck run, they circled the field, both exulting at the speed and freedom. Finally, when Fox began to show sweat around his neck, Brodie slowed him and headed into a grove through which he knew a stream ran. Although it had been frozen since he'd discovered it a month ago, he thought it might offer an opening large enough for the stallion to quench his thirst.

As the horse lowered his head to drink from a small hole in the ice, Brodie became aware of the sounds of the stream's awakening beneath its winter's covering, an early herald of spring. And spring was exactly what Brodie was dreading.

He rode Fox back to the stable at a walk and put him into his stall. As he began to rub the animal down, he noticed the gray hairs appearing amid the red coat.

"How old are you, laddie?" he asked softly. "I've never given it a thought until now. Perhaps we're both getting too long in the tooth for the outlaw life." He paused. "But we don't have any choice, do we?"

****

"Lass, would you mind if I read one of your books?"

"What?" Surprised, she turned from her writing to look at him. He was sitting in a chair by the hearth. It was a bitterly cold morning, and he'd had to add logs to the fire several times to keep the cabin warm.

"I'm asking if I might read one of your stories. I can read, you know."

"I never doubted that you could. I'm simply astonished you'd want to spend time reading a novel."

"Well, not any novel. One of yours. I'd like to know a bit more of what goes on my wife's pretty

150

head." He grinned at her.

"Of course." She opened a drawer of the desk, paused to look over the contents, then drew out a volume. "Perhaps you might enjoy this one." She held it out to him.

He stood and crossed the room to take it from her.

"*Backwoods Bride*." He perused the title. "Is it perhaps a tale of a woman such as yourself?"

"You'll have to read it and find out." She turned back to her work.

****

"Well?" Louisa looked over at him. Casting furtive glances at him over the course of the morning, she'd been amazed to see him absorbed in the book.

"Lass, I said I can read"—he looked over at her—"but not at a great speed. However…"

He stood, placed the book carefully on his chair, opened to the page he had been reading, and went to put another log in the fire.

"However?" She found she was awaiting his opinion with a combination of eagerness and trepidation.

"However." He took up the book and reseated himself. "I'm right taken by the yarn."

"Are you?" A sense of delight coursed through her. "Do you know what the term 'yarn' means?"

"Aye, my mother was a clergyman's daughter. She taught me a bit about books and such. A yarn is a tale with a bit of both truth and fiction."

"And you're finding my book a yarn, not just a silly story? Just what parts do you see as truth?"

"The bits about the love between the man and woman. Lass, you couldn't have captured the reality of those moments any better. That English writer lass had better be prepared for some serious competition."

"Oh, Brodie, I'm delighted." She got to her feet and rushed across the room to kneel before him, to cover his hands with hers as they held the book. "Your approval is so very important to me."

"Well, I'm right glad I've pleased you, my darlin', but I'm no scholar. I could not give you educated reasons for my likin' it. I just know I'm enjoyin' it no end."

"That's the whole purpose of what I write. To give people pleasure, an escape from the harshness of reality."

"You've done that, sure and certain." He bent forward to kiss the top of her head. "Now, you'd best get back to your writin', or a whole lot of people will be missin' out on those lovely moments you're supposed to be conjurin' up. Furthermore, if you keep on kneelin' there, lookin' so beautiful, I fear I'll lose interest in this fine book and be forced to carry the authoress off to the bedroom."

Chuckling, she stood and returned to her desk. Brodie MacMillan definitely was one in a million, she decided as she glanced back at him, once more absorbed in her story. An outlaw who could appreciate a love story was a rare man indeed. Each day she cherished him more.

Chapter Eighteen

Rain beat against the windows while a gale roared about the cabin. March was going out like the proverbial lion. Fighting down the sick feeling the change in weather was engendering, Brodie glanced absently from tuning his fiddle to the early spring storm raging outside. Soon, within days, he'd have to be on his way. Soon he'd have to leave the woman he loved more than life itself and go back on the run. With the snow melting in the rain, the homestead would become accessible, if it weren't already.

His thoughts broke off abruptly. Someone or something was stumbling up the cabin steps.

"Bloody hell…!" Brodie dropped his fiddle onto the table as Louisa swung from her writing.

"Let me in!" a man's voice yelled. "For God's sake, let me in. I'm bleedin' to death!"

"Jonah Parsons." In an instant Brodie was on his feet. "What does that old bugger want?"

As he swung the door open, the man staggered inside. Crusted with freezing rain, he clutched his left arm.

"What are you doin' here?" Brodie faced the new arrival. The man's scraggly beard and eyebrows iced from the storm gave him the appearance of some horrible mythical creature. He could have been Old Man Winter or a weird creature from some fantastic tale designed to terrorize.

"Brodie…Brodie MacMillan, is it you?" He stared up at the younger man. "Most in the village thought you must've died…or fled to the United States."

"Well, I haven't done either. Now whit are you doin' here?"

"The man's injured, Brodie." Louisa stepped forward to take Jonah's arm and help him to a chair by the fire. "It's no time for questions."

"Aye, aye, that's it, mistress." Jonah Parsons grimaced as she assisted him out of his coat, stiff with frozen rain. Beneath it, a ragged, dirty bandage had been wound about his left forearm. "I cut myself something fierce tryin' to chop firewood. I was holdin' a stick…it was bitter cold, the chopping block coated with ice. The ax slipped and landed on my arm. I bound it best I could, but I've heard of men gettin' infection and losin' an arm, so I came to find you with your magic and Injun cures." He looked up appealingly at Louisa.

"How did you find us?" Apprehension coiled in Brodie's gut.

"I'd heard rumors that the witch…that is, Mistress Abbott, was living on this old farm. I had no idea I'd find you here, Brodie."

"You couldn't have walked, not in this condition." Louisa began to unwind the rags from about his wound.

"No, no. I borrowed a mule from the stables in the village. A mule will wade through mud and snow up to his belly, where a horse will panic."

"I hope you told no one your plan?" Brodie wasn't about to let up his inquisition even as Louisa revealed the ugly gash stretching from wrist to elbow.

"No, no, of course not." Jonah flinched as she began to examine the wound that leaked blood.

"Brodie, enough questions." She straightened to frown at him. "Fetch my medical supplies...and that jar of honey on the sideboard. It will stanch the bleeding while I prepare to remedy Mr. Parsons' wound. Then perhaps you should see to the mule. The poor creature must be freezing out in this weather. Put it in the barn."

****

"You stood up to the treatment well, Mr. Parsons." Louisa finished wrapping a clean bandage over the neatly stitched wound and smiled at her patient.

"Aye, well, that brown drink you gave me fair made it easier." He grinned at her from under eyelids grown heavy from the effects of laudanum.

"You'd best lie down on the bed in the corner." She indicated the mattress. "And get some sleep. Good God, what now?"

Jasper had begun to bark and snarl.

Above the noise of the gale, she heard more footsteps rushing up her steps. The door was flung open, and two big men, drenched with rain and ice pellets, pistols drawn, burst inside.

"Ah-ha, you old bastard!" one of them yelled at Jonah. "We figured you knew where we'd find that bit of trash Brodie MacMillan. Where is he, mistress? Tell us, or we'll make short work of that wolf!" He aimed a gun at the snarling Jasper.

"Jasper, quiet." Struggling to remain calm and look innocuous, Louisa put a hand on the animal's head. He subsided to a rumbling growl. "What makes you think Brodie whatever-his-name is here?"

"Because we've heard how he helped the witch

when she came to the village, how they became chummy real fast," he replied. "And because we figured if we watched this old bugger here"—he indicated Jonah—"he'd eventually lead us to the villain. We know he was responsible for letting MacMillan out of jail, even if it was supposed to be the result of his being overpowered."

"He did overpower me!" The older man's voice was a frightened whine. "You've seen the blighter. He's twice as big and not half as old as me. I didn't have a chance."

"Aye, right." The two words were a sneer. "Check the other room, Tom." He indicated the bedroom with its curtained doorway. "He's probably hiding under the bed."

"I won't have you invading my home!" Louisa struggled to slow their progress as the man named Tom brushed past her. When Brodie saw their horses on his way back from the barn, he'd know he had to be cautious. Hopefully, before he came into the cabin, he'd realize the identities of these unwanted visitors and take the opportunity to get away. She had to keep them talking to give him more time.

"Be quiet, mistress, or I'll be forced to shoot that creature you're holding back."

"Nothing here, Clem." His companion came out of the bedroom. "But there are men's clothes about."

"My dead husband's." Louisa countered quickly. "I was planning to give them to the needy the next time I was in the village."

"A likely story! Clem, search the stable. See if there's a big red stallion living there. That'll tell us the bastard isn't far away. He'd never leave without that brute. On your way out, throw in that chain on the verandah. I think it was used to tether the wolf. She can chain the brute up in here. I don't like the way it's looking at me."

An icy-cold nausea seized Louisa. Oh, God, even if he'd managed to get away on Fox, there would still be tracks. The rain couldn't immediately expunge them.

"Would you like some tea?" Louisa took on the role of hostess as the man named Clem went out of the cabin. Anything to slow their progress, possibly even to gain a bit of confidence. "Or perhaps a bowl of stew and some fresh-baked bread?"

"Don't go trying to butter me up, mistress," snapped the man with the gun, but she saw his eyes roaming to the hearth and cupboard.

"But you must be cold and hungry after your long ride."

The door opened, and the man Clem came inside dragging the chain Louisa had used to tie Jasper to the verandah. He threw it at Louisa's feet.

"Tether him in the corner," Tom ordered. "Otherwise I'll be forced to blow his head off. He's worrying me. Clem, get on down to the barn and see if there's any signs that the bastard has been here."

The minutes until the man named Clem returned had to be among the longest in Louisa's life. She helped Jonah to the bed in the corner, removed his boots, and after some protest, his wet breeches. His eyes closed in sleep as she pulled a blanket over him. She was relieved. Unconscious from the effects of the laudanum, the man was incapable of speaking any words that might endanger Brodie.

"Nothing out there." Clem came back into the

cabin. He paused inside the door to brush rain from his coat and stamp mud from his feet. "Nothing except the old man's mule and a big white mare that probably belongs to her." He jerked a mittened thumb toward Louisa.

"No tracks, nothing?"

"A bunch of red hair on the door of the mule's stall."

"Mine." Louisa jumped in, but a moment later realized it was too sudden, too urgent. "The mule butted me against the boards when I was stabling him."

"Clem." Tom was staring at her, eyes narrowed. "Tell me about that hair."

"Long and red, that's all."

"Like this." Louisa pulled her hair from its combs and let it flow down her back.

"Like that?" Tom questioned his companion.

"Well…" To Louisa's disgust Clem stepped forward to grasp her hair in a big, dirty hand. "No, this is softer, way softer." He leered at her over brown teeth as he fondled it before letting his hand drift to her shoulder. He guffawed when Louisa shrugged away.

"A horse's hair from a mane or tail." Tom slammed the fist of his left hand into his right. "Bloody hell, the bastard has been here!" He grabbed Louisa by an arm. "I think it's about time you started telling the truth, my girl!"

"All right, all right!" A plan in mind, Louisa pretended to quail. "He was here…early in the winter. He stole supplies and left."

"And when was this, my fine lady?"

"After Christmas, before the New Year."

"He's wanted for seduction, the randy bastard." He

leaned into her face, breathing a foul stench. "And you're telling me he only wanted supplies, nothing more.?"

"Nothing more." She held her ground. "He was desperate to get away…to Upper Canada. He said he had friends there."

"That stew smells good, Tom, and it's one damnable, long, cold ride back to the village." Clem was gazing toward the hearth.

"Ah, what the hell!" Tom pulled off his coat and seated himself at the table. "Dish us up some of that food, woman. And a bit of bread and tea."

"Of course." She hastened to do his bidding as a snore from Jonah reassured her that the old man wouldn't be a danger with his loose tongue for some time. That, accompanied with the strong possibility that Brodie had managed to get away somehow without leaving a trail, allowed her a measure of comfort. The longer she could keep these nasty bits of work here, the better chance he had of making a complete escape.

As she poured tea into a pair of mugs, overwhelming sadness shadowed her feelings. Brodie had had to make a major run away from the cabin. She'd probably never see him again.

Chapter Nineteen

In trees beyond the barn, Brodie hunched against the driving rain as he held Fox quiet beside him.

Sweet Jesus, what's going on? If either of those great louts harm Louisa, they'll be adding murder to my list of offenses.

A touch on his arm made him whirl. Behind him, Runner held up a hand to warn him to silence.

"I was bringing moose meat," he muttered as he dropped a sack onto the ground. "I saw those men and decided to wait until I knew what they wanted, until I knew if you and Louisa would need my help."

"Much appreciated." A slight sense of relief washed over Brodie as he looked at the tall, strong native man. Knowing he'd have ready assistance if he had to fight the pair in the cabin gave him confidence. "I'm fair goin' mad wonderin' what's happening inside the cabin."

"I'll look in at a window. I'll try not to let them see me, but if they do, they'll just think its another Indian prowling about."

"Good man." Brodie slapped him on a shoulder.

With a curt nod, Runner headed off.

****

The pair gobbled the food, wiped their mouths with the backs of their hands, and stood. As they put on their coats they'd left drying by the hearth, the one named

Clem swung on her.

"You wouldn't be having a bit of whisky or rum about the place?"

"Only a half flask I keep for medical use." She went to a cupboard and took it out. "Please, please don't take it. It's all I have left," she lied.

"Give it here." Tom snatched it from her hand, pulled out the stopper, and quaffed a great drink. He choked, then handed it to his partner, who did the same before offering it back to him. He gulped another mouthful and thrust it into an inner pocket of his coat.

"You'll just have to do without until spring." He leered. "Maybe your Injun friends can make you some kind of joy juice to get you through the long, lonely nights. Folks say you're as cozy with them as your man once was." His companion chuckled. Jasper, now chained in a far corner, muttered a deep growl.

"Let me finish off that furry bastard!" Clem pulled out his pistol and aimed it.

"No!" Louisa inserted herself between man and dog. "Please! He's chained. He can't possibly harm you. He's all I have for protection! That bandit Brodie MacMillan may be lurking somewhere nearby. Surely you wouldn't leave a woman alone under such a circumstance!"

"You've already told us he was here and left you unmolested," Tom retorted. "Go ahead, Clem. Shoot the damned brute."

A face appeared at a window behind the men's backs. A familiar face that looked straight at her, nodded, and vanished.

Runner. And he nodded. Brodie must be safe. Courage flooded through her.

"Harm the wolf and a curse will fall upon you." Louisa stretched out her arms and narrowed her eyes. She struggled to make her words sound like an incantation. "Your teeth will rot, your joints will swell, and your manly parts will shrivel and drop off."

"Good God!" His eyes rounding, the man let his hand holding the weapon drop to his side.

"Ah, Jesus, Clem, she's playacting!" Tom exploded. "Shoot the thing!"

"You shoot him." Clem remained caught in Louisa's stare. "I'm not about to risk having all that stuff she's threatening happen to me just to shoot a nasty cur." He swung to face his companion. "If you're so sure she's playacting, you shoot it."

"Argh! You're timid as an old maid." Tone and expression registering his disgust, Tom shrugged his coat over his shoulders. "No need to go wasting powder and ball on a mangy brute. We'd best be getting back to town. This blasted weather isn't showing any sign of letting up. As for you, mistress…" He narrowed his eyes as he looked at Louisa. "If Brodie MacMillan ever does show up here again, you'd best be taking care. He is wanted for seduction, and he's been on the run for most of the winter. He's probably right hot for a woman about now."

"I'll heed your warning." She drew herself up to face him squarely. "I do have my wolf to keep me safe. When not kept at bay by a pistol, I assure you he can be a savage force."

"No doubt. Take care it doesn't turn on you."

"I shall." She faced him squarely. "Now, I'd advise you to leave. I've herbs to brew."

With a final guffaw from the one named Tom, they

turned and went out into the misery that was a spring storm.

Louisa waited until she heard them ordering their weary horses back down the trail before she rushed to a window to assure herself of their leaving. Once they were out of sight, she pulled on her coat and rushed out of the cabin and across the clearing to the stable. Heart pounding, she burst inside.

In the stall formerly occupied by Fox stood Jonah Parsons' mule contentedly munching hay. Across from it, Snow muttered a welcome.

"Brodie?" She whispered his name, her breath forming a small cloud in the cold air. "Brodie, where are you?"

"Right here, my darlin'." She swung to see him, wet and bedraggled, entering the stable, leading Fox.

"Brodie, how…?"

"I saw those bastards coming. I realized showin' myself would forever brand you an outlaw. I had to take the chance that they'd not dare harm you with Jonah as a witness and with your reputation as a witch. So I took Fox and headed into the trees. Then Runner appeared and offered to check on the situation in the cabin. He said all was well, but if they've so much as hurt a hair on your head, rest assured they'll pay."

"I'm fine, but Clem—the one who came down here looking for you—said he found no tracks."

"A good spruce bough helped to sweep them away."

"And Runner? Where is he?"

"Gone as soon as he knew you were safe. He's like a guardian spirit, showin' up when he's needed. How did you manage to get rid of them?"

"Being confronted with a curse, they fled like chickens from a wolf." She gave him a sly smile. "What good is being branded a witch if you can't put it to good use?"

"You're a minx, sure and certain, Louisa... MacMillan." He went into the stall, took Jonah's mule out to tie next to Snow's stall, and led Fox inside. When he returned, he gathered her into his arms. "Come here, woman."

"You're shaking." She was startled by the tremor in his body. "Are you so cold?" She pulled out from him to look into his cap and coat iced with frozen rain.

"I was just that scared." He looked into her face, his jaw working with a tick. "Louisa, if those bastards had harmed you, if..."

"But they didn't." She put up a hand to stroke his cheek. "We both played our cards perfectly. We're a good team, my darling."

"I believe we are." He cut off her reply by kissing her harder than ever before. When he finally let her breathe again, his words were an apology.

"That wasn't the act of a kind and loving husband." He heaved out a breath. "I apologize."

"No, it definitely wasn't." She smiled up at him. "It was the behavior of a lover, a passionate lover. Let's get ourselves back to the cabin and our bed before the laudanum I gave Jonah wears off. I'm thinking we have a deal of lovemaking to do."

"Aye." He caught her up in his arms and started out of the stable.

"Put me down, you great fool!" she protested, laughing. "Your leg..."

"Is perfectly fine and won't bother me one bit for

what I have in mind."

****

She stood staring at him, a sneer turning her formerly beautiful face into a dark picture of evil while, he, Brodie stood on a scaffold, a rope about his neck, hands tied behind his back. Beside him on the wooden structure, similarly restrained and awaiting their fate, were Harry and Margaret. Below, restrained by soldiers, were the couple's seven stepchildren—Eppie, the baby of the group, screaming, her small face contorted in horror.

"Now you and your friends will pay!" Cassandra Carmody stood with her hand on the lever that would release the trap doors beneath their feet. As she pushed it forward, he awoke, yelling, "No!"

"Brodie, love, what is it?" Drenched in cold sweat, he became aware of Louisa's voice, her hand on his shoulder.

"Sweet Jesus!" He heaved a great breath. "That woman! She's haunting me…even in my sleep."

"You must try to put the creature and her vile schemes out of your mind." Louisa's voice was soft as she brushed damp curls from his forehead. "You must let yourself be possessed by only one woman."

Slowly she moved over him in a gesture so erotic it made him suck in his breath. She ran her hands over his broad chest and down the front of his body. Cassandra Carmody and her witchcraft vanished in a puff of nothingness, replaced by the sensual reality that was his wife.

****

Later, Brodie eased himself out of their bed. He paused to look down at Louisa sleeping peacefully.

Their lovemaking an hour earlier had left him amazed by its passion and intensity. Good God, he loved the woman! But he knew what he had to do. The events of the day and that nightmare had been signs. In the darkness, he dressed and stealthily left the room.

Jasper, lying across the entrance door, raised his head. Brodie gestured the animal to silence. The wolf muttered but once more lowered his head, yellow eyes gleaming in the scant illumination of the fire receding to embers on the hearth.

Silent as a shadow, Brodie moved to the bed where Louisa's patient slumbered. With a move perfected in his bandit days, he clapped a hand over the man's mouth.

Jonah's eyes flew open wide. Held down in Brodie's strong grip, he couldn't struggle. Instead he stared up in mute fear until his expression in the darkness showed he recognized the man looming over him. Putting a finger to his lips, Brodie indicated he was to dress and follow him. Jonah nodded.

While he waited for the old man to struggle into his clothing, Brodie retrieved his sword and pistol. When Jonah joined him, he eased open the door and led the way to the stable.

"I'm leavin', Jonah," he informed his companion once they were inside the barn. "I have to. This place won't be safe anymore. If I stay, I'll be endangerin' Louisa. What I want from you is to stay with her, guard her as best you can if that nasty pair return."

"Aye, aye, Brodie." The old man shook his grizzled head in dismay. "I never was much of a fightin' man, but for you and her what fixed my arm, I'll give my best."

"That's all anyone can do." Brodie slapped him on the back and went into Fox's stall.

"You'll be travelin' awful light." Jonah watched him saddle the stallion. "No food, no extra clothes…"

"I have all I need for the first part of my journey." He touched the hilt of his sword, then the gun in his belt. "I'll get outfitted for my travels farther along."

"You're not plannin' to go back thievin'?" Jonah caught at Brodie's arm as he reached to bridle Fox. "Because if you are, and you get caught…"

"No, I'm not plannin' to go back to my old ways." In the dark stable, he eased the old man's concern. "I'm right fond of the lady inside that cabin. I plan to clear my name and marry her right and proper…in a church with all the trimmin's."

"Good lad!" It was Jonah's turn to slap a back. "You and Harry deserve a decent life. I'll never forget what you did for my miserable whelp of a brother. I'm willin' to risk life and limb for the pair of you. And I'm right sorry for leadin' that miserable scum here."

"You needed help, and you came to the source." Brodie finished with the horse's tack and began to lead him outside into the darkness. He'd become adept at being swift about the chore during his rebel days. "I'm not about to fault you for that." He swung into the saddle to look down at the man who'd followed him outside. "Good luck, Jonah. Take good care of my lady."

"Best I can."

With that less than reassuring remark, Brodie swung Fox away and headed into the forest.

****

As he paused on the edge of the bush, Brodie took

a moment to reflect. It had been an astonishing few months since he'd arrived half frozen on Louisa's doorstep. Brodie MacMillan had become what he'd once never thought again possible…a happy, fulfilled man. Now he had to put it all behind him and ride off into the night like the bandit he was.

He could at least feel relieved on one score. Events of the past week had made it known there was no pregnancy to be concerned about. If things had been different, if theirs had been a normal marriage, he would have been disappointed. As it was, he could feel only relief. He couldn't have left her with a child on the way, no matter what the danger.

He guffawed as he thought how he'd left her guarded by Jonah Parsons. The wolf was a thousand times more reliable. She needed better protection. And he knew just the man for the job. He would go to see Harry, tell him about Louisa, and get his assurance he'd look out for her.

Aye, definitely Harry will take care of her. And I need supplies for the journey I'm about to undertake. A sword and a pistol would be right hard chewin'. Harry will outfit me.

He looked down the rough trail Louisa had told him led to the village twenty miles away. Harry and Margaret's farm and mills wouldn't be that far if he cut across country.

He took one last look at the small homestead outlined against the blackness of the night. Something that felt like a great, jagged stone hurt his chest.

Engulfed with a lost, sick feeling, he nudged Fox down the trail leading into the trees. Happiness was not for such as him. He'd been a bandit. He was an outlaw.

He'd spend the rest of his life on the run.

He'd gone only a few miles when he realized he'd lost direction. The rain and wind had abated, but no stars had appeared. In the blackness, he couldn't get his bearings. He stopped the stallion to consider what he should do.

"You are lost." The voice coming seemingly out of nowhere startled him. His hand instinctively flew to the hilt of his sword as he tried to focus in the direction of the speaker. Fox shied and began to prance.

"You've lost your way." A hand took Fox's bridle, words in a language unintelligible to Brodie calmed the horse, then continued, "Tell me where you wish to go, and I will guide you."

He recognized the voice. Runner. Relief relaxed him. His hand fell away from the weapon.

"I want to go to my friend's mills and farm, the Fowler place. Do you know it?"

"Yes." Runner began to lead a submissive Fox forward. "It is fortunate I decided to stay and watch your cabin. You were headed in the opposite direction."

"Runner, you've been good to Louisa…you and Marie." He had to ask the favor. "Will you continue to watch over her, to see that she's kept safe?"

"You do not have to ask, my friend." The soft, husky voice in the darkness reassured him. "She saved my woman and son when he was born, and her man helped my grandmother leave this world in peace. We would do no less."

"And another favor." He looked down at the outline in the darkness that was the native man.

"Yes?"

"Once I've been gone a week…seven days…guide

Louisa to my friend's farm. Make her know it's my wish that she goes to live with Harry Wallace. You've heard of him. He'll take her in and keep her safe."

"I will."

"A hundred thousand thank-yous." Brodie heaved a sigh and wet dry lips.

Chapter Twenty

"Harry." Brodie entered the barn through the rear entrance.

"Sweet Jesus!" His friend whirled, from where he'd been brushing his mare, to face him. "Brodie…"

"Don't stand there gapin'." Grinning, Brodie strode forward, hand extended. "Come and greet me like a man."

"Brodie." Harry Wallace stared for a moment, then grasped Brodie's hand in a nearly bone-crushing grip. The next instant, he'd pulled him into his arms. "Brodie!"

"Ah, now, don't go takin' on, Hamish." Brodie finally managed to pull free and, using his friend's Highland name, grinned at him. "You must know by now I've more resurrections in me than the good Lord Jesus."

"We thought you were dead! We thought that musketball… The boys and I searched the bush until the snow got too deep. Brodie, how…?"

"A long tale, and one best told once I've had a cup of hot tea, some food, and perhaps a wee dram."

"Aye, aye, come up to the house. Margaret is alone with the girls. The boys are still finishing up in the woods. They're getting ready to drive the winter's logs down to the mill as soon as the stream clears of ice." He swung an arm about Brodie's shoulders as he headed him out of the barn. "Bloody hell, I can't wait to see Eppie's face when…"

"Harry." Brodie stopped him in the barn doorway. "On second thought, maybe I shouldn't go up to the house. I'm still a wanted man. The fewer people who know I'm here the better. I just came to tell you…"

Now that the moment for revealing his wonderful news had arrived, Brodie wasn't sure how to proceed.

"Aye? Not in more trouble, are you?" Harry narrowed his eyes as he looked at his friend.

"No, no." He drew a deep breath and found the words to continue. "It's just that…well, Harry, I've been stayin' with a woman, a rare woman, who saved my life last autumn…and, Harry, we're…married." He felt his face brighten with the joy of the admission.

His friend gaped at him. Then he was laughing, slapping Brodie on the back, hugging him again. "Laddie, I cannae tell you how glad that makes me. I cannae…"

"I hoped it would. That's why I came." He backed off a step after Harry released him. "I wanted you to know…" He couldn't go on.

"You wanted me to know, to relieve me of my guilt." Harry sobered. "You took a great risk to do it, brother."

"Perhaps, but I wanted you to be happy, truly happy, when the new wee one comes." Brodie stopped abruptly. "He hasn't arrived yet, has he?"

"No, no, *she* hasn't put in an appearance." Harry relaxed into a grin. Brodie knew Harry had been teasing his wife about wanting a girl to level off the number of each sex they had as children. "But come up to the house. Margaret and the girls can be trusted to keep your visit a secret. They'll be so verrae, verrae happy to see you. Especially Eppie."

"You're temptin' me beyond resistance. Lead on, Hamish."

"Harry. Remember, it's Harry now." He slapped an arm about his friend's shoulders and headed him for the barn's front entrance.

"Aye, aye." Brodie grinned at him as they headed together toward the big log house. "And Harry..." He stopped them midway. "I've a great favor to ask of you."

"Aye?" Harry turned to him.

"I've asked a native friend...Runner is his name..." Again he paused.

"Aye, I know him. In my position as magistrate, I've used him to run messages. He's a good man. What about him? You've not involved him in one of your daft capers?"

"No, of course not." He faced his friend squarely. "I've asked him to bring Louisa here after I've a week's head start on gettin' away. I'm hopin' you'll take her in and protect her until I...if I can return."

"Do you even have to ask, laddie?" Harry's response was strong with sincerity. "We'll be honored to have your wife join us. And," he said as they continued on toward the house, "she can come in right handy, what with Margaret near due."

****

"Brodie, this is such a wonderful day!" Margaret, seated in a chair by the hearth, her pregnancy far advanced, smiled over at him, the warmth of her expression mirroring her delight in the return of a man she regarded as her brother-in-law.

"Aye, that it is." His belly full of Maggie's fine cooking and warmed by a fire blazing on the hearth, he sat with a tankard treated with whisky in one hand while he balanced a delighted four-year-old golden-haired cherub on his knee.

"Father said we mustn't look every day for you to be coming back, but I knew you would." Eppie snuggled into his chest, and he felt his heart swell. "Mother said we must go to church every week and pray for your safe return. Uncle Edward and Aunt Mary said the same thing. I did, and I knew you'd come. I just knew it."

"Oh, so it's Uncle Edward and Aunt Mary now, is it?" Brodie held her close and teased. "So I'm not the only one that has the honor of such a title?"

"They said that is what we might call them." She pulled out from him and looked up into his face, her expression registering distress. "But, Uncle Brodie, you're our special uncle. You're Father's brother, aren't you?"

Brodie glanced over at Harry seated at a chair at the long table in the middle of the room. They looked at each other, understanding passing between them.

"Eppie, don't badger Uncle Brodie." Margaret started to stir from her seat. "It's time to clear the table."

"Stay where you are, Mother." Bella, the eldest girl and nearly fourteen, stood from a bench at the table. "You must rest. Come, Lizzie." She nudged her twelve-year-old sister. "We'll clean the kitchen."

"Thank you, girls." Margaret settled back into her chair with a sigh. "I must admit I tire more easily these days."

"Small wonder. You're less than three weeks away..." Harry glanced at Eppie.

"If our calculations are anywhere near accurate." She smiled at her husband.

"Father, look!" Bella, who'd been near a window as she washed dishes, was staring out into the dooryard. "Someone's coming."

"Damnation!" Brodie placed the tankard on the floor and leaped to his feet. "I didn't think I'd been followed. I hid Fox in the trees and walked a quarter mile."

"Dunnae greet." Harry got up and went to join his stepdaughter. "Just stay out of sight until we know who it is." He squinted out into the brightness of the early spring evening. "Someone riding a white horse fair lathered up...as if they've come a distance riding hard and, if my eyes don't deceive me, with a wolf by his side."

"Whit?" Brodie bolted from his seat to join him. "Guid God! Louisa!"

In long strides he was out the door and reaching up to assist her as she swung down from Snow.

"You shouldn't have come, lass," he breathed as he stood with his hands on her waist once she'd dismounted. "I told Runner not to bring you here for at least a week. You must not be seen with me. If I'm caught, you could be charged with helpin' a criminal escape, you could be jailed..."

"Brodie MacMillan, we've agreed to be husband and wife, and a wife's place is with her husband." Green eyes brooking no rebuttal, she looked up at him. "Don't go blaming Runner. He tried to stop me. If you're bound for prison, then so am I. But first..."

She turned to face Harry, Maggie, and the two oldest girls, who'd come to stand on the back doorstep of the log house. "Perhaps you'd do me the honor of introducing me to your friends." She turned to them with a dazzling smile. Moving out of Brodie's embrace, she advanced toward them, a hand extended to Harry. "I'm Louisa MacMillan, Brodie's wife. You must be Harry and Margaret Wallace. I'm delighted to meet you."

A chuckle bubbled inside Brodie as he saw the astonished expression on his friends' faces. *Aye, it's best they know us as man and wife. But as soon as possible, we'll pay a visit to Lachlan—or the Rev. Edward Morgan, as he's chosen to call himself—and get the deed done right and proper.*

"A…pleasure…Mrs. MacMillan." Harry, still in the throes of astonishment, accepted her offer. Coming back to himself, he bent gallantly over her hand. "Your servant, ma'am."

Ah, there's the old Highland Harry coming to the top like cream. Brodie watched Louisa and Harry meeting.

"This is my wife, Margaret," Harry continued, indicating the woman at his side.

"I'm delighted to meet you, Mrs. Wallace." Louisa bobbed a respectful curtsey.

"As am I to meet you, Mrs. MacMillan." Margaret's greeting was bright with sincerity.

"These beautiful young ladies must be Isabella and Elizabeth, Brodie's nieces." Louisa turned to the girls. Amused, Brodie watched their mesmerized expressions as she smiled at them. They were meeting the famous witch for the first time. "He's told me many good things about you both."

The door opened again. Eppie, with Precious the Pig waddling beside her, came out of the house.

"Jesus!" Harry, who conscientiously avoided profanity in front of the children, lost control as the wolf turned toward the pair. He swung to block the animal's path. Beside him, Maggie gasped.

"Wait!" Louisa moved between the wolf and the child with the pig. "Hello," she spoke softly as she smiled at the child. "I'm Louisa. Your Uncle Brodie has told me about you and your wonderful friend." She indicated Precious. "This is my companion." She pointed to the wolf. "His name is Jasper."

"Your friend is very big." Eppie stared round-eyed at the animal.

"Yes, but he's also very gentle." Louisa held out a hand. "Come. Meet him."

The child hesitated, then took it. Louisa drew Eppie toward Jasper and slowly placed the small hand beneath his snout.

"Soft," Eppie, accustomed to her pet's prickly skin, breathed in delight. "Precious, come meet Jasper."

"No!" The word exploded from Harry.

Louisa stopped him with a raised hand as she hunkered down between them. The little pig hesitated, then, wiggling its curly tail, sauntered forward. Silence held the group as they watched,

Brodie thought his heart stopped. *Louisa, please know what you're about. I've trusted you with my life, but this is the wee lassie…*

When Precious stopped in front of the big animal, Jasper lowered his head and gingerly stretched his neck to touch the other's snout. His tail, like the pig's, began to wag.

The organ in Brodie's chest began to thump again.

"They're going to be friends!" Eppie cried. "You must be a good fairy." She turned to Louisa, eyes wide.

"That's one of the kinder things people have called me." Louisa smiled. Taking the child's hand again, she stood.

"Come inside, Mrs. MacMillan." Brodie could see Harry was back in form, the charming rogue who'd finessed many a rich lady of her jewels. "You're most welcome. We're finishing up a meal, but I'm sure my guid wife and the girls can find something decent for you to eat. Brodie, you might be taking your wife's mare down to the barn and see to it. It might also be wise to fetch that great red beast of yours from wherever you've hidden him. I'm sure both animals are tired and hungry."

"Yes, of course, Mrs. MacMillan, do come in." Maggie held out an arm to indicate the back door.

Harry winked at Brodie over Louisa's shoulder as he slid an arm around her waist to guide her into the house.

"Come on, Precious and Jasper!" Eppie skipped behind them, urging the animals to follow. "Jasper, we'll get you something to eat, too."

With a guffaw, Brodie took up Snow's reins and headed down to the barn. Relieved that the meeting between wolf and pig was over, he relaxed, but a small smidgeon of something he disliked to think of as jealousy nipped at him. If he didn't know Harry Wallace to be a happily married man, he'd be right annoyed by his attentions to the beautiful Louisa.

Chapter Twenty-One

"More tea, Louisa?" Margaret started to rise at the end of the meal to fetch the pot.

"Please. But allow me, Margaret." She stood and went to the hearth.

A smile tugged at Brodie's lips. It hadn't taken but a single meal together for the two couples to become comfortable, to get to a Christian name basis. Some day, soon he hoped, when he'd been cleared of that ridiculous charge, he'd bring Louisa to live in the small log house he'd built on the opposite side of the valley that encompassed the Fowler holdings. Wallaces, Fowlers, and MacMillans would start their own small, independent community.

But first he had to stop being a fugitive. Once he got Harry alone, they'd discuss what had to be done. Harry was a right smart bugger and the regional magistrate to boot. He'd find a way.

"We need more sugar." Margaret picked up the wooden bowl from the center of the table and pulled herself awkwardly to her feet. "Oh!" The container fell from her hands as she doubled up, her face contorting in agony.

"Lass, what is it?" Harry was instantly at her side, his arm about her.

"I don't know," she gasped. "It's still too early...I think."

"You could have miscalculated." Louise stood and joined Harry. "Harry, I think you'd best take Margaret into your bedroom."

"Do as Louisa says, Harry." Brodie was on feet. "She's right clever about such things. She'll know what's to be done."

"But she's a witch!" The words burst from Lizzie.

"There are no such things, lass!" Harry's words were the harshest he'd ever spoken to one of his daughters. "Now go with your sister and turn down the bed for your mother."

Head hanging, his second oldest stepdaughter turned to obey.

****

"You'd best send the two youngest girls away from the house." Louisa came out of the bedroom, closed the plank door behind her, and spoke softly to Brodie. "Perhaps you and Harry could take them over to that cabin you told me you've built across the stream."

"Whit? Is it time?"

She nodded. "I'll need Isabella to help me. She's already doing as I instructed. The rest of you will just be in the way."

"Verrae guid." He turned to the two girls and Harry. "My guid wife has requested we take ourselves off for a bit...over to my cabin."

"No!" Harry tried to step past the couple at the bedroom door. Louisa stopped him with a hand on his arm.

"Margaret wants you gone, Harry," she said softly. "She doesn't want you to see her in labor."

"But it's my wee one! It's my concern!"

"Harry, if you truly love her, you'll honor her

wishes." Louisa looked up at him with an expression Brodie had come to recognize. No man, woman, or child could refuse Louisa MacMillan when she cast her bewitching gaze over them.

"Verrae well." Harry's broad shoulders slumped, then jerked erect as a muffled cry came from the room. "Sweet Jesus!"

"Go!" Louisa wasted no more reasoning. "Take the children, and go with Brodie. We'll let you know when you may return."

****

"I've never been this afeard in my life." Harry sat slumped in a chair before the fire in Brodie's cabin, rubbing his hands together as he spoke softly. The children, Lizzie and Eppie, were outside riding their pony, Goldbug, in the yard. "Not even when the redcoats were breathin' down my neck, not when…"

"Have another dram." Brodie, sitting opposite him, picked up the flask from beside his chair and held it out to his ashen-faced friend. "It'll steady your nerves."

"Thank you, no. I want to have my wits about me if something goes wrong, if I'm needed…"

"Hamish, Hamish, nothing will go wrong. Margaret is a fine, healthy woman, and my Louisa has all the skills of the best doctor. How often have you heard of a man's leg being saved after takin' a musketball?"

"She did that?"

"Aye. I was about to tell you and Margaret all about it once the bairns were gone to bed. My Louisa can work miracles. Now let us speak of other things for a bit." Brodie wet his lips and fingered his tankard. "Hamish, I've been wonderin'…"

"Aye, come on, lad, spit it out." Harry's words were sharpened with stress. "It's not a time to be meandering with me."

"It's about that charge...of seduction." Brodie stared down into his drink and hoped with all his heart for a good answer to his question. "I was wonderin' if you've managed to get it straightened away...what with you being magistrate and all. Now that I've met Louisa, it's become right important. I want to come back here to live with her, to start a family."

He looked up at Harry, and he guessed his expression mirrored all the fervent desire in his wish.

His friend hesitated.

"Hamish, what is it? Has that Carmody woman blown the offense into something even bigger?"

"No, no." Harry heaved a great sigh that drew back his broad shoulders. "It's not that. Brodie, lad, you know I'd do anything in the world for you...to see you happy with that fine woman, but..."

"But what, but what? Guid God, man, spit it out!"

"I'm no longer magistrate."

"Whit?" Brodie felt as if he'd been struck a blow in the jaw. "Hamish, whit are you sayin'?"

"After your escape, Mistress Carmody sent a message to Fredericton telling of her suspicions that I'd been involved in your escape."

"But you and the boys were at the church..."

"Aye, aye, but it appears her father was a friend of more than a few people of importance in our province's capital. As a result, they've removed me from office. A new magistrate, Captain Caleb Cameron, has been appointed...a hero of the war, I understand. He and his right-hand man, a lad called Duncan MacDougal, and their wives have already arrived and taken up residences. I'm hoping he'll be a fair and decent man."

"Ah, sweet Jesus! This is all my fault." Brodie stood and began to pace the cabin. Finally he stopped short. "How did Margaret take the news? She was so proud of your appointment."

"Margaret's a strong woman, as you know, Brodie MacMillan." Harry looked up at him. "She took it in stride. Well, not exactly in stride." He let a wry grin curl his lips. "She did call Mistress Carmody a few very choice names…when the children were out of hearing."

"Bloody hell!" Brodie sank back onto his chair. "Hamish, I've been nothing but a great millstone about your neck since I came here. I'll be gettin' out of here just as soon as I know Margaret is well."

"And leave the woman you love? Man, you must be daft."

"I'll not put you and your family and her in danger because of what I've done—or have been accused of doin'. I'll be askin' you to take care of Louisa for me. She needs a family and a safe home."

"Brodie…"

Lizzie burst into the cabin. "Father, Eppie wants to let Fox out into the paddock. I told her you and Uncle Brodie said no, but…"

"I'll see to it." Placing his tankard aside, Brodie stood.

"Make the child understand no one must see your horse." Harry's words followed him. "That's why I told you to stable him here in your barn, not at the farm. If that red stallion is spotted…"

"Aye, aye." Brodie dismissed his friend's concerns with a wave of his hand as he snatched up his coat and headed for the door. "Dunnae alarm yourself with such small matters. You've bigger fish to fry. I'll take care of this wee concern."

****

"Father?" Bella, smiling broadly, opened the door of Brodie's log cabin. "Aunt Louisa says you may return now."

Harry bolted from the chair where he'd been sitting before the fire, and a pewter mug that had been in his hands dropped with a dull thud to the plank floor.

"Margaret...your mother...she's well?" He voiced the question to which all four occupants of the room awaited the answer with bated breath.

"She's fine." Bella's smile became smug. "She'd like to see you, Father...alone."

"Aye, aye." He was snatching up his coat and hat as he headed for the door.

"Come on, girls." Brodie reached for his outerwear as his friend bolted down the trail. "We'll follow at a safer pace. I doubt a white-tailed deer could catch up with your father at this moment."

****

Louisa met Harry at the door of the log house. His wild-eyed expression shot straight to her heart. This former Highland outlaw, who'd kept regiments of redcoats at bay and, according to her husband, laughed in the face of the rawest danger, was afraid, perhaps even terrified.

"Margaret...?" The question broke from him in a gasp.

"Very well...considering." Louisa couldn't suppress the smile tugging at her lips.

"Considering? Considering what?"

"Come. Look." She led him to the open bedroom door.

Inside, Margaret lay in the bed smiling, a baby cradled in each arm.

"Whit…?" Harry stared, the word stumbling from his lips.

"Twins, Harry." She looked up at her husband. "Twin boys." Then, frowning slightly, she added, "You aren't disappointed, are you? I know you wanted a girl, and now not one but two boys…"

"Sweet Jesus, lass." He advanced into the room as though in a trance, and Bella, who'd been standing by her mother, moved aside to give him her place. "As if I could ever be disappointed in anything so…so wonderful."

Louisa watched as he dropped down on one knee by the bed, his face mobile with a series of emotions. With a shaking hand, he reached to stroke her cheek. "It's a miracle, my love, a miracle. I could not be more delighted."

As he bent to kiss her, Louisa winked to Bella and inclined her head toward the door. Harry and Margaret needed to be alone with their boys.

Chapter Twenty-Two

"Good morning." Louisa entered the barn, where Brodie was trimming the hooves of a black gelding. She leaned over the side of the stall and smiled down at him.

"Good mornin', lass." He straightened to return the greeting. "And a fine spring one it is."

As memories of their night in his cabin after the birth of the twins came back, a satisfied grin stretched the corners of his mouth. Every moment he was privileged to spend with her was magic. If she was indeed a witch, then she was a good one who'd come to breath joy back into his life.

"Brodie…" She paused and watched her fingers tracing lines on the top of the stall. "I've been thinking."

"Ah, now there're words that can cast a pall over a man's day." He came out of the stall and laid aside his trimming tool to put an arm about her shoulders and plant a kiss on her temple. "Whit is it, my love?"

"I came here planning to convince you to come back to our homestead. I didn't expect to get involved with birthing a pair of babies. The twins and Margaret will need my help for a while." She looked up at him, and he saw her imploring him to understand. "Bella is a fine girl, but she is little more than a child. It's too much responsibility to foist upon her. I'd like to stay on here until Margaret is back on her feet and strong enough to manage this big family."

"And you thought I might be objectin'?" Brodie drew her close. "Love, I understand. We'll stay for as long as you like." Knowing he was lying when he referred to both of them remaining, he kissed her again. "In fact, I wish we could stay forever in my cabin across the stream."

"Brodie, don't." She pulled away and went to rub the nose that Prince the Clydesdale was thrusting out at her. Their own horses were stabled in the barn on Brodie's homestead, hidden in case of visitors. "You know it's what I want as well. Only…" She avoided his gaze.

"Aye, aye." He drew a deep breath and looked down at his boots. "Only I'm an outlaw, a wanted man, a man who's been branded a bandit…a man who will have to go on the run again." He looked at her. "You've made a poor choice, lass."

"Oh, Brodie, no, no, no!" She grasped his arm. "We'll get those false charges dismissed soon. We'll…"

"Aye, aye." He couldn't prevent the note of defeat from coloring his words.

"Good morning, you two." Harry came into the barn. He strode toward them, his mouth stretched in the satisfied grin Brodie didn't think had left his face since the birth of his twin sons. "And a fine one it is, too." He paused, looking from one to the other. "Am I breaking in on a private discussion? If so…" He made as if to leave, but Brodie stopped him.

"No, no, Harry. Louisa was just expressin' her desire to stay on a bit to help Bella and Lizzie with

Margaret and the twins…if you've no objection."

"Objection! Of course not. I'd be delighted. I was beginning to worry about how Margaret would manage with just the young lasses to help her. Thank you, Louisa. Most sincerely, thank you."

"No thanks necessary. It's a joy to spend time with your lovely family."

"Then it's settled. Now to other business." Harry leaned against a beam and narrowed his eyes as he looked over at Brodie.

"Oh, aye?" Suspicion rising, Brodie faced his longtime friend. "Whit is it you have in mind for me, Hamish?"

"Nothing nefarious, my lad. I simply wish to ask a small favor."

"Aye?"

"As you know, my boys have been in the woods cutting logs all winter. Now it's nigh on time for the stream to open. That will mean it's time for them to drive the logs down to our pond on the spring freshet. I'm more than a tad worried about them. James is a man at nineteen, but Sam is a mere lad, only fourteen. I'd take it as a kindness if you would go to our logging camp and urge them to a wee bit of caution."

"In other words, get the hell out of here before I'm discovered." Brodie's words came out harsher than he'd intended.

"Aye, I've no denying that's part of my plan, but the major reason for my suggesting you go is to see to the boys. I was right worried that I couldn't accompany them this spring, what with Margaret about due, and now…"

"And now you want to stay with her and those fine,

wee boys." Brodie turned back into Midnight's stall. "Verrae well, I'll go."

"Today." The single word brooked no contradiction.

"Whit?" He whirled on his friend.

"I said you must go today. Brodie, there's been a wee…accident." Harry busied himself straightening out harness. "As a result, it's best you leave at once."

"What accident?" Brodie caught Harry by an arm.

"Eppie and Lizzie went over to your homestead this morning. They wanted to see Fox again. While Lizzie was fetching him a bucket of water, Eppie decided Fox needed to run free in the paddock…"

"Guid God, never tell me the beast ran the lassie down!" An instant sickness clutched Brodie's gut. "Never tell me…"

"No, no, nothing like that. But before the girls could capture him or come for help, Ezra Gardiner came up the trail in his wagon. He'd mentioned at church last autumn that he wanted to order enough sawn lumber to build a new barn this spring. I believe he may have been coming to place the order. The long and short of it is, he saw Fox."

"Ah, sweet Jesus."

"Aye, sweet Jesus. I was on my way over to your place to see what was keeping the girls when I encountered him. I tried to talk casual, saying we'd found the horse wandering around the place, even hinting he must have found his way home after you'd possibly died from a wound in the bush, but suspicion was written all over his face. Therefore…"

"Therefore, I'd best get myself out of here as fast as possible." Brodie turned to Louisa, a sick, hollow feeling gushing over him. Where one time running from the law had been an exhilarating challenge, a game of sorts, now it fostered a disgusting illness in his gut.

"You'd best not take Fox. If they come lookin' for you—and I'm sure they will—and he's gone, they'll know or least strongly suspect you were here."

"And that would put you and your family in danger as conspirators. Aye, I agree. But leavin' on foot…"

"Take Midnight, the lads' gelding. He's strong and surefooted in mud such as you'll encounter on the way to our logging camp. You shouldn't have any trouble following the marks left by the sled runners the last time Geordie came out for supplies."

"I'll go and pack provisions." Louisa turned to leave, but Brodie caught her by an arm.

"I'm right sorry, lass." He looked down into her green eyes, the apology coming from his heart. "I shouldn't have married you. It wasn't fair to make you a bandit's bride."

"Brodie, I knew you were some sort of outlaw the moment I found you wounded and half-frozen on my doorstep." She met his gaze squarely. "That didn't stop my taking you in, or loving you. Nothing has changed."

"I'll leave you two alone." Harry headed out of the barn. "But, mind, only for a few short moments. Time's of the essence."

****

A half hour later, Brodie swung into Midnight's saddle, bags of supplies tied behind it, and paused to look down at Louisa standing close to the gelding's shoulder, a shawl pulled tight about her body to ward off the cold east wind of the April day…and the bitter chill in her heart.

"Farewell, my love." He bent down to pull her close as she rose on tiptoes to give him one last kiss. "All will be well."

"I know." She touched his cheek before stepping away from the horse.

"Go, go!" Harry slapped the animal on the rump, making it dance in anticipation of a good run.

"Aye." Brodie touched his forelock in a salute to the three young girls on the doorstep before releasing his mount into a full gallop down the hill and across the bridge toward the road leading to the logging camp.

"Uncle Brodie!" Eppie ran from the porch to pursue him.

"No, no, lassie." Harry strode after the little girl and scooped her up in his arms. "You cannae go with your uncle, lassie. He'll be back…soon."

"Uncle Brodie, Uncle Brodie!" the child stretched out her arms after the disappearing rider, his name a wail.

Louisa understood the little girl's distress. Something inside her shriveled. What if she never saw him again? First Neil, then her child, and now Brodie…

"He'll be fine." Harry stepped up beside Louisa, the child now sniveling softly, still in his arms. "He's one tough, resourceful lad."

"I know." She tried to sound as confident as her companion, but she heard the shakiness of insecurity in the two words.

"Take courage, lass." Harry placed his youngest stepdaughter on the ground as her sisters came forward to take her hands and lead her back to the house. "He's said he had more resurrections than the good Lord Jesus, and I'm inclined to believe him." He put an arm about her shoulders and grinned down at her.

"That sounds like Brodie. We'll hope he's correct."

****

So once again I'm banished, sent away from everything that means life to me.

Brodie let Midnight pick his pace as they headed down the rutted wagon road into the woods. He supposed he should be grateful for having escaped the law on so many occasions, but he was weary, tired of running and hiding, of never feeling safe, of not having had the opportunity to properly marry the woman he loved, to have a home and children with her.

The thought of him and Louisa never being able to have a life together discouraged him to the core of his soul. What he wanted seemed so simple, would be so easy for most men.

When the gelding stumbled over a tree root, he returned his attention to the animal.

"Easy, my fine laddie," he cautioned the animal. "I'm no more accustomed to you than you are to me. We must both give a care."

As if in answer, the horse stopped, threw up his head, and snorted.

"Whit is it, laddie?" His hand went to the butt of the pistol he carried stuck in his belt. Bobcats were not uncommon in the area and, quite possibly, some hungry fresh-from-hibernation bears were already roaming the forest in search for food.

When Runner emerged from among the trees a moment later, he heaved a gust of relief.

"You gave me a right start, laddie. You have a way of turnin' up sudden as a gust of wind but a lot more quiet."

"I'll help your friend Harry and his family watch over your woman." He rubbed Midnight's nose as the horse nuzzled him. "But you must take care. Talk in the village is that the Carmody woman is still out to take revenge on you and your friends."

"I appreciate your concern." Brodie shifted in the saddle. "But I'll be fine. I've a skill at avoidin' pursuers, but if you'd help in lookin' out for Louisa, that would mean the world to me. You probably know the villagers call her a witch."

"Fools!" Brodie was startled to hear the vehemence in the normally soft-spoken man's voice. "They cannot recognize a great healer such as your woman. They rob themselves of her skills."

"I agree, but old fears and superstitions cast long shadows. Now, I'd best be on my way. It's cold and damp. I want to get to the lads' loggin' camp and a warm fire."

Chapter Twenty-Three

"But I don't like beets!" Eppie's protest was a mournful whine as she sat on the floor holding the doll Harry had purchased for her the previous summer, her pig lying with the white wolf beside her. "Mother knows I don't like beets!"

"The root cellar is running low, Eppie." Bella knelt beside the child. "Aunt Louisa has to cook what is left. In a few days there will be fiddleheads along the stream. You and I will go picking them. You like fiddleheads, don't you?"

"I like fiddleheads, too." Louisa placed the pot of beets on the sideboard to cool. "We'll have some soon, Eppie, but for now we have to make the best of what we have. Beets can be tasty with salt and butter, can't they, Bella?"

"They can. Now, Eppie, you must stop your whining and be a good girl for Aunt Louisa. Mother wouldn't want you to act like a spoiled baby, would she? We're fortunate Aunt Louisa is here to help us, so we must be as good as gold."

"All right." Eppie returned her attention to the doll. "But I want maple syrup on my bread."

"And you shall have it." Louisa left her chore and knelt by the child. "You deserve a treat. You've been a very good girl."

"Don't go spoiling the lass." Harry, who'd entered

in time to hear the exchange, pulled off his coat and hat and hung them on a peg by the door. "She's got young brothers now…"

Louisa caught him by the arm and propelled him back outside.

"Whit?" He looked down at her, his forehead furrowing.

"That's just the problem." Louisa hissed up at him. "She has two new brothers, her beloved Uncle Brodie has left, and she's feeling sad and confused. We have to allow her time to become accustomed to the changes…gently."

Harry hesitated before letting a slow smile ease across his features.

"You're a wise woman, Louisa MacMillan. It's a blessing you've come to guide a great oaf like me who has scant experience at being a father, and alone…until Margaret is able to take up one of the reins again."

"You're doing well, for a former Highland outlaw, Hamish Wallace." Louisa winked at him before turning to go back inside the log house.

****

"Aunt Louisa!" Bella's gasp made Louisa turn from where she'd returned to preparing the midday meal to see the girl staring out the open door. She'd gone to fill the wash basin bucket but now stood staring at something as if transfixed.

"What is it, dear?" Wiping her hands on one of Margaret's aprons she was wearing, she went to stand beside her. A smile broke over her face.

"Runner, welcome!" She greeted the tall, broad-shouldered brave. "Come in. We're about to have a meal. Please join us. Bella…" She turned to the transfixed child by her side. "This is my friend Runner. He's been most kind and helpful to your Uncle Brodie and me."

"I cannot stay." His grim expression told her he was on a mission. "In the village I've learned soldiers are about to come here seeking you and your man."

"Oh, no!" Louisa caught her breath. "Bella, run down to the mill and get your father. We must prepare." She looked at the native man standing with arms crossed on his chest. "A most sincere thank you, Runner, but now you must leave. I don't want you indicated as helping us."

"I'll take the wolf and the pig to the barn and stay there…in case I'm needed." He turned and strode off toward the structure.

****

"Bloody hell!" Harry looked out the window a half hour later. "Soldiers comin' over the rise beyond the mill. That's a mite sooner than I'd expected. Thank God your native friend gave us warning and that Brodie's gone."

Louisa went to join him. "At least a half dozen. What possible resistance can they be expecting?"

"That blessed Ezra Gardiner!" Harry's hands clenched into fists as he turned away. "I knew he didn't believe me when I told him I'd found the horse wanderin' about the place."

"Father, I'm sorry…" Lizzie looked up at him, eyes wide. "If I'd stopped Eppie from letting Fox loose…"

"Not your fault, lass." Harry put a big hand on the child's shoulder. "Now I have to figure a way out of this pickle. They mustn't find you here, Louisa, but there's no time for you to leave unobserved."

"I've had an idea." She turned to the three girls staring at her and their father, eyes filled with fear. "Upstairs quickly, all three of you. Harry," she snatched up the pot of beets as the children scuttled to obey. "Tell them there's sickness in the house, and they're to search at their own risk."

"Verrae well." He headed for the door. "I do hope you know what you're about, my girl."

****

"Sweet mother of God!" Hidden behind the door of the girls' bedroom, Louisa flattened herself against the wall and listened. "It's the plague they've got...or something worse!"

The sound of boots scrambling down the stairs and someone falling in the frantic process made her smile. As the front door of the log house slammed on the soldiers' retreat, she emerged, a finger to her lips as she looked down at the three children in their beds, their faces stained with beet juice. Portions of the vegetable peelings clung to their countenances.

"They've got some god-awful disease, Sergeant," Louisa heard one of the soldiers yelling. "I never seed the likes. Their faces are a terrible dark red and great patches of their skin are fallin' away!"

"What are you playing at, Wallace?" the sergeant's voice boomed up to them. "Letting my men be exposed to whatever bloody illness you have in your house? Do you want to infect the entire community?"

"You entered the house against my wishes, Sergeant." Harry's words were calm and even. "You cannot possibly blame me for any consequences of such an act of violation."

Leather creaked; the men were remounting.

"You haven't heard the last of this, Wallace. Once those brats are recovered or buried, we'll be back. You may count it."

"I'll be right here, waiting."

As the sound of hooves galloping away reached the bedroom, the three girls scrambled from their beds, giggling.

"That was so clever, Aunt Louisa." Bella chuckled.

"It's fortunate I'd just cooked those beets, isn't it, Eppie?" Louisa put an arm around the youngest. "I can't think of any other vegetable capable of making you three look so inflicted with a horrible plague. Now come downstairs and wash it off before your mother sees you. Fortunately, she and the twins appear to have slept through most of this, but now I hear a bit of wailing from the boys. I imagine the noise of those ruffians clattering up the stairs has awakened all three."

As they came down the stairs, Harry reentered the house. He stopped short as he saw them.

"Dear Mother of God! Whit…?"

"Aunt Louisa made us look sick." Eppie ran to him, holding up her arms to be picked up. "It scared the daylights out of those men."

"Well, you do look a sight." Harry bounced her up into his arms. "I confess, I'd be afeard of the lot of you if I didn't know it was a disguise. Louisa?" He turned to her. "What of you? I see no stains or beet skins on you."

"I hid behind the door in the girls' room." She returned to her work at the cupboard. "I assumed that once they entered and saw the girls, they'd run like rabbits."

"Louisa, Harry, what is going on? Come in here and explain all the noise." Maggie's voice from the bedroom made all five occupants of the room exchange conspiratorial grins.

"Mother will be so surprised, won't she, Father?" Eppie chuckled.

"Aye, that she will." Harry replaced her on the floor. "Now, you and your sisters wash your faces and run on down to the barn. There's a gentleman hiding out there who deserves a good meal and our sincere thanks."

Chapter Twenty-Four

"Louisa, I wish you'd stay here in the night." Harry sat alone by the fire. The children and his wife were all abed as she finished up chores at the sideboard. "I don't like you going over to Brodie's cabin alone in the gloaming. I can sleep on the floor here by the hearth, and you can use the little room where Brodie once slept."

"I'll be quite all right, Harry, never fear. You need your rest. Until Margaret and the twins can welcome you back into the bedroom, I insist you use the cubicle and sleep in comfort. It's not an easy task running the farm without your sons to help and with your eldest daughters busy with tending the babies."

"Aye, aye, I couldn't agree with you more." He looked down at his hands. "Runnin' this place without my lads and lassies is one big chore. But"—he grinned up at her—"I wouldn't be anywhere else in the world for a king's ransom."

"I know." She crossed the room and took a shawl from a peg by the door. Swinging it about her head and shoulders, she turned back to him. "Bar the door after me, and don't forget to bank the fire before you retire. It may be the month of May, but there's still a brisk chill in the air."

"Aye, aye, Mistress." Harry saluted her orders. "I shall do all that is required as the master of the house.

But wait." He went to the sideboard and lighted a lantern. "Take this with you."

"Very well." She accepted his offering before stepping out into the chill of the early spring night. "But it's not necessary. Jasper and I will find the way. Jasper?" She turned to the wolf dozing by the hearth. "Up on your paws."

As she started down the hill and across the bridge, long shadows stretched out from the mill and trees. The weaving light of the lantern cast weird silhouettes. Soon it would be pitch dark. A shiver washed over her. She would be glad to get to Brodie's cabin...their cabin...get a fire blazing on the hearth, the door barred against the night. Not usually apprehensive of being alone in the hours of darkness, Louisa was disconcerted at finding herself in that state.

It's missing Brodie, worried about what might happen to him.

Still the feeling persisted as she made her way up the opposite hill and down the lane to the cabin, Jasper close by her side. At the door, she placed the lantern on the small verandah and paused. The wolf muttered a snarl, hackles rising. The rope that had held the door closed, the rope she'd put in place that morning, hung loose.

Her heart banging at her ribs, she reached to put the fastening back in place. If someone was inside, he'd be trapped. She'd go back to the log house across the valley and summon Harry.

She was reaching for the rope when the door burst open. In the light of the lantern she saw the ragged, bearded, drink-reddened face of a man she didn't recognize. He held a pistol leveled at her chest. Jasper snarled and crouched to spring.

"Stop him, or he's dead!" the man grated.

"Jasper, stop!" Louisa seized a handful of fur at the back of the wolf's neck, knowing that wouldn't stop the animal physically. She could only hope he'd listen to her command, or one of them was about to die.

****

"They say as how you have magic powers." The man held the pistol leveled at her as she knelt by the hearth building up a fire. Jasper, shut securely in the stable, yelped and growled. Would Harry hear and perhaps come? The hope was slight. If he did, he'd most likely attribute the noise to some wild animal. She had to find her own way out of this quandary.

"They do say that." She stood as a blaze flared up. A plan was forming in her mind.

"You see this arm?" He shrugged to indicate his paralyzed right appendage. "I want you to cure it with your magic. My name is Michael Kelly."

"Should I know you?'' She fought to remain calm.

"That bastard Brodie MacMillan did this to me in the fight with Joe Carmody and his men. I've been watching this place off and on for months, hoping to find him here. But I missed him. He must have gone on the run again. Then I saw you. Mistress Carmody's men have been telling tales in the village of a doxy with gold-red hair they suspect of hiding MacMillan. A witch, they said, who could heal as well as make curses. You have to be her. So I decided you'd make payment for what that bit of Highland leavings did to me. You'll fix it or die." With his left hand, he shook the pistol in her face.

"You have no proof Brodie MacMillan injured

you. My husband described the battle between Joseph Carmody's men and his. There were many shots fired. No one could be sure where each originated."

"Aye, well, I do…in my gut. It was either him or his outlaw friend Harry Wallace. Either way, you're honor bound to repair the damage. Now get to it."

"Very well." She picked up the lantern and headed into the small bedroom.

"Hi, there!" He followed her, pistol at the ready. "Don't go getting any idea about fetching a weapon."

"If I'm to help you, I have to get my potions." She picked up the small bag of medical supplies she'd brought with her from her cabin and returned to the main room.

"Drink all of this tonight before you retire." She withdrew a small bottle of dark red liquid and handed it to him. "It will give you a wonderful rest. When the first crop of onions appears later this spring, you must eat a dozen without vomiting them up. If you expel a single one, the cure will not work."

"Oh, aye?" His eyes narrowed suspiciously in the lantern light. "You're certain sure it will cure me?"

"On my honor as a sorceress."

"All right, then." He shoved the bottle into his pocket. "But you'd better not be lyin' to me, woman."

Stuffing the pistol inside his belt, he left the cabin. Moments later Louisa heard a horse galloping down the lane to the village road.

She stood still, listening until the sound passed out of earshot. Then, for a few moments, she remained in place, breathing deeply in and out to quell the trembling in her hands before heading out to the barn to release Jasper.

She wouldn't tell Harry about the incident, she decided, as with the wolf once more inside the cabin she barred the door. He had enough on his mind. And, she suppressed a chuckle, Michael Kelly would be fittingly punished when he tried to eat those onions. No living being could possibly contain a dozen and not be violently ill. Therefore, the man would have no recourse regarding her described cure.

Chapter Twenty-Five

"They're coming!" Lizzie burst into the log house where her father and mother were finishing their midday meal. "I heard logs crashing together and the boys cursing and laughing. Come on, Bella and Eppie!"

"Cursing, are they, by God?" As the three girls dashed out of the house, Harry, grinning broadly, got to his feet. "I'll be having a wee talk to them about that."

"You'd best watch your own language, Harry Wallace," Margaret rebuked. "I doubt you're in the mood to do much reprimanding, at any rate, since you haven't seen them in over two months. Your joy at hearing them coming safe home is written all over your face."

"Aye, aye, you're right, my darling." He looked over at Louisa. "The twins are sleeping. Would you mind keeping an eye on them while Margaret and I go down to greet our boys?"

"Of course not. Go." She watched as the couple snatched up coats and hastened out into the bright May sunshine.

She understands him. Louisa, getting up from where she'd been kneeling by the hearth, felt warmth spread through her. *Margaret understands Harry as I understand Brodie. It must be wonderful to have that intimacy with the blessing of a home and children...*

She wondered when Brodie would arrive with the

team and the gelding Midnight. She missed him to the depths of her soul.

No point in wasting time hoping. I'd best be seeing to food, and a goodly amount of it. Those young men will be hungry as lions after that long log drive downriver.

Through an open window at the front of the log house came the shouts of the young arrivals rising above the rush of water and thunks of colliding logs as she turned back to the counter and a basket of potatoes. She was peeling her third when she heard the door open softly behind her. Whirling, she felt her breath charge up her throat. Brodie, in shabby, drenched, woolen clothing, stood grinning at her.

"Hello, lass."

"Brodie!"

The woman branded as a witch flew into his arms.

"How did you get here *now*?" she finally managed to ask. "I thought you were bringing the horses and wagon."

"Aye, well, when I saw how treacherous a log drive can be, I talked young Samuel into driving the horses." He quirked a corner of his mouth. "Furthermore, when I saw the fun it could be, dancin' from log to log, chancin' a drenchin' in an ice cold stream…"

"Brodie MacMillan, I believe you'll always need a bit of adventure in your life." Smiling, she cocked her head to look at him.

"Aye, aye, and with you by my side, I have a feelin' I'll never want for any." After another close hug and deep kiss, he drew her out to his arms' length and looked seriously down into her face. "Now to the next order of business. I want us to be married right and proper as soon as my friend Lachlan, the local minister, can do the deed. What do you say?"

"I say yes, oh, yes, my fine Highland laddie."

****

"I'm right nervous, Harry." Brodie, dressed in some of Harry's finery he'd brought with him from the Old Country, struggled to stand still as his friend adjusted his neckcloth. They were in his cabin across the valley from the farmhouse where the bride and her lady attendants were preparing for the wedding.

"That's normal." Harry finished and stepped back to admire his handiwork. "I remember I was right uneasy the day Margaret and I were wed. Turned out to be the best thing I've ever done. It will be for you as well, my brother." He clasped Brodie's shoulder in a hard grip and grinned at him. "James, how does your uncle look? Good enough for your Aunt Louisa?"

"Very nice." James, in similar finery, was nervously adjusting his waistcoat. Not accustomed to such clothing, his discomfort was obvious.

"James, I declare, you look as nervous as Brodie." Harry grinned at his eldest stepson.

"I've never stood witness at a wedding, Father." James wet his lips. "I don't want to ruin things by doing something wrong."

"All you have to do, laddie, is stand up at the front of the church with your uncle and catch him if he tries to make a run for it…or faints."

"Neither of which will happen." Grinning, Brodie slapped a hand on the young man's shoulder. "You must not go takin' your father too seriously."

"Still, I want everything to be right for you." James

207

faced his uncle, such sincerity in his blue eyes Brodie felt a lump forming in his throat.

"It will be, laddie. Never fear, it will be," he was quick to reassure him. "I only wish it didn't have to take place in the dead of night, that we can't have guests, that it has to be a bloody secret when I want to shout it from a rooftop that Louisa Abbott is marryin' me proper and makin' me the happiest of men."

"Soon, soon. We'll get all this nastiness cleared away, and the pair of you can set up house right here, with Louisa and Margaret talking housekeeping, and children, till they fair drive us to distraction." Harry's grin had broadened as he spoke.

"That will be a fine day, Harry, something that would make me feel I'd tumbled into a wee bit of heaven."

"It will happen. Now." His friend turned away and reached for a coat thrown over a chair. "Put yourself into this last bit of my old finery, and let us be off. I've the horses saddled and waiting. Lachlan has informed me we're to be at the church well before the women. I hope Geordie remembers to put blankets over the seats of the wagon to keep the ladies from snagging their gowns on the planks."

****

The log house across the small valley was a hive of activity. The three girls had rags wound into their curls in the hope of bringing order to their coiffures. Margaret was busy piling Louisa's hair into an artistic design about her head, while Bella and Lizzie bundled the twins into blankets and urged Eppie to leave off playing on the floor with Jasper and Precious in her good dress.

"Margaret." Louisa caught one of Margaret's hands in hers to stop her working on her hair. "Am I doing the right thing?" she asked softly below the hearing of the chattering children. "Am I putting Brodie at greater risk by marrying him openly? Would he not be safer running free on his own?"

"Possibly." Margaret turned her friend to face her. "But he's weary of running. And he loves you so very much, Louisa. You know his history. His life has not infrequently been an unhappy one. You've changed all that. He's a good man. He deserves a woman like you."

"You really believe that's true?" She gazed deep into Margaret's eyes.

"Yes, I do, with all my heart. I'm sure every bride feels uneasy on the eve of her wedding. I know I did when I was about to marry Harry, but it's been the best decision I ever made. Now." Margaret returned to her task. "We must finish up our preparations."

"Thank you, Margaret." Louisa heaved a sigh of relief. "I do love him so."

"Mother, Eppie won't stop playing on the floor with the animals." Lizzie's voice was querulous. "She's going to be dirty! And she says she doesn't want to leave Jasper and Precious here."

"See what you have to look forward to." Margaret finished her task and faced her friend with a smile. "I'm betting it won't be all that long before you and Brodie have your very own such brood."

****

As the strains of "Ave Maria" wafted softly from Geordie's fiddle, Brodie turned where he stood beside James at the front of the small, candlelit church and felt his breath catch in his throat. Louisa on Harry's arm had entered and paused, a vision in a gown of soft green, apple blossoms twined in her golden-red hair that seemed to shimmer in the flickering candlelight.

An angel. God in heaven, she's an angel. Can I be deservin' of all this wonder and beauty?

Then she was by his side, casting him a glance so full of emotion and understanding he thought he'd burst with joy. *Louisa, my love, my darlin' love.* The magic of it swirled around in his heart and mind and spirit.

Hearing Lachlan's voice, he forced himself out of the spell cast by her eyes and prepared to respond.

"Who gives this woman to be wed to this man?" Lachlan was asking.

"I..." Harry began, but at that moment the door at the rear of the church burst open. A half dozen militia men led by a burly sergeant burst inside, muskets drawn.

"Caught you at last, you wily bastard!" their leader yelled. "Tryin' to seduce another with your bandit ways!"

"Whit's the meaning of this?" Harry, accustomed to assuming command, moved Louisa behind him and faced the soldiers. "This is a family wedding in a sacred place. You've no right..."

"We've every right...a warrant for this outlaw's arrest!" The sergeant pulled a piece of dirty paper from his jacket and waved it toward the group at the front of the church.

"Not in my church you don't!" Lachlan came striding forward. "This is a holy place, not to be defiled by the likes of you. All here are in sanctuary."

"Stay out of our way, minister!" The sergeant thrust his drink-reddened face into Lachlan's belligerent one. "There're rumors floating around this region about you and your lovely wife's past in Scotland. You'd best keep out of my way, or I may just be tempted to seek a warrant for her arrest as well as your own."

"Bastards!" James made a start toward the soldiers, his three brothers rising in the pews to come to his aid.

"Hold, lads, easy." Harry raised an admonishing hand as the soldiers swung their muskets on his sons. "We'll get nowhere by squabbling. Now, Sergeant…" He turned to the officer, and Brodie saw his friend metamorphose into the suave Highland Harry who'd charmed many an Englishman in his time. "Let me see your warrant. I was the magistrate for this district, and as such can decipher official documents. I must be certain you've got the correct man in your sights."

"Right here." The officer shoved toward him the paper he'd been brandishing toward him. "You'll see there's a new charge, as well. Bastardry."

"Bastardry!" Brodie's response was a bellow. "I never touched the woman! I never…"

"Oh, you did much more than touch, Brodie MacMillan." Her voice made all turn toward the rear of the church, where Cassandra Carmody stood, wearing a loose cape. "Now I'm with child, and you'll pay. I'll definitely see you pay."

"Harry, it's a blatant lie." Brodie swung toward his friend. "I swear…"

"Mother!" Bella's cry drew everyone's attention to Margaret, who'd slumped from her seat to the floor. Her eyes closed, she appeared in a dead faint. "Mother! Oh, help me, please!" Bella sank on her knees beside the woman, the twin baby she held clutched in her arms. "Father, Father, come quickly! I think she may be dead!"

Brodie recognized the ruse. As attention focused on Margaret, he made a dash for the open church door. Before he'd gotten halfway down the aisle, one of the soldiers drew back a musket butt and smashed him on the side of the head.

Stars whirled before his eyes for a moment; then for a long time he saw and knew nothing.

****

"I ought to take you all off to jail!" the sergeant barked as his men dragged an unconscious Brodie from the church. Beside him, other soldiers held muskets leveled at the group. "Especially you, madam, and you, young lady, for perpetrating such a farce in an attempt to allow a criminal to escape," he spat at Margaret and Bella.

"Here now, you'll not go talking to my wife and daughter in such a manner." Harry stepped forward to stop the man's verbal attack.

Louisa, seated on a bench beside Margaret, one arm around her and the other around Bella standing next to her, felt a sudden urge to vomit. She, who'd nursed the sick and wounded through all kinds of hideousness, had become ill at the sight of her beloved Brodie being wounded and dragged away to prison.

We should never have come here. We should never have tried to have a normal marriage. We were tempted by the prospect of too much happiness...so much happiness it was not for such as us...a bandit and his witch bride.

"I bid you good evening." With a smirk twisting her lips, Cassandra Carmody dropped the group a mocking curtsey and followed the others outside.

As Margaret made to rush after her, Harry caught his wife about the waist and held her back.

"No, no, lass, that is not the way!"

"Let me go, Harry! I'll not let that creature ruin Brodie and Louisa's lives!"

"You won't be helping by pummeling the woman." He held his struggling wife in a strong grip. "Do you want our children to end up with no mother, while you rot in prison?"

She stopped protesting, but her green eyes held all the threat of a cat about to attack.

Silence fell over the church. The only sounds were those of the soldiers and their prisoner leaving. When retreating hooves marked their departure, the Reverend Edward Morgan spoke.

"Verrae well." He drew himself up to his six-foot-four-inch height and placed his hands on his hips covered with the white surplice he'd donned to perform the ceremony. "Now we must begin our plan to free our brother. Gather around."

He startled Louisa with this new stance. A hard, determined new outlook had come over his countenance. This was no longer the affable clergyman she'd been introduced to a few days previous. This was Lachlan Cameron, the outlaw leader Brodie had described to her.

As they obeyed, Louisa was further astonished at how quickly her friends set about laying out a plot that would free her husband. Brodie had the best and truest of friends. These former Highland outlaws remained a clannish lot not to be trifled with.

"I heard the new magistrate was a privateer during the war." Robert spoke. "Maybe he'll listen to us. When

I was in the village yesterday, folks were talking about how Captain Caleb Cameron and the man who was his first mate were holy terrors aboard their ship they called the *Lady Ghost*. They said Captain Cameron got captured once and that the Americans only managed to hold him for a day before he escaped. They said…"

"You mustn't put much store in village gossip, lad." Lachlan put an arm around the young man's broad shoulders. "What we need now is a plan, a clever plan that will free Brodie and not land any of the rest of us in prison. Harry, you've the look of a man who has a plot brewing. Would you care to enlighten us?"

Chapter Twenty-Six

"Good morning to you, Sergeant." Harry stepped into the magistrate's office, his most affable expression in place, Louisa by his side. "How are you and your fine troop this lovely spring morning?"

"Don't go giving me any of your Highland blarney," Sergeant Patrick O'Leary snapped as he looked up from behind the cluttered desk, and the two soldiers slumped into chairs in a corner snapped to their feet, muskets leveled at the pair. "You can play the charming bastard when it suits you, the whole village knows that, but underneath you're nothing but a highwayman, a Highland rebel who will be facing the noose if ever he dares show his face back in the Old Country. And as for this one..." He stood, his belly straining the buttons of his soiled uniform as he pointed at Louisa. "The village has declared her a witch."

"Now, now, Sergeant," Harry continued in the same calm, friendly tone, although Louisa saw his jaw jerk in a tick that she guessed indicated contained outrage. "You've the look of a clever man, a sophisticated man, not someone who goes believing local gossip and superstition. Mrs. MacMillan here is a healer of unusual skill, someone for certain sure this community could use. She's recently delivered my wife of fine twin boys. That's why we've come. We'll be holding a christening party day after tomorrow. We'd be honored if you and your fine group of men can attend."

"Stop trying to charm yourself into my good graces, Wallace. I'm not about to be won over. I can imagine what's behind this invitation. While we're all attending the baptizing of your two little bastards, your horde of stepsons and this woman will sneak down here to release my prisoner. Do you think I'm a complete fool?"

"Certainly not, certainly not," Harry kept on in his friendly vein. "If you decide to attend"—he glanced at the three soldiers and grinned in a comradely manner— "there'll be food and drink aplenty, maybe even a few pretty young women who'll be looking for partners in the dancing that will follow. Gentlemen, I bid you good day."

When his fingers went under her elbow to guide her to the door, Louisa recognized the tension in them as they seized her harder than necessary. It was taking every bit of restraint Harry Wallace possessed to turn away from these arrogant, ignorant creatures with a semblance of continued goodwill. She understood. Getting into an outright confrontation with the authorities would do little to further their case.

But as he assisted her onto Snow, she caught the muttered words, "Sons of bitches, miserable devil's spawn!" and, looking down at him, saw outrage in his face.

"It's no use trying to deal with the likes of them." Louisa made an effort to console him. "Anyway, I have an idea. Remember Robert's telling us he'd heard in the village about the new magistrate? A former ship's captain who fought for these colonies during the recent war…a man who was a bit of a rogue in his day, who'd spent time, even if briefly, in prison. Perhaps we might appeal to him. Perhaps…"

"I'd heard of Captain Caleb Cameron and his exploits before Robert's tales." Harry swung aboard Scotia and turned his mare to face hers. "He might be respectable as the church now, but he and his former first mate, Duncan MacDougal, were right devils at sea. They called Captain Cameron 'the Sea Wolf.' In fact, when he was captured at one point during the war, the Americans regarded it as a major victory. And Robert had the last part of the story correct. He spent time in a New Hampshire prison before escaping."

"All the more reason for him to appreciate Brodie's plight." She swung her mount about. "He has a fine house upriver, but James has told me he spends most of his days at his shipbuilding operation in the opposite direction, at the far end of the village. I'm going to see him."

****

Louisa stood holding Snow's reins as she gazed about, hoping to locate someone who could find the infamous Captain Cameron for her. Harry had remained aboard Scotia. She understood. A man who'd often been on the run, he stayed at the ready. Mounted, he'd have the advantage if anything in this proposed meeting didn't work out.

She looked about the construction area. The place was a veritable beehive of activity, with dozens of workers engaged in the building of three ships in various stages of construction. This Captain Caleb Cameron and his partner, his former first mate Duncan MacDougal, were obviously making a success of their venture with money they'd reputedly gleaned as a result of their years of privateering.

"Can I help ya, mistress?" Tipping his stained hat, a worker, dirty and sweating, approached her.

"I…that is, we…" She gestured to Harry. "We'd like to see Captain Cameron."

"I'll try to locate him, ma'am. Wait here." He strode off, back into the center of activity.

"Louisa, don't place all your hopes in this man." Harry frowned down at her. "To the best of my knowledge, he is an Englishman."

"As am I." She cast him a wry glance. "Well, Englishwoman. Don't paint us all with the same color, Harry Wallace. Some of us can be rogues as infamous as any Scotsman."

"Point taken." Harry touched his hat brim.

"At any rate, it's worth trying." She held her ground and watched as a tall, sandy-haired, broad-shouldered man came toward them, hat in hand, a cordial smile on his handsome face.

"Ya wanted to see Captain Cameron?" he asked.

"Yes. Might you be he?"

"No, lass, no." The Highland brogue broke over his words. "I'm Duncan MacDougal, his foreman. The captain is engaged at the moment. He sent me in his stead. And you would be?"

"Louisa MacMillan."

"Your servant, ma'am." He bowed. "Your companion needs no introduction. He's well known in this community. A pleasure to finally meet you, Mr. Wallace." A twinkle in his eyes, he held up a hand to the man on the horse. "I believe we've got a wee bit of a common background."

"From the sound of your words, yes, indeed, Mr. MacDougal."

A wave of relief coursed through Louisa as she caught the warmth coming into Harry's words. Perhaps here she'd find sympathy for her cause.

"Might we step off a bit and have a word?" Harry indicated a place on the edge of the shipyard near a stand of trees.

"I see no reason why not." With a sweep of his hand to indicate the way, Duncan MacDougal started in the direction indicated.

****

"So the lady's intended has been wrongfully accused of seduction…and now of fathering a child on a lady to whom he was not wed?" The big Scotsman leaned against a pile of lumber and spoke when Harry had finished. "The first charge I'm no stranger to…nor is Captain Cameron. We found ourselves in a similar circumstance a while back."

"What did you do?" Louisa's words came out more eagerly, more intensely, than she'd intended.

"Well, now, mistress, I don't reckon you'd sanction our solution." A corner of his mouth quirked as he squinted at her in the sunlight.

"Which was? Please, Mr. MacDougal, we're desperate."

"The captain and I married our accusers. Fortunately, it has all worked out right fine."

"Well, there's one solution out the window." Harry swung to the ground as Louisa felt hope fade. She'd thought this man might have an answer to the problem. The best to have come out of the interview was that apparently Harry had come to trust him.

"Don't despair." Duncan MacDougal pulled himself upright. "I'll go and fetch Cal...Captain Cameron. He's a right sly bugger...excuse me, ma'am. He might have a solution."

"I thought you two were a team, that together the pair of you gave the Americans a hell of a time to catch your ship." Harry stopped him as he turned to leave. "Tales of your exploits have reached even this outpost."

"Aye, well, we did give the Americans a fair run, but Cal was always the brains. I was more the muscle, the one who could take a blow with a belaying pin and keep on going. Even had a chunk of meat shot off my side with a musket. My guid wife sewed me up and now I'm right as rain. Wait here."

****

Shortly, Duncan MacDougal returned, a tall handsome man with curling black hair showing beneath his hat by his side.

"Mrs. MacMillan, Mr. Wallace, may I have the pleasure of introducing you to my friend and partner in this as well as various previous activities, Captain Caleb Cameron." The big Scotsman grinned. "Cal, meet Mrs. MacMillan and Harry Wallace." He leaned close to his friend and continued sotto voce, "The latter is suspected to be the infamous Highland Harry."

"Your servant, ma'am." The captain inclined his head to Louisa. "I am an admirer of yours, sir." He turned to Harry. "My friend"—he jerked his head to indicate Duncan—"has told me tales of your daring in the Scottish cause."

"Aye, well, we'd best leave that bit aside as history." With a sly grin, Harry accepted the hand Caleb extended to him. "At the moment, Louisa...Mrs.

MacMillan and I…have an immediate problem. Louisa thought that you, with your past daring exploits, might be willing to assist us."

"I believe I know something of your dilemma already." The captain crossed his arms on his broad chest. "That was your friend who was brought before me late last evening, accused of seduction and, as a result, fathering a child with a lady to whom he was not married?"

"Aye, aye. He's innocent of both charges, but that Carmody woman is determined to ruin both him and me. She's using Brodie to accomplish her nefarious ends."

"So, Cal, what do you suggest?" Duncan squinted over at his friend. "You must be able to come up with some plot to free Brodie MacMillan. You were right good at that during the war…or maybe you'd like to dash off home to consult Ann?" As a scowl darkened Caleb's face, Duncan continued, his face twitching to contain a grin. "His wife Ann was fair good at getting us out of scrapes when we were privateering aboard the *Lady Ghost*."

"I don't have to consult my wife," Caleb snapped. "I have an idea in mind, but it will involve your taking a journey to the American border. I know you're not partial to horseback riding."

"Haven't I always obeyed your orders, Captain?" The big Scotsman smirked. "Even the distasteful ones, even the ones that could have shoved my neck into the noose."

"Aye, that you have." He leaned into the group and spoke softly, "Now here's the plan."

Chapter Twenty-Seven

"On your feet, MacMillan. This is no time to be dozing."

Grimacing, Brodie struggled into wakefulness. His head still caused him misery from the blow he'd received in the church. In the darkness of his second night in the jail, he saw a man entering the cell area, a low burning lantern in hand. As he became able to focus, he recognized the man who'd stood beside the magistrate when the official had sentenced him to his present fate.

"Aye, aye." He staggered to his feet. "Whit has that woman accused me of now? There's not much left except murder. Am I to be hanged at dawn?"

"Nothing like that." The newcomer inserted the key into the lock. A moment later, the door swung open, and he thrust clothing he carried over one arm toward the prisoner. "Change into these. Your friend Harry is wanting his finery back."

"Is that all? Well, I'll be more than happy. These fancy things aren't my idea of comfortable dress."

He began to strip off the outfit he'd worn for his wedding. A wedding that had been so miserably interrupted. As he changed, he thought of Louisa and how she must be faring. She'd come to the jail the previous morning but had been denied entrance by Cassandra Carmondy's two bodyguards, who'd been standing watch outside. Through the glassless window high up on the cell wall, he'd heard her calm voice trying to convince the pair she had no intention of attempting to free him, but they'd finally managed to turn her away.

Clever Louisa. She'd recognized the pointlessness of the momentary situation, but he'd no doubt she was a long way from giving up. By now she'd be plotting something…something that would hopefully free him to be with her once more. But for the present… He pulled on the last of the garments, which he discovered were his own, and handed Harry's out to the man.

"Come along." The man's hissed whisper astonished him. He swung the door fully open. "There's no time to waste."

"Whit…?" Brodie hesitated. Were those two bastards the Carmody woman had in her employ waiting outside to shoot him down?

"Your wife, your friend Harry Wallace…Highland Harry…and my friend have come up with a scheme that will see you free until we can get these charges straightened out. Now, come along. I've horses waiting."

Highland Harry. So Harry had let this man know his true identity. He could guess at least part of the reason. The lad's Scottish accent colored every word he spoke.

"My name is Duncan MacDougal. I don't believe we've been properly introduced." He held out a big hand.

"A pleasure, Mr. MacDougal. But I think we'd best get the hell away from here."

Shoving his shirttail into his trousers, he made

haste to follow Caleb Cameron's friend out of the jail.

In the office, he found one of Cassandra Carmody's henchmen slumped over the desk. He glanced the question at his companion.

"Not all that loyal to their mistress where a fine brandy—laced with a secret flavoring of laudanum—is concerned." A corner of the other man's mouth curled with a contemptuous smirk. "Come along. We've got to hit the trail."

"We?"

"I'll be coming with you. I'll explain along the way." He dropped the clothes Brodie had been wearing into a dark corner and kicked them out of sight behind some shelves. "Best to let anyone who chooses to come after us think you'll be easy to spot wearing that finery."

****

Behind the jail, a pair of horses waited, supplies tied behind their saddles. The men swung aboard and walked them off into the trees. A short distance from the village, Duncan, who was leading the way, turned out along a well-worn road.

"Where are we going?" Brodie could wait no longer for an explanation.

"To the American border. That's as far as I'll escort you. Harry said to make sure you obeyed his instructions this time." He patted the pistol he had tucked in his belt. "Don't go trying to run off. I'm a right fair shot. I can knock a leg from under a man or a horse a good distance off, even in the dark."

"But how will my escape be explained?"

"My friend, Captain Cameron the magistrate, will tell the tale in the morning that he received an urgent request from the lieutenant governor. That illustrious official declared that you be brought to Fredericton to face justice in the provincial capital. Wishing to keep in that gentleman's good books, Captain Cameron decided not to wait for morning but to send me off immediately with the prisoner."

"And you think people will believe that yarn?" Brodie couldn't keep the skepticism out of his voice.

"I do. During the war, the lieutenant governor and Cal struck up an acquaintance. It's well known in Riverhaven that he got his appointment as magistrate because of His Excellency Stacy Smyth's regard for the captain. It will seem perfectly plausible that he should send instructions personally to a man he's come to regard as a friend."

"I sincerely hope so, Mr. MacDougal. I'd hate to see your friend lose his position as my friend Harry did, because of me."

"Don't concern yourself, Mr. MacMillan. Captain Caleb Cameron, occasionally with the aid of his clever wife, has been getting us in and out of slippery situations for years. Now, put your heels to that horse and let us be off. The border is a good long ride, and I'm hoping to be back in Riverhaven before the end of the week."

****

As dawn began to brighten the sky above the trees, Duncan stopped his horse and held up a hand to indicate Brodie was to do the same. He swung to the ground, rummaged in one of his saddle bags, and produced a pair of manacles.

"You'll have to wear these from here on." He approached his companion. "Hold down your hands."

"Whit! Are you daft?" Brodie stared down at the man who, up until the moment, had appeared to be his rescuer. "Bloody hell, man, you're really taking me to Fredericton as a prisoner! Two-faced bastard!"

Brodie kicked his horse's sides, but Duncan MacDougal, former privateer, was quick. He grabbed the animal's bridle and managed by sheer strength to prevent it from bolting.

"Hold, there!" he ordered. "That's not my intention at all. Listen, and I'll explain."

Looking down at the man, Brodie saw no duplicity, no deception in the man's face. He reined in his prancing mount.

"Explain."

"It's getting on to daylight. If we're met on the road, you must appear to be my prisoner."

"Aye, aye." Brodie heaved out the two words, his companion's logic becoming clear. "Verrae well." He held down his hands. "Your prisoner I'll be."

"Furthermore..." Duncan quirked him a sly grin as he fastened the restraints in place. "Your friend Harry didn't want to take any chance of your deciding to run back to your lady. He said you'd previously ignored his advice and tried to return to the grave of your first wife. He felt that a living, breathing beauty would offer even greater temptation."

"Sweet Jesus! Harry doesn't trust me? After all we've been through together, after all..."

"After, I've been given to understand, you've acted as a loose cannon on more than one occasion." Duncan MacDougal finished fastening the manacles and paused to look up at him.

"Aye, well, there might be a wee bit of truth in

that." Brodie heaved a sigh and let a corner of his mouth curl. "Now." He straightened in the saddle and adjusted the reins. "Let's be off, then, laddie. The sooner we get to the border, the sooner I'll be free of these." He rattled the restraints, making his horse shy and prance. "Quite right, my fine lady." He patted the mare's neck as best he could. "Damn, annoying nuisance."

****

As darkness fell, Duncan headed their horses off the trail into a grove with a brook gurgling through it.

"We'll stop for the night." He swung to the ground. "The horses need rest. We can let them graze in that meadow off there a bit and water them at the stream. As for myself"—he stretched cramped muscles—"I'll be right glad for food and a bit of sleep." He turned to Brodie. "Get down and relieve yourself, if you feel the need. I'll be unloading the horses and setting up camp."

"You're not afeard I'll make a break for it?" Brodie swung to the ground and rolled tired shoulders.

"The captain once accused me of having eyes in the back of my head." Duncan began to unfasten saddle bags and drop them to the ground. "I reckon you wouldn't get far…not with me having been given that recommendation and having control of the horses and the key to those manacles."

"Aye, aye." Brodie headed off into the trees. "Anyway, why would I try to get away? You broke me out of prison and now you're guiding me to safety. It would be a right ungrateful move."

"Logically, you shouldn't." Duncan became involved in spreading out supplies. "But I've seen your wife. She's enough to make a man throw common

227

sense to the wind…much like my own." From where he'd hunkered down over their supplies, he glanced up at Brodie. "So never say I don't understand your inclinations."

"I didn't know you were married." Surprised by the revelation, Brodie turned back.

"Aye, aye, to a real spitfire if ever there was one." Brodie watched as a broad grin spread over his companion's face. "And a tongue to match. I'm going to have no end of a challenge to keep our wee daughter from picking up some of her mother's colorful language."

"You've a child, as well?" Brodie stared. "Man, you're takin' a devil of a risk doin' what you are to help me. If Captain Cameron fails to convince Cassandra Carmody and her pair of picaroons with his tale of the lieutenant governor's request to bring me to Fredericton, you'll be in serious trouble."

"Ah, but you don't know the captain as I do." Duncan opened a bag of provisions and began to spread them out. "He's one clever bastard. Now, off with you and do what you must. And while you're about it, see if you can find something to use as firewood."

****

They sat beside the fire they'd used to cook a meager meal and watched the flames die to embers.

"Fancy a wee dram before we take our rest?" Duncan drew a flask from a saddle bag and held it up to Brodie.

"Aye, aye, that I would, but should you be sharin' it with a prisoner?"

"I don't consider you my prisoner." Duncan pulled the cork free with his teeth and took a swallow before continuing. "I'm simply keeping one unpredictable…so I've been told…bastard out of harm's way until the mess into which he's gotten himself can be cleared away." He handed the flask to Brodie.

"Aye, I guess that's true enough." Brodie took a drink. "Ah, that is fine stuff. Good Scotch whisky if ever I tasted it."

"That it is." Taking it back after Brodie had had another quaff, Duncan enjoyed one more mouthful, banged the cork back in place with the heel of his hand, and put it back into the saddle bag. "Mustn't let ourselves get under the influence," he said as he got to his feet. "But, damnation, I needed it. My arse is fair sore from all this riding. I'm a sailor, you understand, not a blessed jockey."

"I've heard you're a seaman, and a fair to middlin' good one." Brodie watched as his companion took up another of their traveling bags. "First mate on the captain's ship the *Lady Ghost*, the story goes. And the queen of privateerin' vessels she was, by all accounts."

"You heard right." He turned back to Brodie, another manacle in his hand. "Now, my fine lad, if you'll move closer to that big pine, I'll be trussin' you to it for the night."

"Whit?" Brodie stared at the chain restraint. "God in heaven, man, you don't mean that!"

"I most certainly do. You've the makings of a boon companion, Brodie MacMillan, but from all I've heard you'd not be above taking advantage of me while I sleep and making a run for it. So…" He rattled the chains.

With a resigned sigh, Brodie edged closer to the tree Duncan had indicated.

"Hell of a thing, a reputation," he muttered as his guard snapped a manacle about one of his ankles and secured the chain around the trunk. "Mine surely has gotten me into some damn uncomfortable situations."

Chapter Twenty-Eight

"Harry!" Edward Morgan, astride one of his Percherons, galloped into the stable yard and reined to a skidding halt in front of the barn as Harry emerged. "We've got trouble in the village! A disaster, if you will!" He slid to the ground, his white shirt open at the throat, dark coat thick with the dirt of a hard ride.

"Whit is it, laddie?" Harry caught the prancing horse's bridle. "Guid God, man, you look as if the plague of Egypt has struck."

"Verrae nearly." Broad chest heaving, the clergyman let his Highland accent override the English one he'd cultivated so carefully since coming to the valley. "A ship flying the yellow flag of illness arrived in the river early this morning. The magistrate ordered the captain to off load all sick passengers and crew onto the quarantine island a bit downriver. Harry, I rode along the shore and discovered that there are dozens of sick and dying out there...and no one to help."

"Sweet Jesus!" Harry looked at Louisa, who'd come out of the barn carrying a bucket of milk. "All of Riverhaven might be at risk if even one infected person gets ashore!"

"What is being done to prevent the spread?" Louisa faced the distraught clergyman.

"When I left, militia men were patrolling the beach in case any try to escape from the island, but there are families living nearby who, I fear, may become afflicted. That island is too near the community to be a safe quarantine. Furthermore, the soldiers were threatening to desert their posts, fearful of becoming ill from a breeze off the island blowing the sickness over them."

"Harry, I'll need medicines from my cabin." Louisa turned to him. "You'll have to go. Ride to the village and find Jonah Parsons. He knows the way. He'll guide you."

"Louisa, you can't seriously be thinking of trying to help those people…"

"Definitely. Now saddle your horse and mine. I'll go to the house and gather what I have with me and what you have available that I believe might help. When you return from my homestead, bring the medicines to the shore and fire a shot. Don't come any closer. After you're a safe distance away, I'll come in and get them." Milk sloshing out of the pail, she broke into a run toward the house. "I'll change my clothes and be on my way."

"Lass!" Harry strode after her and caught her by an arm. "If I allow you to undertake this work and you fall ill, Brodie will never forgive me. I've already been responsible for his losing his first wife…"

"I had the fever some years ago. Neil reckoned that once a person has had it and survives, they have but scant chance of getting it again. As for Brodie?" She gently shrugged off his restraining hand and continued toward the house. "He'd expect me to do no less. Now go! There's not a moment to waste."

"I'll be coming with you, lass," the clergyman called after her. "I dare say you'll be needing help."

232

"Lachlan, you're a married man." Harry used his friend's Highland name as he faced him. "You'll be risking your life…"

"It's no more than my duty as a minister, Harry. My wife will manage. Remember, she was a Highland outlaw once, too."

"Verrae well. I can see there's no reasoning with a stubborn Scotsman. Help me saddle the horses."

Harry strode into the barn, Edward Morgan close behind him. Inside they saw James had paused in brushing his gelding Midnight and was reaching for a saddle cloth.

"I'm coming with you, Uncle Edward," he said.

"Lad…" Harry began to protest, but the determined look in his stepson's blue eyes stopped him.

"Take care, my boy," he said softly as he went to saddle his mare.

****

On the small island, inside the shed that housed the sick and dying, Louisa faced a terrible display of bodies lying on the dirt floor, some clutching blankets about them, others only their ragged clothing. The stench was overwhelming. Some of the stricken were moaning, others lay horribly still.

Louisa placed what medical supplies she'd been able to muster on a dirty table near the door and turned to James and Edward, who'd followed her inside. The men carried what blankets they'd been able to bring from the farm and beg from villagers. The latter had been a scant collection, most residents unwilling to help people they saw as bringing death to their community.

"Come with me," she murmured to her companions. "Bring the blankets."

Edward nodded. They would be needed to wrap the dead and remove them.

Louisa moved among the stricken, kneeling beside each individual. When she stood, she frequently turned to the two men and shook her head to indicate death had overtaken the person. Edward knelt beside each victim and bowed his head in prayer. Out of the corner of her eye, Louisa saw James swallow hard on each of these occasions. She admired his fortitude as he managed to recover after each such incident and move to help the clergyman remove the body from the shed.

He's a strong, compassionate man. He'll do well in whatever he attempts in life.

****

Hours later, she stepped outside into the drizzle of a foggy spring evening and drew a deep breath in an effort to rid her lungs of the putrid air. From around the corner of the shed came the sounds of someone vomiting. James. After working steadily beside her and Edward throughout the long day, a few moments previous he'd rushed outside.

She leaned back against the crude structure that had become her hospital and listened to Edward comforting a dying woman with a prayer. The former Highland outlaw was a man of deep compassion and empathy. She hoped he wouldn't fall ill. She needed him by her side.

She also needed to know that Brodie had escaped, that the plan Harry and Captain Cameron had concocted had worked. As she drew another deep breath and prepared to go back inside, two horsemen appeared on shore beside the soldiers who were keeping the island under quarantine.

"Mrs. MacMillan," the first called, and she recognized Captain Cameron. "How can we help?"

"Keep the villagers away. We need no more sick in our care."

"Very well. Mr. MacDougal?" He turned to his companion. "Issue such orders to these men. I don't care if you're not their sergeant. They're duty bound to obey. You'll be acting on my behalf as magistrate."

"Aye, aye, Captain." Duncan touched his cap in acknowledgement. "Mrs. MacMillan," he called before turning his horse away, "all is well."

"Thank you, Mr. MacDougal. Most sincerely, thank you." Feeling as if a huge weight had been lifted from her shoulders, Louisa raised a hand to him before returning to her duties in the shed.

****

Louisa sank down onto an overturned bucket outside the fish shed. It had been a week since she, Edward, and James had come to help the victims. Her body ached as exhaustion threatened to overwhelm her, but she knew she'd done her best. Those she couldn't save had passed, those she'd been able to help were well on the mend. The ship that had brought this unfortunate group had sailed that morning, disinfected with brimstone. The captain had been so eager to get away he'd opted to sail with ballast rather than wait for a cargo of lumber. The guards on shore had been dismissed from duty.

James came out of the building to lean a broad shoulder against the door frame. His white shirt was dirty and sweat-stained, but he managed a weary grin.

"We did our best, Aunt Louisa, didn't we," he said. "Do you think the worst is over?"

"Yes, we did, and if you're speaking of the sickness, I believe the most dreadful is indeed behind us. But I have a feeling"—she looked up at him, the first smile she'd been able to muster in days making small curls at the corners of her mouth—"your mother won't be greeting me with any pleasure for allowing you to help your uncle and me."

"I could do no less." He straightened to his full height. "If Uncle Brodie had been available, he'd have done the same. I wanted to begin to repay the debt our family owes him for saving Eppie some time back."

"Brodie saved Eppie?" She hadn't heard of it.

"One day when Father was away, some of Joe Carmody's men, with Michael Kelly leading them, rode out to our farm. They would have run Eppie and quite possibly Mother down if Uncle Brodie hadn't arrived on the scene, waving his sword and yelling like a banshee. Scared them clear off our land."

"That sounds like Brodie." She stood and rubbed her hands down the front of her stained apron. The thought of Michael Kelly trying to eat those raw onions gave her renewed pleasure. "I must get back to work. There's still bathing and cleaning to do."

The minister, his shirt filthy, his face gaunt, shrugged past James in the doorway, put his hands on his hips, and drew in a deep breath.

"This has been quite a battle." He turned to the pair by the door. "Worse than fighting off a regiment of redcoats."

"You're weary, Uncle Edward." James went to put a hand on the older man's shoulder. "You'd best clean up and go back to your family."

"Aye, aye. But only if you and Louisa are certain

sure you can manage."

"We'll do very well." Louisa smiled up at him. "The danger has passed. Once those remaining are well enough to leave, which should be in a day or two, all that will remain to be done will be to fumigate this building."

"I think we should burn it." James's expression was grim as he looked at the dilapidated gray building behind them.

"Perhaps, but if I were to do it…" Louisa didn't finish.

"Aye, aye." The minister looked over at her. "No need to drag up old memories. I'll wait until you've gone back to the farm. Then I'll set it aflame. If the villagers choose to brand me a warlock, so be it."

"Thank you, Edward. I think that would be best. A new structure should be built to house any more sick that come to the area aboard ships. This one is worse than a hovel."

"I'll go, then." He wiped a hand across his wet brow. "I'll swim ashore. It'll give me a good wash, clothes and all. I won't risk Iona and the wee lass catching this miserable sickness. You did well, lad." He held out a hand to James. "You've done your family and your community proud."

"It was no more than Papa…and Father…would have expected of me."

"Of course." Edward Morgan nodded to the young man, turned and walked toward the water. They watched as he waded in until depth set him swimming. He headed for the beach in long, sure strokes.

Louisa leaned back against the side of the shed and looked at James, who was watching him leave. The young man admired the minister in no small way. She wondered…

"Look!" James turned toward the village as a horseman burst into view, riding full speed toward them. He drew rein on the shore. He was leading Snow, saddled and bridled. When they'd gone out to the island, Louisa and James had left their horses at a stable. Edward had sent his mount galloping back toward the manse with a slap on its rump.

"It's one of those great brutes Mistress Carmody has guarding her," James muttered. Louisa saw his hands knotting into fists at his side.

"Don't, James, please!" Louisa moved to stand beside him. "We're not armed but"—she indicated the pistol in the man's belt—"he is."

"You're to come with me, healing woman," the man bellowed.

"Why?" Louisa faced him across the water. "Are you in need of medical assistance?"

"Not me, but my mistress. She's come down with the fever. She sent me to fetch you."

"Cassandra Carmody has the fever? How can that be? She never once came near the ship or this island."

"I don't know. All I know is that I'm to fetch you…any way that I can." He put his hand suggestively to the pistol in his belt.

"Now, just a minute!" James made to move forward, but Louisa caught at his arm.

"It's all right, James. I'll go. You can manage alone here for an hour or so." She turned to the man on the horse. "Give me a moment to collect what supplies I need."

An idea taking shape, she stepped back inside the

shed to the table near the door, where she kept bottles and flasks of remedies, and began to sort through them.

"Aunt Louisa, you can't go with that brute! It may be a trap!" James followed her, a deep frown wrinkling his forehead.

"And it may not be." She began to collect supplies into a bag. "It may be an opportunity to get your uncle cleared of those ridiculous charges she's laid against him. I'll be back as soon as possible."

"All right, but if you don't return shortly…"

"Don't worry. I will. Now you'd best get to the chores at hand. We still have a few patients left to care for."

As soon as he left her alone, she found paper and one of the bits of a pencil she'd used to keep track of patients. Taking a fresh sheet, she began to write.

Shortly, she was in the small skiff she, James, and Edward had used to get to the island and was rowing toward shore.

****

Louisa, mounted on Snow, her bag of medical provisions tied to her saddle, followed Clem to the mansion on the rise above the village.

"I'll see to the horse." Her companion reached down a meaty hand for the reins as she dismounted. When she gave him an apprehensive look, he continued, "I'm not about to steal the creature. Where could a bloke hide something as white at that?"

"Very well." She handed the horse over to him and untied her bag. "But mind I find her ready and waiting when I've finished with your mistress…ready and waiting and fit as a fiddle…or else…" She narrowed her eyes and gave him what she hoped was a witchly glare.

"Aye, aye, that you will." The words came out with an apprehension, even a trace of fear, that told her she'd accomplished her purpose. Clem wasn't about to risk any kind of curse being put upon him over a horse.

Repressing a sly smirk, she went up the steps and into the house. Inside she found a frightened young maidservant fluttering about.

"Thank God you've come, mistress." The girl dropped a quick curtsey. "She's been moanin' and groanin' something fierce."

"Can you tell me what your mistress has eaten recently?" On the ride to the house, an idea had occurred to her. Since Cassandra hadn't been near the fever shed, she doubted the woman was suffering from the disease. There were other possibilities.

"Ah, she has some strange cravings, mistress. Yesterday she longed for a wine she said bubbled…"

"Champagne."

"Aye, that was it. And something called caviar. Do you know what that is, mistress? Fish eggs! Imagine longing for anything so vile."

"Mistress Carmody is a sophisticated woman of the world. Her tastes are exotic."

"Yesterday, she made Tom ride out to find oysters. Oysters! At this time of year. Everyone knows it's folly to eat the things at this time of year. But she insisted."

"And did Tom succeed in finding oysters?" A diagnosis flashed into Louisa's mind.

"Aye, that he did…although he had to pay a fisherman a terrible sum to rake up a bunch. The man knew they'd not be safe to eat until September."

"Only in months with an 'r' in them, so the story

goes." Louisa remembered the adage. "May isn't one of those." She started for the stairs.

"Will you be needin' my help, mistress?" The girl fingered her snowy apron and gazed after Louisa with large, frightened eyes.

"No, thank you…" She looked the question down at her.

"Lily, mistress. My name is Lily."

"Well, Lily, you may stay down here. I'll call out if I need you. Don't be afraid. I feel certain your mistress isn't suffering from the same sickness as the people who came in on that ship. You're quite safe."

"Thank you, mistress." Lily's shoulders slumped with relief. Brightening, she turned away with a spritely manner. "I'll have Cook make you a nice pot of tea for when you're finished above."

****

Moaning, the woman lay in the luxurious bed of a room with curtains drawn, her long, black hair spread over snowy pillows, a pair of candles and a small fire on the hearth providing the only illumination. Louisa couldn't help thinking what a small bit of heaven such a place of repose would have been for those recovering in that miserable shed on the island.

"Miss Carmody?" She advanced across the room to stand beside the woman in the bed. "You sent for me?"

"You're supposed to be a witch, a magic healer." Cassandra Carmody looked up at her from a face deathly pale. "Make me well. Make me well, and I'll see you're rewarded. I'll be generous, I promise."

Her body began to jerk with great spasms.

"I will." She put her bag onto a bedside table. "But first…" She grabbed the covering Cassandra clutched

241

to her throat and flung it back. "Just as I knew!" she said triumphantly. "Your belly is as flat as mine! You're not carrying my husband's child. He's never so much as touched you, has he!"

"Never mind all that. Get on with healing me."

"Not so quickly. My services come at a price."

"Name it and you shall have it." Cassandra clutched her middle and groaned. "I've already told you."

"Very well. In the presence of your maid and cook, who'll act as witnesses, you're to sign a paper exonerating Brodie MacMillan of the charges of seducing you and fathering this nonexistent child. You'll state that you lied, that he never laid a hand on you except to aid you home after your riding accident."

"Exonerate the bastard? Exonerate..." Another bout of heaving overtook her. She retched into a basin beside the bed.

"Then I must take my leave. Good day to you, Miss Carmody." She picked up her medical bag.

"Wait, wait! Don't go! Give me the damned document, and I'll sign it!"

Feeling smug to the core, Louisa went to the top of the stairs and called for the maid to come and bring the cook with her. On her return to the room, she removed from her bag the carefully worded document she'd written in the fever shed, and smoothed it out on a bedside table.

****

Louisa gathered her medicines into her valise. Although pale and gaunt, her patient was resting comfortably. Food poisoning had passed naturally with only slight assistance from her cures, Louisa knew.

Nevertheless, she wasn't about to let Cassandra Carmody believe her seemingly miraculous recovery had been little more than the result of giving her an emetic to make her vomit up tainted oysters. She wanted to keep the woman in her debt as long as possible, even if the document she'd tucked into her bag held all the repayment she required. Cassandra Carmody was not a woman to be trusted.

"I'll be going now." She drew back her shoulders and thought how weary, how very, very weary she was. She needed a decent meal and a long, long sleep, but first she had to deliver that document to Captain Caleb Cameron, the magistrate. She wouldn't risk the woman in the bed rallying sufficiently to send her thugs to retrieve it.

"Go." *No thanks from this creature.* "You've got what you wanted. Now get out of my sight."

"Of course." She nodded curtly and headed for the door. Before she stepped out into the corridor, she glanced back at the woman in the bed. Although weakened by her recent illness, the woman's dark eyes flashed out such venom Louisa felt something deep in her gut jerk and roil.

Cassandra Carmody wasn't yet finished punishing her husband and his friends. Not yet.

Chapter Twenty-Nine

"Well, Mr. MacDougal, it looks as if you'll be heading back to the American border." Captain Caleb Cameron finished examining the document Louisa had laid before him and looked up at his former first mate. "This paper clears our friend Brodie MacMillan of any crimes against Mistress Cassandra Carmody. He's a free man, free to return to his wife and our community. You can set out at first light."

"Ah, Cal!" The big Scotsman's response was a moaning protest. "I'm right happy to hear Brodie's been cleared, but isn't there someone else you can send to fetch him? My backside..." He glanced at Louisa. "Excuse me, ma'am. It's just now healing up from that last ride. I'm a sailor, not a blessed jockey. My nether parts weren't made for jouncing about on a horse."

"The Fowler boys and Harry Wallace are all busy at their mill, and I'm not about to send this lady off alone into the wilds of New Brunswick. Nor will I trust Jonah Parsons with the task. It would take him a month, with the speed he rides on that mule he borrows. Furthermore, I doubt he'd be able to find his way. You can navigate on land as well as on water. I shouldn't have to remind you you're my deputy. It's your duty. Furthermore, how else would you expect to travel in this country, in a curricle or a barouche? This isn't England, you know."

"Bloody hell! Excuse me again, mistress." Duncan glanced over at Louisa. "I'll go, but if I suffer permanent injury…"

"I have a soothing elixir you might get your wife to apply on your return." Louisa gave him a coy smile. "The effects can be most pleasant."

"Oh, aye?" He looked over at her, catching her double meaning. "Aye, well, then." He drew himself up. "I'd best be finding a decent horse first thing in the morning and be heading off, hadn't I?"

****

Nursing an ale, Brodie MacMillan sat in the Anchor and Arms in Calais, Maine. Liquor had lost its power to sooth. Still he had found no other way to pass the time.

Sweet Jesus, what's keeping Harry from getting me cleared of those daft charges? Has a happy marriage and nine children softened his brain, his ability to scheme the way out of any situation? I need Louisa. I need to get back to her before I go mad.

"I be lookin' fer one Charles Bonnie." A scrubbily bearded man in dirty, disheveled clothing appeared in the tavern doorway. "I has a message for him."

"Here." Responding to his alias, Brodie raised a hand. *Dear God, let this be the news I need.*

"I have a message for ya." The vagabond approached the table, a grubby piece of paper clutched in his dirty hand. "A fella on the far side of the river gave this to me. Said if I delivered it to the right fella, he'd reward me handsome."

"Give it here." On his feet, Brodie made to snatch it.

"Not so fast, laddie." Pulling it back, the man

245

wrinkled his face into a smug smirk, bloodshot eyes narrowing slyly. "First I'll see the color of your coin."

"First I'll see that message, or it's my fist in your face you'll be seeing."

"All right, all right." The man hesitated only briefly before handing over the paper.

"Your clever wife has gotten the charges against you dismissed. You can come home."

There was no signature. Brodie wasn't surprised. The paper might have fallen into the wrong hands and anyone indicated in a signature could be found guilty of aiding a fugitive. Recognizing Harry's handwriting assured him of the legitimacy of the document.

"Where is this gentleman who gave you the note?" His heart pounding, Brodie grasped the man by the shoulders.

"Like I told you…other side of the river, straight across from here."

"Guid, verrae guid. Thank you, laddie." Brodie fumbled in his waistcoat pocket and drew out a couple of gold coins. He dropped them into the man's dirty palm. Duncan had given him a small bag full of them when the two men parted at the American border.

"From Harry," he'd explained. "To keep you from starvation."

Typical of his friend's generosity, there'd been a lot more than enough to keep him in food.

"Thank you most kindly, sir. You're a gentleman."

Brodie barely heard him. He was headed out of the tavern at a run.

****

"Get a move on, you great lout!" Brodie yelled ahead at Duncan.

246

They were riding across the province, Duncan navigating.

"I told you I near got lost going home the last time," the former first mate snapped back. "Finding the way through all these blessed trees isn't the same as navigating with a clear sky overhead. I'm a sailor, not a bloody hunting guide."

"Aye, aye, well, that's obvious," Brodie muttered.

"Look." Duncan swung his horse awkwardly back toward his companion. "I'm right eager to get back to my wife, too, but getting us good and confused isn't going to help."

"Sorry, sorry." Brodie shook his head, annoyed with himself. Duncan MacDougal, who hated traveling on horseback, was on his fourth ride across the province, and all on his behalf. He had no right to berate at him.

"Aye, well, you'll soon be home." Duncan pulled off his hat and wiped sweat from his brow with the back of his forearm. "If my calculations are right, and I'm almost certain sure they are, we should be hitting the wagon road into Riverhaven within the hour."

"Guid, guid." Brodie fought down his impatience. "It's a right warm day. I hear a brook gurglin' not far off to the right. What say we stop and wet our whistles? I reckon as how these horses could do with a drink, as well."

Gunshot rent the air.

"Sweet Jesus!" Duncan fought to control his terrified horse.

"Ride!" Brodie kicked his horse into action, but as a second shot followed the first, he slumped over the animal's neck as it charged off into the bush.

"Brodie!" Duncan tried to bring his mount under control to follow. As the mare reared, Duncan MacDougal, yelling curses, was tossed into a thicket.

Chapter Thirty

"Louisa, I have a gift for you." Carrying a brightly colored quilt over his arm, Harry came into the log house. "When I went into the village today, the ladies presented me with this bedcover. They said it was by way of saying thanks for saving everyone who lives there. They claim it was your doing that prevented not a single resident from contracting that dreadful fever."

"It's beautiful!" Margaret fingered an edge while Louisa turned from where she'd been gazing out the window to look at the gift. "Oh, Louisa, it will be lovely on your bed."

"They went so far as to suggest it might be thought of as a wedding gift." Harry was all-out grinning by that time. "It appears they've become comfortable with the idea of your marrying into their midst. Now all we need is the groom."

"Still no word of Brodie?"

"No, lass. I'm right sorry." Harry's response was soft, his Highland accent heavy.

"I'm sure he'll be here soon." Margaret touched Louisa's arm. "We're going to have a fine wedding when he arrives. Iona—I suppose I should get accustomed to calling her Mary, since she's chosen to stay with her new name—will be decorating the church with flowers, and my girls and I will prepare a lovely feast."

"Lass, I fear you missed out on such festivities yourself, what with us dashing off to get Lachlan to marry us in haste." Harry put an arm about Maggie's shoulders.

"Do I look as if I have any regrets?" She smiled up at him. "I have a wonderful husband, two healthy sons, and seven fine stepchildren. What more could a woman want?"

"Perhaps a little more leisure time to take a stroll with that wonderful husband?" Blue eyes teasing, he looked down at her.

"And she shall have it." Louisa held the quilt to her breast, her eyes sparkling. "The girls are picking strawberries, the boys are busy in the mill, and your two healthy sons are sleeping. So be off with you. As I've just been given credit for saving an entire village, I think I can be trusted to watch over your twins while you two go on a romantic walk this lovely afternoon."

"Thank you, Louisa." Harry seized his wife's hand. "Come along, my love. I've a great desire to court the most beautiful woman in the province."

"Oh, my, Harry Wallace, you do have a way with words." Giggling, Maggie snatched up her bonnet, and together they hurried out of the house.

****

Hooves. Hooves coming up the hill into the dooryard at a full gallop. Could it be…?

Still holding the bed covering, she swallowed hard and hoped as she went to the window. Her heart plummeted when she saw only Duncan MacDougal and Edward Morgan dismounting from the clergyman's Percherons in the dooryard.

When they entered, their expressions brought the

nausea of despair welling into her stomach.

"Louisa, I'm afraid we have unpleasant news." Edward Morgan stepped forward. "Perhaps you'd best sit down." He guided her to one of the rocking chairs by the hearth.

"It's Brodie, isn't it?"

"There was an accident on the trail back from the United States." Duncan MacDougal spoke while the minister dropped on one knee by her chair. "We were ambushed. Brodie appeared to have been hit by one of the shots."

"Oh, God!" Trembling washed over her as she stared up at the man. Then, "What do you mean, 'appeared'? Aren't you certain?" She jumped to her feet to glare at him. "Didn't you stop to find out what happened to him? Didn't you…"

"His horse bolted at the gunfire. It took off like a thing possessed, with Brodie slumped over its neck." The agony the account of the incident was causing him made him speak hesitantly, brokenly. "I'm a right poor excuse for a rider. Panicked by the noise, my beast reared and threw me into the bush. I couldn't catch the miserable brute. I decided my best plan would be to walk to the road to Riverhaven and get help. Once on the trail, I managed to beg a wagon ride into the village. My horse hadn't yet arrived back at the stable by the time I got there. I rode one of the minister's horses to get here."

"Dear God!" Louisa slumped back in the chair. Edward took the quilt from her hands and drew it about her shoulders.

"Duncan, over in that cupboard above the dresser you'll find a flask of Harry's best brandy," he said.

"Pour out a goodly measure and bring it here."

"Oh, aye." The big Scotsman was quick to comply.

He was handing her a cup half full of it when more hoof beats announced another arrival.

A moment later, Brodie MacMillan, sweaty and dirt-streaked, burst into the log house.

"I'm back, love." He paused in the doorway, a broad grin on his face, hands on his hips. For a moment Louisa fancied he glowed like a miracle before he strode across the room to pull her from the chair and into his arms.

And then they were kissing, kissing as if there should be no end to the greeting, no end to the joy of their reunion.

"Guid God, lad, how?" Duncan MacDougal breathed out the query when Brodie finally let his wife come up for air. "I thought certain sure you were dead…at best, carried off somewhere by that daft beastie to die."

"I have to admit, that first pistol shot took me a wee bit by surprise." He grinned over at his former companion. "The second one gave me an idea. Being so close to Riverhaven, I had a good notion that it was those two louts of the Carmody woman, out to get me. So I faked being hit. Two shots told me they'd have to reload. By that time, I'd be well away. I was confident they wouldn't harm you, what with you bein' the magistrate's right-hand man. Anyway, it was me they were after."

"So whit did you do?" Duncan stared at him as if he still wasn't sure it was Brodie MacMillan he was staring at and not his ghost.

"I pretended to be shot and kicked my horse to a

run. Although he wasn't swift like Fox, he did manage to get me a fair distance away. I think, from some of the thrashin' around I heard for a bit in the bush behind me, that those dastardly devils tried to follow me, but I ride right well, as you know. Once I was out of their sight, I could straighten up in the saddle and put distance between us."

"I'm glad your man is home, Mrs. MacMillan." The former sailor grinned. "I will even consider forgiving him for being responsible for me being tossed on my backside when those louts took a shot at him. Now, I reckon the Reverend Morgan and I should be leaving you alone to have a proper reunion. But, ma'am, you did promise me that ointment, and I'm fair sore from riding for miles and miles and then being tossed."

"Yes, of course." She eased out of Brodie's embrace to go to a cupboard. She removed a small jar and handed it to him. "Slight recompense, Mr. MacDougal, for all you've done for Brodie. If there's ever anything I can do for you or your family, I will be delighted to help."

"This will do nicely, thank you, ma'am." With a wink, he turned toward the door. "Now I must be on my way. I have a wife who's waiting as well." He held up the jar. "And perhaps even a bit of fun in the offing. Come along, Minister. We're no longer needed here."

"Aye." Edward Morgan paused to smile at the pair. "God bless you both. Brodie, I'm delighted to say you appear to have more lives than a cat, but in the future, try not to press your luck."

"Oh, aye. From now on I'll be mild and meek." He winked, and Louisa couldn't help scoffing. She knew that for the man she'd chosen, mild and meek would never be an apt description.

"Enjoy that ointment, Dunc," Brodie called after him.

"Brodie!" Louisa gave him a nudge. "That's hardly an appropriate comment to a man regarding his time with his wife…especially with a clergyman present."

"Oh, isn't it!" He caught her up in his arms and swung her about off the floor. "Well, my love, I'm plannin' for us to enjoy ourselves as well." He let her regain her feet and kissed her again. "Now we're off to the privacy of our own cabin to have a proper reunion."

"Oh, Brodie, no!" She stopped him as he began to pull her toward the door. "I'm watching the twins. Margaret and Harry wanted a little time alone together, and the children are all otherwise engaged. We must wait until they come back."

"You picked a fine time to play nanny." He heaved an exasperated sigh. "But I've waited weeks and weeks. I guess I can manage a bit longer. What's this?" He picked up the quilt that had fallen to the floor.

"A gift from the women of Riverhaven."

"A gift? Why? What have you been up to in my absence? How has this change of attitude come about?"

"We'll talk about it later." Louisa wasn't about to dampen their reunion by the story of how she, James, and Edward Morgan had risked their lives to stop an outbreak of fever in the village. She turned toward the bedroom as a small wail indicated one of the twins was awake. "Right now I have to fulfill my duty as nursery maid."

"I'll go. I'm right eager to see my nephews."

As he strode into the adjoining room, Louisa

looked down at the quilt he'd left in the chair. Her life should be perfect...acceptance by the villagers, and her beloved Brodie home and a free man. But she couldn't dismiss the remembrance of that evil look Cassandra Carmody had cast at her as she'd left the woman's bedroom. This attack on her husband as he was about to return home a free man was evidence that Cassandra Carmody wasn't finished with them yet. She and Brodie still weren't out from under the woman's wicked pall.

"Louisa, love." Brodie's voice from the bedroom made her put disturbing thoughts aside as she went to join him.

"I've got this one." Cradling one of the twins in his arms as carefully as if the baby were the rarest of treasures, Brodie was gazing down at the child with such tenderness it made Louisa's heart ache. Her husband deserved one of his own, and hopefully soon.... "But now the other one is natterin'."

"You're doing just fine, Mr. MacMillan." Louisa picked up the second baby. "You'll make an excellent father."

"Aye, some day soon, I'm hopin'. But first we have to get married in a church. Now that the village women have seen fit to accept you, we must let them see you properly wed." He looked down at the small bundle in his arms. "I missed the christenin'. What did Harry and Margaret choose to name them?"

"This fine fellow"—Louisa looked down at the baby in her arms—"is William Harry Wallace, named for the children's birth father and of course for Harry. The little boy you're holding is Adam Brodie."

When her husband looked up at her, the expression

of astonished delight on his face struck Louisa with the force of a sunbeam after a stormy day.

She hastened to continue while she still could. "Adam because he's Margaret and Harry's first child— he was born before William. And, of course, Brodie for his uncle."

"I cannae believe I've been so honored." Brodie's words choked with emotion as he stared at the tiny face. Blinking, he looked up at her. "But Harry and Margaret have used up all the proper family names. Whit will we do when we have bairns?"

"We'll have a girl, perhaps." Louisa smiled. "We should be able to find a name for a wee lass."

Chapter Thirty-One

The little church was filled to capacity. It appeared the entire community had crowded inside to wish Brodie and his bride well. Standing near the altar, Brodie experienced a warm glow spread over him. This was indeed a wonderful day, the day he and Louisa would publicly become man and wife, a day after which they'd truly be a married couple legally and in the eyes of God.

He had to admit a portion of his happiness was derived from what this show of community acceptance would have for Harry and particularly his wife Margaret. They'd had to drive off alone to a poor excuse for a wedding. Now he and Louisa would vindicate the presence of all of their family in the valley by this publicly supported event.

The first notes of a soft ballad wafted through the little church as Geordie drew his bow across his fiddle. Brodie turned toward the rear doors and felt his breath lump in his throat.

Entering the church on his best friend's arm was a vision in an emerald green gown overlaid with lace so pure, white, and fine it would have suited an angel. Tiny white blossoms that looked like snowflakes intermingled with the artistically arranged golden-red mass of her curls. Dear God, what had he ever done to deserve such a vision?

As she came slowly up the aisle on Harry's arm, in step with Geordie's heartfelt music, Brodie had to blink to keep tears of joy at bay.

Don't go disgracin' yourself, laddie. This is her day. Make it perfect as best you can.

As she stopped beside him, from somewhere in the midst of the spell her beauty had cast over him, he heard the Reverend Edward Morgan asking who gave this woman to be married to this man. Harry's gruff-with-emotion response, "I do," brought Brodie back to the moment.

And then she was smiling up at him, making his entire being surge with joy. Finally, this remarkable woman and he, Brodie MacMillan, former bandit, would be one, a couple in the eyes of God and this new land they'd chosen to call home.

****

A half hour later, as he and his new bride stood on the church steps receiving congratulations, Brodie glanced across the grounds, beyond where tables had been laid with food and drink for the celebration of their union, and saw her.

Mounted on a midnight black horse and dressed in a riding outfit and hat equally dark, Cassandra Carmody rode slowly out of the trees beyond the festivities and reined to a halt. Her two mounted bodyguards stopped behind her. Her haughty gaze fell on the couple in a look that in Brodie's vernacular could have curdled cream.

The bitch isn't done with me yet...not by a long shot.

The thought cast a pall over his previously perfect day. A slight tug at the arm his bride held made him look down at her. Her expression brought all the happiness flooding back. And after she'd looked toward the woman on the black horse, staring unflinchingly at her for a moment pregnant with meaning, and returned her gaze full of love and understanding on Brodie, he relaxed. Together he and Louisa could meet any trouble this vindictive woman would thrust upon them. They were an invincible team.

The guests, apparently noticing the newlyweds' distracted glaze, turned one by one until all were facing the interloping woman. Silence fell.

With a movement so sudden it startled even Brodie, Cassandra Carmody kicked her horse into a gallop. Thrashing through the crowd, slashing at them with her riding crop, she raced to the church steps to pull the animal to a skidding halt before the couple and their assembled family members.

"So you're married...a bandit and a witch." She held her cavorting horse before them, dark eyes sparking with hatred. "No doubt you think you've found perfect bliss. But you will pay, you and all this ragtag assembly you allowed to steal from my father. Don't rest easy in your bed this night, Brodie MacMillan. I haven't finished with you...and yours...yet. Not by a long measure."

She spun the prancing, snorting horse around and whipped it back into a run through the guests. They stumbled out of her way. Cries and yells of outrage followed her.

Once she and her bodyguards had vanished down the trail, an uneasy murmur began to rise from the guests.

"Come along, friends." Harry, his arm around

Margaret on the church steps, called out. "Don't let one bitter woman spoil this day. There's much food and drink to enjoy. Later my son Geordie will provide music for dancing. Let's get to the business for which we assembled...to celebrate Brodie and Louisa's special day."

"Aye, aye!" Brodie looked down to see James turn to the crowd and raise a fisted hand into the air. "To the tables! Time to drink a toast to my uncle's beautiful bride...and a new aunt for my brothers, sisters, and me!"

Chuckles and finally good-natured laughter broke out among the guests as they went to take their seats on the benches beside the tables laden with food and drink.

Good lad. Brodie winked down at James before the young man turned away to join the revelers. *He'll be a fine man like his stepfather and, most likely, his birth father as well. But that witch woman...I know she meant it when she said she's not done with me yet.*

****

"Much as I hate to leave, love, I am a workin' man, and I've been ignorin' my duties too long." With a sigh, Brodie eased out of Louisa's arms and swung his feet over the edge of the bed in his log house. "I'm a partner in the Fowler-Wallace Mills. As their millwright, I'd best be gettin' back on the job."

"Yes, I suppose you must." Smiling languidly, she reached to run a finger down the spine of his bare back.

"Lass, lass, don't tempt me." He swung back to place a kiss on her forehead. "I have to go to work." He got to his feet and began to gather up his clothing. "You may not be a witch, but you do have mystical powers over me."

"Well, then, I'll release you from my spell and let you get on with your duties." Naked, she slipped from the bed and gathered up her robe. "But first, like any good wife, I'll make your breakfast." She pushed her arms into her garment, gave him a quick peck on the cheek, and headed into the kitchen.

Brodie watched her go, a slow grin coming to his face. He was a happy man, an entirely happy man. He snatched up his shirt and pulled it over his head.

If only the specter of Cassandra Carmody wouldn't keep rising up to cast a long, dark shadow over our happiness.

Once dressed, he followed her into the cabin's main room, where she was building up the fire for their breakfast tea.

"And what will you be doin' today while your man labors in the heat?" He paused to look out a window into what he saw as shaping up to be a hot summer day.

"After I set this cabin to rights, I may go over to visit Margaret and see if I can be of use to her and the girls. If not, I'll return here and get to my writing. I'm falling woefully behind because of your doings these past few months, my fine lad. I want to have my stories ready to go to the publisher in London in November."

"You know you don't have to work for gold any longer." He went to put his hands on her shoulders. "I'm not a poor man. I share the income from the mills with Harry and his family. And, like Harry, I didnae leave the Highlands without a bit of booty."

"Brodie MacMillan, are you suggesting I become your kept woman?"

"Lass…"

"I know that's not what you meant." She kissed

him lightly on a cheek. "I love to write. It's been part of my life and dreams since I was a young girl. Will you go denying me that pleasure?"

"No, no, never. If it makes you happy, if you find joy in the work, I'll never want you to stop. When the bairns start to arrive, rest assured I'll do my duty and care for them to allow you time for your pursuit."

"You're a rare man indeed." She slipped out of his embrace and returned to breakfast preparation. "I'm delighted I managed to bewitch you into my life."

"You did that indeed, my enchantress. But you must promise me one thing."

"What?" She turned to him, surprised.

"You must be verrae, verrae careful. I don't believe we've heard or seen the last of Cassandra Carmody."

"I will. I'm not about to go turning my back on the woman. But, Brodie, you know what I've been thinking? How wonderful it would be if Runner, Marie, and their child would agree to visit us here. I do miss them."

"Perhaps they will in time, love. They're not yet comfortable in surroundings such as these. We must accept the fact that our ways are not theirs."

Chapter Thirty-Two

Louisa sat at the table, savoring her second cup of tea. Brodie had gone off to work at the mill in the valley. She was content and pleased with the arrangement. She liked having Harry and Margaret and their growing family nearby. She savored the thought of their making a small but thriving rural community together. Now she, Brodie, and hopefully their children would be part of it.

Bringing herself out of her daydreams, she knew she had to address more immediate concerns. She looked around the basic, thoroughly masculine room and decided it was in need of a woman's touch. Back at her cabin she had dishes, curtains, bedding, and other bric-a-brac that would brighten the place no end.

A decision made, she stood. As soon as she'd cleared away the breakfast dishes and made up the bed, she'd saddle Snow and ride back to the cabin. Harry had retrieved her medical supplies at the time of the fever outbreak, but he'd been on a desperate mission and hadn't taken time to gather up any personal items. With luck, her wagon would still be at the homestead, unscathed. She'd load it up with her possessions, harness her mare to it, and bring them back to her new, permanent home.

She'd leave a note for Brodie. If she went down to the mill to tell him her plan, she knew he'd insist on accompanying her. She didn't want him leaving his job to ride as her guard. After his extended absence, his skills as a millwright were much needed. She could manage on her own. Lord knew, she'd done it before. Surely Cassandra Carmody and her pair of brutes wouldn't be watching them still.

"Jasper, you stay here," she ordered the animal. "It's a hot day. You'll get too warm running through the bush beside Snow. Brodie will be home at midday and let you out for a run."

Leaving the wolf muttering his disappointment, she went out, closing the door and securing it with its rope fastening to keep the animal inside.

****

Brodie came back to the log house at midday. He was dirty and hungry, but eager to see his bride. As he arrived at the cabin, he was greeted by the door tied shut with its rope and Jasper's whining from inside. An eerie coldness chilled him to the bone.

The wolf leaped up on him as he opened the door.

"Down, Jasper. Easy, boy. Where is our lady?"

He saw the note on the table and snatched it up. Gone to collect her things from the cabin. Alone. The chill turned to a freezing fear.

"You stay here," he ordered the wolf. "You'll just be a great nuisance tryin' to keep up with me in this heat." Leaving Jasper once more yowling out his disappointment, Brodie snatched up his sword belt and ran to the stable.

Within minutes he'd saddled Fox and was off at a dead run.

****

He was nearing the clearing in which her

homestead was situated. Much as impulse urged him to rush forward, he recognized the possible folly of such a move. Perhaps marriage had tamed him; the idea slid across his mind. Or made him wiser. As he approached through an alder thicket, he held Fox to a cautious walk.

Sweet Jesus!

Coming within view of the clearing that held the homestead, he saw a sight that made his heart seize. Tied with her hands above her head to a verandah beam was his wife. Standing at the bottom of the steps before a blazing fire was Cassandra Carmody.

Fox chose that moment to snort.

"You can come out, Brodie MacMillan." The woman's words were a taunt. "Your horse is too brilliant a red to be disguised by a few branches. Come out where you can watch my triumph." In one hand she held a pistol leveled in his direction, in the other a dry branch. She thrust the top of the latter into the flames.

"Whale oil burns so well, doesn't it? I've doused the verandah with it." She held the torch aloft as he advanced into view.

"What do you want?" he asked, his voice gruff, fear making his head swim as he saw the darkness on the boards around his wife's feet. He walked his horse slowly forward, his stomach roiling.

"You and Harry Wallace murdered my father." She stared at him with such hatred as he'd never before seen. "In return, I've ruined Harry Wallace...taken away what he and that tavern wench of a wife valued most...respectability. Now I'll ruin you. I'll take away what means most to you!"

She flung the torch into the oil on the verandah steps, and the dry wood burst into flames.

"Burn, witch, burn!" she screamed, dancing back from the conflagration.

"No!" Brodie pulled his sword from its scabbard and kicked Fox into a run across the clearing to the cabin. The horse charged toward the woman at the bottom of the steps. As he bolted, she raised her pistol and fired. The stallion screamed and dropped on top of her, blood spurting from a wound in his chest. As the horse fell, he leaped clear and vaulted to the verandah.

"No, Brodie, run! Save yourself!" Louisa screamed as flames licked around her ankles.

"Never!" With a slice of his sword he severed the rope that held her to the rafter, clutched her up into his arms, and leaped to the ground. There he rolled them both about to extinguish any fire that had caught into their clothing.

Finally, together, they staggered to their feet. The cabin was in flames.

"Fox!" Brodie released his wife to run to the fallen stallion. The animal's eyes rolled. He snorted and gasped. To one side of him lay Cassandra Carmody, staring lifelessly up into the sky, a sneer on her face. The stallion had saved Brodie. Now his own life was ebbing.

"Fox." Brodie dropped to his knees beside the animal's head. "Oh, laddie."

Louisa knelt beside them. She made no attempt at comfort. There could be none.

With his master's tears streaming down as the man lay prostrate on the ground beside him, his arm about the animal's neck, the great Scottish stallion died.

****

Together they pulled Cassandra Carmody's body

from beneath the dead animal and laid it in the back of Louisa's wagon. As the cabin roof collapsed into a mass of flame, the heavens opened and a great deluge poured down. The rain would keep the fire from spreading to the bush. Brodie turned and headed for the stable. He was only vaguely aware that Louisa followed him. When he grasped a shovel and saw her reaching for another, he knew she understood, that she would share in the painful obligation.

****

Together they stood beside the stallion's grave. It had been a long, exhausting task in the rain to dig a pit large enough for the animal, but Louisa knew it was one Brodie had to complete. She watched as her husband threw a last shovelful of earth over the mound. They hadn't spoken during the work. Louisa knew, like Brodie, that some grief was too sharp, too deep for words.

Brodie stuck the shovel into the earth and, with both hands on the top of the handle, dropped his forehead onto them. His broad shoulders shook.

Louisa let him have his grief. When he finally raised his face, her heart lurched at the tearstains straggling through the dirt of fire and burial. She knew it was time to go to him.

****

Later, as he drove Louisa's wagon back toward the village, where Brodie had said they must deliver Cassandra Carmody's body to the magistrate, he told her Fox's story.

"He came out of the mist one day after I lost Annie and our child, after our mill had been burned and I'd decided to take to the road to find Lachlan's—

Edward's—band of rebels." He handled the reins lightly as Snow picked her way down the rutted trail. "Saddled and bridled, he just appeared in front of me, a great saber slash in his shoulder, drenched with sweat and blood. At first, he shied away, his eyes showing white, even rearing up at me, flailing with his hooves. But I spoke softly to him, telling him we were both hurting…" He paused and glanced at Louisa. "Sounds daft, I know."

"Not at all." She touched his arm in the dirty, ragged shirt. "I spoke much the same to Jasper when he came to my door shortly after I lost Neil and our baby."

"Well." He returned his gaze out over the horse's back as he continued. "The long and short of it is that he finally quieted and allowed me to clean his wound." He drew a deep breath. "He followed me about for the next two days and nights. When I deemed he was well enough to bear a rider, we set off to find Edward's merry band of rogues."

He flashed her a weak smile. "The rest you know. That stallion has stood by me through more tight places than I care to recall. He's fought with me and been wounded on more than one occasion. We shared a wildness in our souls. I'll be getting a stonemason to make a grave marker for him, Louisa. A marker that will forever show the place where lies the bravest of the brave…a loyal friend who gave his life for his master."

"You should do no less." Louisa removed her hand from his arm. Tonight, after the rest of the duties of this horrific day were behind them, she'd hold him and let him ease his pain in her arms.

Chapter Thirty-Three

Brodie sat on a bench amid the cacophony of the Wallace log house and let the merry family confusion swirl around him. Moving between hearth, table, and sideboards, his wife, Margaret, and Mary were chatting as they prepared a midday meal. On the floor on a rug removed from the paths of the busy women sat Eppie, Edward and Mary's toddler Iona, Precious the pig, and Jasper the wolf. Settled in the pair of rocking chairs frequently used by Margaret and Harry, Lizzie and Bella each held a twin.

Ah, yes, quite the remarkable domestic scene, one that he, Brodie MacMillan former outlaw, never thought he'd be privileged to enjoy. If only he could shut out the ugliness that Cassandra Carmody had brought into his life, the vision of Fox dying to save him and Louisa, if only...

The sound of a wagon and horses arriving in the dooryard brought the memories still more poignantly to mind. Edward Morgan, Harry, and his four stepsons had left early in the morning to bury her body in the churchyard. They had not asked Brodie to join them. They'd known he could not again be exposed to the woman, even in death.

A silence had fallen over the room at the sound.

"Let's get food on the table. They'll be hungry." Margaret brought the group back to the moment. It was time to move on.

****

The two men and four boys entered the house. They'd put the horses away and washed at the stand by the door before coming inside. Their entry caused another hiatus.

"We've done the deed," the clergyman said finally. "It's over." He crossed the room to put an arm about his wife and kiss her on the temple. "Now." He heaved a deep breath after another short silence. "I see we have a fine repast awaiting us." He let a smile brighten his broad, handsome face. "I'll say a brief grace, and we'll have at it, shall we? It's time to be thankful that we're all once more together, hale and hearty."

****

Later, after the meal was finished, while the women were clearing away, Edward motioned Harry and Brodie outside, away from the happy, boisterous noise and confusion of children and washing up.

"Brodie, I have a wee inkling of how you might be feeling." The minister clapped a big hand on his friend's shoulder as they paused in the dooryard. "It's understandable."

"I cannae forgive the woman, Lachlan." Brodie faced the clergyman. "Although you expect it of me, although I know it's the Christian thing to do, I cannae, although you'll tell me how wrong that is. She tried to have me imprisoned, and nearly killed my wife. She murdered Fox."

"Now, there you're wrong, laddie." Edward met his gaze squarely. "Cassandra Carmody hurt you to the quick, did everything in her power to destroy you out of a vicious sense of revenge. It's natural that you aren't yet ready to forgive. Forgiveness comes like a gentle rain, and there's no way of rushing it. It can take days, weeks, perhaps even years. But rest assured, Brodie MacMillan, it will come. It has to come to a man as good and decent as you."

"I hope...and pray...you're right, Lachlan. Carryin' hatred is a heavy load."

"Uncle Brodie!" Eppie burst out of the house, followed by the rest of the gathered family and friends. "Uncle Brodie, we have a surprise for you! A big, big surprise!"

"Oh, aye?" His somber mood vanished as the child he adored rushed up to him. He caught her up in his arms. "Whit may I ask do you have in store for me? More rhubarb pie? While it was delicious, I don't think I could down another piece. Too much dinner."

"No, no, not pie! Better, better. Put me down." She squirmed in his grip, and he eased her to the ground. She grasped his hand as his wife and their friends gathered around him, smiling and laughing.

"Close your eyes, Uncle Brodie," the child insisted. "I'm going to take you to see your surprise."

As he was led blindly across the barnyard, Brodie stumbled a few times. Finally he felt himself bump into a fence rail.

"You can look now." Eppie told him.

Brodie looked. And couldn't believe his eyes.

Standing in the paddock beside Scotia was a foal...a beautiful little red filly.

"We've named her Vixen...in honor of her father," Louisa said softly.

"She...she's Fox's foal?" Brodie stared, frozen in surprised delight.

"Aye." Grinning, Harry moved forward to slap him on the shoulder. "That great nuisance got at my mare somehow. You're looking at the result—a filly, thanks be to God. And leave it to him…this is the wrong time of year for a newborn, but when did the creature ever do anything that was usual."

As Brodie continued to stare, the families broke into applause.

"You'll have to train her up to be like Fox, Uncle Brodie." Samuel grinned as everyone assembled around him to look at the little mare. "Father says she won't be as big, being a filly and all, but still…"

"This is one wonderful day!" Brodie pulled Louisa close to kiss her on the temple and then turned to the assemblage. "A wonderful, wonderful day!"

"Like a phoenix, the gallant beast has risen from his ashes in the body of this lovely creature." Margaret smiled.

"Well, well." Brodie shook his head, emotion robbing him of further words, his eyes bright with unshed tears. "The lad lives on. You've named rightly." He managed to control his emotions sufficiently to look around at his family and friends. "If she's at all like her sire, she'll be a rare lass, to be sure."

As if on cue, the filly kicked up her heels, gave a sharp little whinny, and set off at a gallop across the pasture.

"Does that answer your question, laddie?" Harry slapped him on a shoulder, grinning.

"Aye, aye, indeed it does. I can see I'll have my work cut out makin' a lady of this one."

"Perhaps you'll be busy making a lady out of more than one new family member." Louisa came to his side and smiled up at him.

"Louisa?" He could only gape. Could his wife be telling him…?

In answer, she nodded.

A cheer went up from the assemblage as Brodie caught his wife in his arms to kiss her.

"Now aren't you glad I made you come out and see the witch, that day in town?" Samuel grinned at his uncle.

"Aye, laddie, for that I'll be forever in your debt." Holding Louisa close, he grinned at the lad.

Brazen Brodie had found absolute happiness with his bandit's bride.

A word about the author...

Award-winning author of over 35 published books, Gail is a graduate of Queen's University and a four-time winner of Maxwell Medals for her dog books. Two of her Riverhaven Rogues historical novels have won awards in the Canadian Romance Writers Maple Leaf Contest.

Visit Gail at:

macgail@nbnet.nb.ca